To Lesley
With love
Emily Royal
x

HENRY'S BRIDE

London Libertines, Book One

by Emily Royal

Dedication

For Jasmine, who is a better person than her mother and who, with luck, on reading this, will pledge to look after me in my infirmity.

Acknowledgements

This book would not have seen the light of day without the support of my family and friends.

Big thanks to my fabulous tribe, the Beta Buddies, who read the rough drafts. An extra huge hug to Sarah Painter for the writing sessions complete with tea, pizza and wine, which helped me over the final editing hurdle.

To Violetta and all at Dragonblade, thank you for having so much faith in this book, for your invaluable feedback and the beautiful cover.

To my high school mathematics teacher, you made me believe it's cool for a girl to be numerate and my heroine thanks you. I'm also grateful to the Romantic Novelists' Association who provided an early critique through their New Writers' Scheme, and encouraged me to take writing seriously.

And finally, to Neil, Jasmine, and Frankie – no words can express how much your encouragement means to me.

PROLOGUE

WITH HIS BODY humming from the afterglow of pleasurable release, Henry Drayton, Marquis of Ravenwell, straightened his cravat and descended the stone steps outside the brothel entrance. Betty ran one of the more exclusive bawdy houses, catering to tastes few men could afford. Discretion was favored over publicity, and he glanced up and down the street before setting off. The sun had yet to rise, and few would be up and about this early except men like him who sought a willing female body to relieve the tedium of polite society.

Lights flickered in the top stories of the terraced houses he passed, servants enduring the cold while donning their uniforms to embark on their duties. Tasks like setting the water to boil, laying the fireplaces so their masters and mistresses met the new day with warmth, comfort, and fresh tea, unaware of the toil that had gone into preparing their breakfast.

The doors of a townhouse ahead opened, and the cloaked figure of a woman stepped out.

Henry stopped in his tracks. What the devil was a servant doing using the front entrance? Or was she a doxy paying a visit to the master of the house?

A shaft of sunlight stretched across the street, illuminating her face as if the sunrise had waited for her. Intelligent eyes the color of emeralds brought a splash of life to her otherwise drab appearance.

With a furtive glance that mirrored Henry's own, she set off at a pace too fast for a lady, but lacking the urgency of a thief.

Her figure was discernible even beneath her cloak; a frame lacking the brittleness prized among society ladies. Her body glowed with the curves and tones of health and vitality. Henry's own body tightened with lust, and he set off in her wake.

Which bawdy house did she belong to? Or was she a courtesan? Currently between mistresses, Henry was looking for another. Perhaps she was in need of a protector. Not only in terms of a man's relationship with his mistress, but someone to warn her of the dangers of wandering about the streets of London unaccompanied.

Maybe she courted danger on purpose.

The woman turned into Hyde Park, and her pace slowed. She stopped at a tree and ran her palm over the bark, fingers caressing the texture as if she drew strength and joy from Mother Nature. Her eyes were closed, the light of the dawn emphasizing the contentment in her face, lips upturned in a peaceful smile as if she had come home.

Male voices called out, and she jerked back, continuing along the path and then disappearing into the park.

Before Henry could follow her, two men appeared. They wore the familiar garb of the Bow Street Runners and carried a body between them. Icy fingers caressed the back of Henry's neck.

It was a woman. Water dripped off her clothes and hair which hung lifeless, dark stains spreading across the Runners' red waistcoats. Her face was bloated, evidence she had been in the water for several hours. Her head lay at an unnatural angle, bruises dark against her pale skin.

Someone had broken her neck.

Henry hailed the runners. "What do you have there?"

The taller man spoke. "Just another doxy, sir. Nothing to concern yourself with."

"Aren't *you* concerned?"

"Of course. It's our job to investigate."

"How did you find her?"

"Some lad told us about a body. Reckon she's been floating in the Serpentine all night. Probably indulged on gin and fell in. You know what their sort's like. We had three of them last month."

"That may be," Henry said, "but even I can see the marks on her neck."

"Them type like it rough." The man nudged his companion. "Come on, John, the sooner we deal with this brass, the sooner we can have a brew."

He tipped his hat at Henry. "Mind how you go, sir. London's a dangerous place at night."

Henry nodded. Dangerous indeed. Yet these men dismissed the death of a whore as an inconvenience which kept them from their tea. These women were people, too.

As was Jenny.

Jenny.

A prostitute like any other but for one thing; she was the mother of Henry's child.

If these men were to be believed, the woman in their arms hadn't been the first body they'd discovered. If they didn't care, perhaps Henry should look into the matter himself. He owed it to Jenny even though she'd long since died. Betty may have heard something. Only last night she'd mentioned the disappearance of one of her girls, though she rarely spoke of her fears, possessing the talent only the best woman of her sort had, revealing little of herself, concentrating only on the needs of the men she serviced.

But he'd have to be careful. A man investigating murders in London put his life at risk. It was fortunate he had no loved ones who might be endangered by association. Perhaps, then, it was not time to find a mistress just yet.

A pity. The intriguing creature he'd followed into the park might have provided an excellent diversion for the Season.

CHAPTER ONE

"**G**OOD GRIEF, LOOK at *her!*"

"Is it me, Dom, or are debutantes getting uglier each Season?"

Henry shifted his attention from the company—unmarried ladies whose muscles tensed at the sight of him—to his friends, Rupert and Dominic, who gestured toward a group of unattached ladies at the edge of the ballroom.

Two sat apart from the rest. The one on the left was the Honorable Andrea Elliot. Recently betrothed to an American privateer, she lacked the air of desperation which clung to most debutantes. Henry didn't recognize her companion.

"A plain, plump little thing," Dominic laughed. "That pink is hideous, and the expression on her face could curdle milk."

"Given her prospects, I'm not surprised she's miserable," Rupert said.

She wore a discontented expression, her mouth downturned, brow creased into a frown, and body slumped forward. Her marked contrast to the ocean of elegance in the room was enough to incite curiosity, even if it rendered her unpalatable.

Henry voiced his curiosity. "What prospects?"

"That's Miss Claybone, née Smith." Rupert relished the emphasis on *Smith*. "Her father's a baronet, but it's a new title. The mother has blue blood, though French, and she's trying to further her ambitions through her daughters."

"As is every mother in the room," Henry said.

Rupert laughed. "She'll have difficulty getting *that* one off her hands. Perhaps I'll have some sport with her. I'm rather partial to a fine set of curves."

As Henry watched her, she lifted her head and their eyes met. His breath caught in his throat. They were the eyes of the woman he'd followed into the park. Deep oceans of green punctuated by sparkles of gold radiated a sharp intelligence. They seemed to look right inside him and find him wanting. He shifted his legs at the surge of heat in his groin.

"She's not worth your notice, Rupe," he said. "Where's the sport in tormenting a mouse when there's bigger game to be had?"

Her eyes hardened and she looked away.

"It's all right for you, Dray," Rupert said. "Your quarry's in the room. I'm sure the countess awaits your pleasure. And hers."

Henry ran a hand through his hair—thick, black locks which women seemed to enjoy burying their hands in while he pleasured them. His gaze fell on their hosts, the Earl and Countess of Darlington. The countess caught his eye and lifted her lips into a seductive smile. Nearby stood Lady Holmestead, arm-in-arm with her husband.

Perhaps he'd have some sport tonight after all.

"THERE THEY ARE, Jeanie. The worst rakes of the ton."

Jeanette looked away from the crowd—row upon row of bright, vibrant silks shimmering against each other, sparkling headdresses and glittering jewels—and turned her attention on her friend. Andrea Elliott looked every part the society lady, her yellow silk gown complementing her classic beauty to perfection. Pale blonde hair fashioned into soft curls and dotted with pearls, framed a face flushed a delicate shade of rose and eyes the color of cornflowers. No wonder she'd secured an offer of marriage less than a week into her first season. To Jeanette, Andrea was a jewel among society, for she possessed intelligence, independence, and wit, and had managed to attract the attention and secure the hand of the only man in society Jeanette deemed worthy of her.

"I thought all men were rakes, Andy," Jeanette said, "except your Mr. O'Reilly."

"Ah, dearest Theodore! Pity he's not titled, but I love him regardless."

Jeanette sighed. "You're unique among your class, for you care nothing for their nonsense."

"I find it entertaining," Andrea said. "For example, those three are infamous debauchers, but look how the women lift their heads when they enter the room. The biggest and best catches of the day! I swear, if your mama had a butterfly net, she'd be running across the ballroom now."

"I doubt that, Andy. If she caught me running, she'd have an attack of the vapors."

Andrea giggled. "Luckily you're of little consequence to attract their notice. And just as well. I hear most of the fallen women in London have them to thank for it. Their tastes include half the married ladies in this room…" She lowered her voice, "…and they frequent bawdy houses to relieve their more *sophisticated* passions."

"Who are they?" Jeanette said.

"Surely you're not interested?"

"Of course not, but at the very least, I ought to know the names of those I should avoid."

Andrea lowered her voice. "The small brown-haired chap is the Honorable Dominic Hartford, eldest son of Viscount Hartford. The blonde fellow is Rupert Beaumont, Viscount Oakville."

"And the darker one?"

"That, my dear, is Lord Ravenwell. He's to inherit a dukedom from his cousin. They say he has more children than any other man in London. Quite the achievement."

"Not one to be proud of. What of the mothers of his children?"

"A man of his status can do whatever he likes, Jeanie, without making the slightest ripple in his reputation."

Jeanette shook her head. "Pity the women caught in the ripples."

The three men looked perfectly comfortable in their surroundings, an environment Jeanette found both alien and hostile. Her gaze lingered on Lord Ravenwell; tall, broad-shouldered, with a toned, athletic build accentuated by his form-fitting dark jacket and pale cream breeches, right down to his calfskin boots.

His hair was longer than socially acceptable, brushing his shoulders in thick black waves. His features exuded breeding, the strong jaw, straight nose, and dark lashes which framed his brilliant blue eyes. His gaze met hers, and a knowing smile curled at the corner of his lush, sensual mouth. What might it be like to be claimed by those lips, to feel his breath on her skin?

Deep longing pulsed in her stomach. How could he master her body from a single glance?

She dropped her gaze to break the spell. It was an unjust world where men ruled the lives of others through circumstances of birth rather than merit. How could she hope to survive in it?

"Jeanette."

Mama's voice made her sit up almost instinctively.

"Don't forget Colonel Chambers."

Mama had tried to persuade Hugh Chambers, the youngest son of the Duke of Bowborough, to offer for the first dance, with thinly veiled comments about how sons of dukes should fraternize with daughters of French aristocrats, oblivious to the titters of onlookers hungry for objects of ridicule and subjects of gossip. To avoid further embarrassment, Jeanette had sought refuge among the wallflowers where man rarely ventured.

Mama fanned herself. "Take a turn about the room. You'll not fill your dance card chattering in the corner. And hold your stomach in. That gown is supposed to hide, not exaggerate, your curves."

To attract a husband, a lady had to appear emaciated, have porcelain skin, and a meek disposition, which was valued over wit or kindness.

Jeanette pulled a face at Mama's retreating back. "I don't know why she doesn't have the size of my dowry embroidered onto this horrible pink gown. Papa could secure a ring through my nose and parade me about the room."

Andrea stifled a giggle. "You see this ball as a cattle market?"

Jeanette eyed up the brightly colored gowns milling about, feathers nodding in the air, the women seemingly desperate to out-feather each other in terms of height. A wicked idea formed in her mind and she leaned toward her friend.

"Watch the women, Andy. See how they flick their fans? A cow in season will approach the bull and show him how—available—she is, by flicking her tail just so. *Come hither, virile creature. I'm ready for you.*"

Andrea waved her fan as a blush deepened on her cheeks.

"Now to the men," Jeanette continued, "one must inspect a bull before placing a bid."

"Would you inspect their teeth?"

"My dear, Andy," Jeanette said, biting her lip to temper the urge to laugh, "a bull is not prized for his *teeth*."

"What is he prized for?"

Andrea, curse her! How did she manage it? Eyes wide with mock innocence, the merest glint of wickedness in their expression. A lifetime in the aristocracy had taught her complete self-control, a quality Jeanette lacked. Andrea lifted an eyebrow in challenge.

Go on, Jeanie, make me laugh.

"When inspecting a bull, you'd look at the same place as you would a cow when checking her udders," Jeanette said.

To her credit, Andrea's composure remained, though she continued to fan herself.

"Of course, Andy, men and women differ from cattle. The udders are somewhat higher on a woman's body. When inspecting a man, we must look further down."

"What if you're caught l-looking?" Andrea stuttered.

"Men are too easily distracted. Look at Lady Darlington over there. I'll wager the Earl of Strathdean is so enthralled by her décolletage that she could perform a manual inspection of his—accoutrements—unnoticed."

Andrea's composure shattered and an unladylike snort burst from her nostrils. Jeanette threw back her head, no longer able to contain the tide of mirth which exploded from her throat. Disapproving voices drifted across the room.

"For shame!"

"How unsightly…"

"My dear, Miss Elliott." A masculine voice with an exotic timbre broke through the unpleasantries as Mister O'Reilly approached. Andrea stood with the fluidity of a well-schooled lady and took her betrothed's hand for the first dance.

Jeanette's chance to escape had come. Mama was nowhere to be seen, and Papa would be playing at cards somewhere. With nobody's attention on her, she could go where she chose. The best remedy for an empty dance card was fresh air, and she moved toward the terrace doors and slipped outside.

The evening light cast a warm pink glow on the gardens, but the manicured lawn compared unfavorably to the meadows Jeanette had grown up with. The shrubs had been stifled into shapes deemed acceptable to society, constrained by clippers as much as Jeanette was restricted by the strips of bone in her corset. Did the shrubs also struggle to breathe?

The only asymmetrical shapes were the trees surrounding the garden. They had the audacity to sprout branches at irregular angles, Mother Nature flouting the mastery of man.

Good for her.

Voices filtered across the night air.

"He's the greatest catch in London, Caroline. He must be looking for a wife. I hear he's disposed of his mistress."

"Very handsomely Lizzie, no doubt."

"He's a generous patron, even if they never last more than a few months."

"Generous in coin?"

"And other matters. Imagine what it'd be like to snare him!"

"He'd not keep faith with his wife."

"Who cares? He's richer than Croesus and has a title. Felicia is to be envied having secured him for the first dance."

"Hrumpf! Felicia Long must have played on his sympathy. Her face is so horse-like, she has to avoid the stallions when the mares at her Papa's stable are in season."

Jeanette smiled to herself, Ladies Caroline Sandton and Elizabeth De Witt, both unmarried. One more season and they'd qualify as wallflowers. Or rather, nettles.

Jeanette's skin tightened on hearing her name.

"Did you see Miss Claybone? Or should I say, *Smith*. She has no shame!"

"What was Lady Darlington thinking of, inviting her sort! No amount of wealth or title bestowed on that family will remove the stench of trade."

"I disapprove of these new titles. They encourage those of low birth to rub shoulders with their betters! What next? Must we take supper with the chambermaids?"

"And the mother! Fancies herself eligible for entry into Almack's just because she's an émigré, of which thousands roam the streets. I hear she worked as a seamstress before marrying."

"How could she possibly snare a gentleman for a husband?"

"Hardly a gentleman, Caroline. Sir Robert's nothing but a cattle farmer."

"I wonder if he has a similar problem to Viscount Long and has to keep his daughter away from the cowshed?"

"I hear she has two sisters."

"Oh Lord! You mean to say next season we'll see more Smiths littering the place, trying to claim that a moderate accomplishment at the pianoforte makes up for an upbringing in the gutter?"

Their laughter resumed before they turned their attentions onto another—Lady Ashurst's youngest daughter who, according to Lady Caroline, sang like a constipated crow.

Jeanette gritted her teeth. How dare those women laugh at her, and at Papa! He was a hard-working, kind man. All his employees and servants looked up to him. How many of those preening peacocks could say the same about *their* servants? Did they even know whose lives depended on them?

Fighting the urge to run and hide, she returned inside. Papa always said an obstacle must be faced and scaled, with a head held high.

A shape moved near the terrace doors. Jeanette blinked and it disappeared. A trick of the light, or shadow cast from within the ballroom where people were dancing. She slipped inside, bypassing the dancers until she reached her destination, a table laden with a punchbowl where a footman stood to attention.

Holding her hand up to deflect his offer of help, she filled a glass, a watered-down mixture of brandy and lemonade, and swallowed it in one gulp before taking another. The epitome of discretion, the footman remained still. After filling her glass a third time, she murmured under her breath, then drained the contents.

"Prize bloody bitches."

She slammed the glass on the table. The footman continued to stare straight ahead and Jeanette let out a giggle.

A deep voice from behind made her jump.

"I'm sorry, madam, I didn't quite catch what you said."

Jeanette turned and came face to face with a broad chest. She tipped her head up and looked into the blue eyes of Lord Ravenwell.

CHAPTER TWO

"I SAID, PRIZE bloody bitches."

Lord Ravenwell cocked an eyebrow toward the punchbowl. "Perhaps you've had enough of that?"

"Not nearly enough." Jeanette refilled her glass.

"Don't you know a lady should never partake of more than three glasses of punch in an evening?"

The harsh words from the gossips on the terrace still stung.

"Then find a *lady* to bestow your words of wisdom on. They're wasted on me."

His eyes narrowed before he took the glass out of her hand.

"May I inquire if you're engaged for the next dance?"

Jeanette snorted. "No, I'm not. Nor any other dance tonight." She tried to retrieve her glass, but his hand curled around her wrist, an action which conveyed strength, purpose, and domination. They were the fingers of a man who knew what he wanted and took it. A man who women would willingly give themselves to.

He caressed her skin with his thumb. The casual gesture sent a flame through her body, awakening previously unknown sensations, and the breath caught in her throat.

His mouth curled into a knowing smile. She was no match for him, a connoisseur of seduction.

"Sweeting, is that how you offer yourself to a man, by playing his sympathies?"

She snatched her hand away, her cheeks flaming. Insufferable, conceited man! That pristine waistcoat of his needed a little dousing.

"Don't flatter yourself," she said. "I'll offer you a glass of punch, though perhaps not in the manner in which a *lady* would bestow it."

A smile of amusement danced in his eyes. "I prefer to taste my punch rather than wear it. At least my valet would prefer it. Perhaps you've had one glass too many."

"I doubt that. If a real drink were available, I could match you glass for glass."

"I only wish to match you step for step on the dance floor."

Now he was teasing her.

"You've mistaken me for someone else."

"No, Miss Claybone," he said, his tongue curling round her name as if savoring a sweetmeat. "And my name is…"

"Ravenwell," she interrupted. "I know *who* and *what* you are."

The warmth in his eyes turned to frost.

"Are you ashamed to dance with me, Miss Claybone?"

She held his gaze. "I'm ashamed of nothing."

"Then prove it."

He led her onto the dance floor where couples were lining up. Whispers fluttered through the company like leaves in the breeze. Any moment, Mama's voice would bluster through them, dissipating the leaves in a whirlwind of desperation.

A few steps into the dance, he broke the silence between them.

"Are you enjoying the dance? You seem accomplished, considering…"

"…my lack of breeding?"

"I meant no disrespect."

Arrogant man! Did he think her a fool?

"For the past two years I've endured lessons in deportment," she said. "A silly word which describes nothing more complex than the placing of one foot in front of the other in an acceptable fashion."

"You must admit, it would be ridiculous to call it a lesson in foot placement, Miss Claybone."

"I would rather call it what it is."

"Yes, I believe you would." His mouth twitched into a smile.

"In that case," she said saucily, "we should rename all the lessons ladies are subjected to. 'Eyelash fluttering', 'fan waving', and worst of all…"

Jeanette's voice broke off as they were separated in the dance for a few steps. Out of the corner of her eye, she noticed Mama's excited gestures which almost knocked the feathers off her neighbor's headdress.

"You were saying?"

Interrupted from her thoughts, she saw he was looking directly at her.

"Worst of all is the lesson in husband-catching. We're taught that tongues and brains are not required, merely a large dowry and a small mind. So, we prance around in neatly aligned rows while the real world is outside. Why this is called *le bon ton,* I've no idea. It should be called *le ton terrible.* For if a woman fails to succeed, Heaven help her."

"Are you sure you want to see the world outside, Miss Claybone? It can be unpleasant."

"What would you know of unpleasantness? Where were you educated?"

He arched an eyebrow. "I had a tutor, then progressed to Eton and Oxford."

"My education took place in Papa's office until two years ago it regressed into the parlor to learn the accomplishments of a lady."

"A fine education for a young woman."

"Music, perhaps, but mathematics was denied me. Before, I could put myself to use helping Papa with his accounts."

"A job for servants! I wouldn't sully *my* hands with it. My steward sees to mine."

"Which confirms my view that an education is wasted on a gentleman when others could put it to better use."

"Others such as yourself?"

"Why not? I'll wager you can't perform a simple mathematical sum on paper, let alone in your head."

"And you can?" he laughed.

How dare he mock her! "Of course."

"All right then, Miss Claybone. I have seventeen staff in my townhouse. If I paid them each twelve guineas, how much would that be?"

"Two hundred and four guineas. Can't you think of a better challenge?"

"That was too quick. How do I know you've answered correctly?"

"Surely your Oxford education equips you to work it out."

"Do you enjoy this kind of challenge? Hardly ladylike."

His smile had disappeared. How many times had Mama told her men didn't like women who were too clever for their own good?

She shook her head. What did she care for the opinion of a rake who would doubtless be seducing several women to their ruin tonight?

Well, none of them will be me.

She sighed. "For the greater part of my life, Lord Ravenwell, I've been free. I have only recently been confined to the prison while society awaits my incarceration in the cage.

"You're talking in riddles again."

"Freedom is the life I had at home," she explained. "The prison is the ton. Surely, I don't have to explain what the cage represents. Of course, you wouldn't see it as such, given what little difference it would make to your life."

"You mean matrimony?"

"Men call it 'the parson's noose' yet your lives are hardly affected. You'll continue to indulge in your exploits."

"Exploits?"

16

"Come, sir! As a rakehell, you understand me, and as a gentleman, you wouldn't embarrass me by asking me to elaborate on the details."

The urge to break through his aristocratic expression got the better of her, and she threw him a wicked smile. "Be careful what you ask, Lord Ravenwell. I grew up on a farm, as I'm sure the gossips have told you."

"Details?"

He squeezed her hand and his eyes darkened with a predatory look. He drew out his tongue and licked his lips, those full, sensual lips. Her chest tightened, and she looked away.

"Your methods won't work on me, Lord Ravenwell."

"Is that another challenge, sweeting?"

At that moment, they were separated again. Elizabeth De Witt walked past Jeanette and turned her back. Whether or not Jeanette had secured the attention of the most desirable man in the room, she was still an outsider in this little circle of the wealthy and titled.

How long would it take for this charade to play out for Mama to realize she had no hope of securing a position in society? In the meantime, Jeanette must suffer their sneers.

"So, sir," she said, coming into contact with her dance partner again, "do you think I belong in society?"

"No," he said shortly, "you lack the characteristics."

"Such as?"

"Wealth, breeding, classic beauty."

She pressed her lips together. Though insulting, he spoke the truth.

"You also lack stupidity," he added.

"A quality I'll manage without."

They continued the dance in silence. Conversation would serve no purpose other than to confirm the vast distinction of rank between them. Lord Ravenwell possessed a wealth of opportunities which were denied her; opportunities he'd squander as a member of the idle rich.

The dance concluded and he bowed.

"Tell me, Miss Claybone, how did you perform that calculation so quickly?"

"As with anything, the observation of human behavior for example, one must look for patterns," she replied. "Three seventeens are fifty-one. Twelve seventeens are therefore the same as four fifty-ones, hence two-hundred-and-four."

"I'm impressed."

"If you're impressed by a woman's intelligence, Lord Ravenwell, I'd suggest *you* lack the qualities society expects in a gentleman."

Declining his offer to escort her to her seat, Jeanette curtsied and left him on the floor. She had no intention of dancing again. Lord Ravenwell had humiliated her beyond recall, and though she had enjoyed some sport with him, she'd felt her inferiority keenly. She would never fit in. Heaven help her if anyone asked her for her hand.

She must never secure the attention of a man of the ton.

⊰⊱⊰⊱⊰⊱

HENRY SAUNTERED OVER to join Rupert by the terrace doors, ignoring the expectant expressions on the faces of the ladies he passed on the way.

"Where's Dominic?"

"Leading Felicia Long out for the next dance."

"The premier heiress of the Season."

"Is that why you snagged her for the first dance, Dray?"

Henry shrugged and reached for a glass of champagne from a passing footman.

"Talking of dancing, Dray, what on earth were you doing with Miss Claybone?"

Jeanette Claybone. That pink gown had done nothing to flatter her figure, but she'd proved a surprisingly engaging dance partner.

He should have left her to her punch, but anger had gripped him when he'd heard those gossipmongers belittling her. Her eyes had been dulled by pain when she'd brushed past him on the terrace.

A sense of pride had warmed his blood at her lively responses to him. Most ladies would have retreated to a corner in floods of tears. But not her. She'd drunk enough to floor every woman and half the men in the room, then matched him in a duel of wits.

Such a pity she was so far beneath him! She might prove an interesting prospect for a dalliance, but she struck him as a virtuous woman, though she cursed like a man. Henry only carried on with dissatisfied wives who understood the rules. No attachments or love, only pleasure.

Father's foolish exploits had taught Henry that to love a woman led to financial ruin. Father had made no secret of the love he bore Henry's mother who had possessed that soulless beauty which defined perfection among society. On realizing that love was unrequited, Father had tried to buy love elsewhere. But the courtesans he'd lavished his wealth on only traded their bodies; their hearts were not for sale.

Father had been weak by letting his heart rule his head. And Henry had to live with the consequences. He would never let a woman rule his heart. There was no room in his world for that particular organ, not even for a woman as intriguing as Jeanette Claybone.

"I suspect there's a delectable, ripe peach-of-a-body underneath that pink gown," Rupert continued. "I've a mind to take a bite."

Rupert licked his lips, and a familiar hungry look deepened in his eyes. In his desperation to keep pace with Henry's own conquests, Rupert had entered the life of a rake with too much relish and too little discretion. Many angry fathers' pockets had been lined as a result, and others injured in duels fighting for their daughters' honor.

"Rupe, leave Miss Claybone alone. There are better sweetmeats to savor."

Rupert lifted his eyebrows. "You're surely not interested, Dray?"

Henry took a gulp of his champagne. "Of course not. Besides, I'm more than accommodated tonight."

"Betty's?"

"No, not a bawdy house. But I must visit Betty's at some point. I hear another of her women have gone missing."

"There are whores aplenty, Dray. Hundreds of women fallen on hard times. Let the runners deal with it."

Women fallen on hard times…

A month ago, he might have agreed with Rupert. But the image of the dead girl had haunted his dreams.

And his conscience. After all, he enjoyed the services women such as her provided, as did his friends. But what of the women themselves? What of their happiness?

What had *she* said? *If a woman fails to succeed, then Heaven help her.*

Out of the corner of his eye, he caught Lady Darlington smiling at him. The diversion of half an hour between Sophia's thighs would restore his spirits.

STRAIGHTENING HIS CRAVAT, Henry closed the study door and blew Sophia a kiss. The noise in the dining room was, thankfully, enough to mask Sophia's shrieks of pleasure as he'd taken her on Lord Darlington's polished mahogany desk. In Henry's eyes he was performing a service to Darlington, and the other husbands he cuckolded. Thanks to his attentions, their wives were content.

And there's nothing so bad as a discontented wife.

Entering the dining hall, he heard Lady Claybone admonishing her husband. If he needed a reminder to avoid the parson's noose, it was right before him, donned in purple silk with an excess of lace adorning its ample bosom.

Discontented mother. She turned her attention to Jeanette, scolding her over the food on her plate. Sir Robert cast a brief look of solidarity to his daughter. A good-hearted man, but ruled by his wife.

That would never happen to Henry.

Lady Darlington arrived, patting her hairstyle.

"Time for a little music" she trilled. Definitely *not* a discontented wife. She took her husband's arm and smiled, her face still flushed from exertion. Beautiful, vibrant, and charming, no wonder Lord Darlington looked at her with slavish devotion.

Half an hour later, Henry sat, bored with the array of insipid sonatas, each one followed by polite applause and the ardent clapping of an adoring mama, the next mama determined to out-clap the last. By the time Lady Claybone pushed Jeanette forward, most of the company had regrouped in the ballroom, while the rest sat in small groups chatting among themselves.

Henry's eyes were closed as Jeanette started to play, but after a few bars, he sat up, recognizing the Scarlatti Sonata. Never before had it stirred such emotion in him. She seemed to express her own melancholy as her fingers ran over the keyboard. When she finished, a few gloved hands rippled in applause. Her chest rose and fell in a sigh.

"That was too gloomy. I told you to play the *Mozart...*"

"I'm not in the mood for Mozart, Mama."

A nearby group of ladies giggled, and Henry shushed them. Jeanette looked up and their eyes met momentarily before she looked away.

Lady Holmestead moved into his sight. Doubtless Louisa wished to compare notes on his prowess with Sophia Darlington when the night was over. Ten minutes later, he found himself returning to Lord Darlington's study, this time to cuckold Lord Holmestead.

21

HELPING LOUISA OFF the desk, Henry jumped at an angry voice outside the door.

"Henry, my husband mustn't catch me here!"

"Hush, darling, they won't come in." He kissed Louisa to silence her retort, and she purred seductively, rubbing her hand across his breeches. He felt a pull in his groin at the memory of the way she'd quivered and moaned as he'd thrust into her.

The door handle rattled, dousing his passion. Of all the places...

Quickly and unceremoniously, he grasped Louisa by the waist, pulled her to the ground, and rolled underneath Darlington's desk, taking her with him.

Just in time. The door swung open, casting a ray of light across the rug. Another couple had come to the same idea as he had. Two pairs of feet appeared, inches away from Henry's nose. He gave Louisa a warning squeeze but she remained still.

"Papa, I don't care!" The woman's voice carried traces of a regional accent.

The man's accent was much stronger. "Jeanie, love, your mama depends on you to elevate our position in society."

"Society can go to hell!"

"Jeanette Frances Claybone, do you want a thrashing?"

"I'm not Jeanette Frances Claybone! I'm Jeanie Smith. We had a good life before. I helped you with the business. I had a purpose."

"You have a purpose now, love."

"To spend my time gossiping with shallow creatures who only care whether they're dressed in the latest fashionable shade of blue or this horrible pink?"

"Your mama is trying to secure a good marriage for you, Jeanette. You should show her—us—more respect."

The woman sighed. "It's not easy. These people don't like us and I don't like them."

"Promise me you'll make an effort at the Holmestead party. Mama worked hard to secure our invitation. Come here, love."

After a moment's silence, Henry heard a rustle of silk and a sigh, and he imagined Sir Robert comforting his daughter. What might it be like to embrace those curves?

"Your mama loves you, Jeanie. She wants you to have the security and comforts she was denied. She lost everything when she fled to England. You can only understand the horrors of poverty if you live it. Your Mama won't admit it, but it's her greatest fear. She'll do anything in her power to ensure you never find yourself destitute."

"Could you ask her not to try so hard, Papa? In turn, I'll promise to try harder."

"There's my girl. Come on, chin up as we say in the ton."

Henry heard a muffled laugh before the door opened and shut.

Louisa twisted her body round and tipped her head up until their lips met. "What about a rematch, Henry darling? Under the desk rather than on it?"

"Another time." Henry helped her to her feet before straightening her lace tuck, his fingers lingering over the dip between her breasts.

"So, they're invited to your house party?"

"William thinks highly of Sir Robert. He may be a commoner, but at least his wife was an aristocrat rather than a doxy."

Henry sighed. "I presume you mean Charlotte Winters."

Louisa gave him a saucy smile. "*Charlotte*, is it? But I suppose given your—patronage—of her, you'd exhibit more familiarity than most. I hear she serviced many men before she snared Sir Daniel."

"That's not fair, Louisa darling. What Charlotte and I did is no different to what you and I are doing."

"Except that I am married, whereas she was paid." Louisa offered her lips to him. "Did she give you as much pleasure as I?"

"Of course not."

Louisa's brown eyes, dark with female satisfaction, smiled at him, but he could not shake the image of a different pair of eyes from his mind: Miss Claybone's—dark green, gazing soulfully across the room, forging an invisible connection between them.

He had no wish to see history repeat itself.

Charlotte Winters had been ruined, reportedly by Viscount De Blanchard, during her first season five years ago. With no other choice, she had entered the life of a courtesan to earn a living. It was only by virtue of her last patron being smitten enough to offer for her hand that she'd been able to restore her position in society. Though being a knight, rather than a baronet, marriage to Sir Daniel was hardly a complete restoration.

If Jeanette Claybone were similarly ruined, she might not be as lucky as Charlotte. At all costs, Rupert must be persuaded to abandon his pursuit of her.

Henry kissed Louisa before leaving the study for the second time that evening.

CHAPTER THREE

"THERE'S NOTHING SO attractive as a virile man astride a powerful piece of horseflesh. I do admire a magnificent beast."

Lady Darlington didn't bother to lower her voice as Henry and his friends rode past. She flashed Henry a smile while walking arm-in-arm with Felicia Long. Felicia at least had the grace to blush before casting Henry a hopeful glance.

Henry spurred his horse into a trot. Rupert and Dominic followed, chuckling. Dear God, it was almost worth finding a wife just to remove himself from the attention of all those desperate, unattached women.

To his annoyance, he caught Miss Claybone's name on Rupert's lips. A fortnight after the Darlington ball, Rupert's intentions had only intensified.

"She's a challenge," Rupert said, "which makes the prize all the sweeter."

Dominic laughed. "Why don't we place a wager on it at White's?"

Rupert nodded. "One hundred guineas say I'll have taken residence between those luscious thighs before the month is out. What say you, Dray?"

"I say you're wasting your time, Rupe," Henry said, irritably. "Even ignoring your difference in station, she's too clever for you. You hardly opened your books at Oxford. You'd have nothing to talk about."

It was an open secret that Rupert's father, the late viscount, had secured his son's third-class degree via a generous donation to modernize the library at Worcester College.

Rupert snorted. "A few love poems will do the trick. I don't expect to spend much time *talking* to her."

Rupert wasn't giving up. Henry needed to change strategy.

"Very well," Henry said, "but if I help you, I expect to profit from it. If you succeed in seducing her, then *you* must pay *me* two hundred guineas."

"Done! I'll secure the spoils by the end of the Holmestead house party."

"That's less than a month away."

Rupert grinned. "I like a challenge."

The two men shook hands. Rupert was an extravagant fool who only managed to stay solvent by virtue of an excellent steward and the Beaumont estate having been placed into trust. After his gaming expenses and money spent on his current mistress, Rupert had little to spare. He'd soon realize the value of keeping his two hundred. Jeanette's virtue was safe.

A scream echoed across the park, followed by a splash. The friends spurred their horses into a canter until they came upon a small crowd on the banks of the Serpentine.

"She's fallen in!"

"Someone help her!"

Rupert dismounted and handed Henry his reins. "Let me through!"

The crowd parted to reveal a sniveling child at the water's edge.

"My top!" he wailed.

A woman emerged from the water's surface, a child's toy in her hand. "I have it!"

"Good God, madam!" Rupert cried. "Are you all right?"

She threw back her head and laughed. Henry would recognize that laugh anywhere.

Miss Claybone stood in the middle of the Serpentine, hair in disarray, water dripping off her gown.

⋙⋘

JEANETTE SPAT WATER from her mouth. *Disgusting!* The child gave her a grin, and she winked back and held out the toy.

The child's nanny, an iron-gray haired woman, snatched the toy from her.

"Come, Thomas."

"We must thank the lady, Miss Brown," the child said.

"You'll do no such thing!"

He gave Jeanette an apologetic smile, and the nanny tugged at his arm.

"Thomas! We don't converse with her sort."

"It's not contagious!" Jeanette yelled at the nanny's retreating back.

Murmurs of admonishment rippled through the onlookers. *Let them rot.*

"All right, ladies. You've had your entertainment. Now leave."

The crowd obeyed the new voice and dispersed, whispering to each other about farm folk tainting the pure waters of London. Hardly pure, the Serpentine was a murky shade of green; mud swirled in the waters around her legs.

The newcomer approached the water's edge and held out his hand. He looked familiar—light blonde hair, pale blue eyes, and a benign smile of friendship, well-dressed in a dark brown coat, cream breeches, and highly polished riding boots.

She took his hand. The skin was warm and smooth; a hand which, unlike Papa's, knew nothing of manual labor.

"What were you thinking, madam?"

"The child dropped his toy in the water and nobody would help him."

"His mama would have given him another one."

"He wanted *that* one. His nanny didn't have the wit to see he was about to jump in after it."

He removed his coat and wrapped it around her shoulders. "We should get you home before you catch a chill."

"Good Lord, Oakville, what are you doing? You'll ruin your coat!"

A deep voice came from behind, its owner sitting astride an enormous black stallion.

Lord Ravenwell.

His fingers curled around the reins. The memory of those hands on her skin sent a shiver through her—strong, dominant hands taking mastery of everything they touched. He stared directly at her, his eyes darkening. How could a man be so *intimidating*? He lifted an eyebrow, then looked away dismissively. Rudely reminded of their difference in rank, she turned back to the man who had come to her aid.

"I think you should leave me, sir, your friend is waiting. I'll have your coat returned if you would give me your name?"

"Rupert, Viscount Oakville." He bowed. "And you are?"

"Jeanette Claybone."

Footsteps clicked along the path. Andrea appeared, dragging her fiancé behind her.

"Jeanie! What on earth are you doing?"

"Miss Claybone," Theodore said, "you look like one of my deckhands after he's walked the plank."

Tall, dark, and unshaven, clad in black and sporting no cravat, Theodore O'Reilly looked every inch the rogue. And he needed to. The seas were rife with ruffians, ships were ambushed, the thirst for riches driving the unscrupulous to piracy. He'd even spoken of women being sold into slavery and spirited across the ocean, never to be seen again.

But looks deceived. Kind, considerate, and utterly devoted to Andrea, when they married, doubtless he'd flout tradition and display an un-aristocratic degree of fidelity toward his wife.

Would Jeanette ever find a man to love *her* as much?

Theodore turned a disapproving eye on Oakville. "Did this fellow push you in?"

"No, Mister O'Reilly," she laughed, "he fished me out."

Rupert bowed to O'Reilly before addressing Jeanette.

"Miss Claybone, may I escort you home?

"There's no need, sir, I have my friends. But let me shake your hand."

He took her hand and kissed it, his warm breath sending a whisper of heat across her skin.

"May I call on you, Miss Claybone?"

She smiled in response, but her body tightened at the notion someone else watched her. Keeping her gaze focused on anything but the man who towered over her sitting astride his powerful horse, she turned her back and set off home with her friends.

CHAPTER FOUR

H ENRY SPOTTED RUPERT at White's the next day.

"Dray! I've lodged my bet. You need to sign the ledger."

Henry lifted a finger to the butler who approached him, bet book in one hand, a glass of brandy in the other. He took the brandy and sat next to his friend.

"You mean to pursue this?"

"You stand to win if I succeed."

The butler opened the book. Three bets had already been lodged that morning. Rumor had it that the Duke of Bowborough had placed a bet of two thousand guineas, that Emilia, Countess of Strathdean, would give her husband an heir by the end of the following year. The cash-strapped duke then tried to bribe several rakes into seducing her.

It was no rumor. Henry himself had been offered one hundred guineas by the duke. Though it would have been the easiest hundred to acquire, he had no desire to seduce on request or father another illegitimate child. Men were supposed to pay the women, not the other way round.

Henry eyed the bet which had been placed before his. Rupert had persuaded Dominic to part with three hundred if he managed to debauch Miss Claybone before the end of the Holmestead house party. *Damn.* Rupert now had financial incentive.

"How do you suggest I start my seduction?" Rupert asked.

"She has a fondness for music and books." Henry smiled at the memory of their conversation at the ball. "...and a talent for mathematics."

Rupert rolled his eyes. "Mathematics? Lord save me."

"You've got *no* chance."

Rupert drained his glass. "Nonsense. I'll wager she already sees me as a something of a savior. Are you sure *you* don't want her?"

"Don't be ridiculous."

The image of Jeanette in the water assaulted Henry's mind, that lush body rising from the water like a nymph. Her gown had clung to her form, exposing every curve; two dark pink nipples had been visible beneath the white muslin. Boldly, she had met his gaze, and he'd looked away to hide the lust in his eyes as he'd listened to every word she had said to Rupert, seemingly thinking nothing of the fact that she'd saved a child's life.

With such a woman in his home, heart, and bed, a man's life would be far from dull. He closed his eyes, relishing the notion. An equal in wit and intelligence, so unlike the fawning society misses; but she was not for him. He could not afford even the slightest risk to his heart.

"She strikes me as a woman whose ideals of morality surpass yours," he said, sipping his drink to hide the lust in his voice. "If I were you, I'd give up."

"Absolutely not," Rupert said. "I'm determined to have her."

Henry's skin itched, and the brandy glass threatened to shatter in his grip. He must ensure Rupert failed.

"MISS CLAYBONE! WHAT a delight to see you looking so well."

Turning her attention from the violinists tuning their instruments, Jeanette looked up from her seat. Oakville stood before her, his mild blue eyes twinkling in the candlelight.

"Lord Oakville! I had no idea you were coming to the concert."

"I adore music, and the countess always procures the best musicians for her soirees. I trust you're recovered from your accident."

"I can't understand why such a fuss was made of it," she said. "The sea's much colder than the Serpentine."

His eyes crinkled into a smile. "Is there anything you're afraid of?"

"Society."

"Society only frightens us when we face it alone, Miss Claybone. You need never be alone if you permitted me to escort you."

"Jeanette…"

A finger dug into her ribs.

Mama.

"Oh, forgive me," Jeanette said. "Mama, this is Viscount Oakville."

"How delightful!" she exclaimed.

"Charmed to meet you, Lady Claybone." Oakville lifted Mama's hand and kissed it. "Might I have the pleasure of your daughter's company at supper?"

"She'd be delighted, wouldn't you, Jeanette?"

He bowed and rejoined his party. A dark-haired man stood at the edge of the room, his back to her. He turned as Oakville approached him.

Lord Ravenwell. He smiled at his friend before he spotted Jeanette, and then his smile disappeared. Even at a distance, contempt exuded from his stance. An uncomfortable heat bloomed in her cheeks. Was there so much in her to be despised? His eyes darkened, the raw power of his gaze rendering her immobile.

A group of ladies approached him, the feathers in their headdresses bobbing with excitement as they vied for his attention. Turning to Felicia Long at his side, his smile returned, though his eyes remained cold and hard.

The Countess of Strathdean's voice carried across the room as she announced the start of the concert. Among the scraping of chairs,

Jeanette resumed her attention on the musicians, forcing herself to refrain from looking behind her where she had an uncomfortable feeling she was being watched.

During the interval, Viscount Oakville approached, brandishing two plates of food.

"I took the liberty of finding you something to eat. I'd recommend the chicken."

"You're most kind."

"Not at all," he said. "I wish to know you better. We have much in common."

"Such as?"

"A love of music. I've heard some of my favorite pieces tonight."

How pleasant to have a fellow admirer of music! Oakville seemed so unlike his friends. His objective was to enjoy the music rather than be seen in society to assert his dominance over everyone in the room.

"Did you prefer the Bach or the Vivaldi?"

"Oh…" he hesitated. "It's difficult to distinguish between them. I like poetry also. Shakespeare's sonnets are a joy to read."

"Which is your favorite?"

"I cannot single one out. The world of literature is a veritable treasure trove, is it not? I'm excessively fond of the written word."

Jeanette took a bite of the chicken. "I prefer music to literature. Music transports you to a world of your own creation. The written word leaves less to the imagination. But with music, the story can begin, and end, in any manner you desire."

Oakville waved a footman over who took their plates. He reached for Jeanette's hand and ran a light finger along her wrist.

"You're not what I expected, Miss Claybone. I'm pleasantly surprised."

"What did you expect?"

"I had no idea, but my friends and I are used to ladies who prefer *not* to dive into the Serpentine on a Sunday afternoon."

As if on cue, a tall shape moved into her eyeline. Ravenwell leaned against the doorframe with an air of arrogance as if the entire party were beneath his notice.

Not the entire party. Only Jeanette. Brow creased into a frown, he glared in her direction, dismissing an approaching footman with a shake of his head.

Jeanette leaned toward her companion. "Tell me, Lord Oakville, what is it that your friend finds to dislike so much?"

"Ravenwell?" Oakville let out a laugh. "He dislikes most things."

Ravenwell's frown deepened. The hand holding his wineglass tensed, knuckles whitening. Rather than display his usual air of contempt, tonight he seemed out of sorts, angry, even. Perhaps he disapproved of her being here.

Why should she be denied the pleasure of music she appreciated and understood better than he?

"Perhaps he dislikes the music."

Oakville snorted. "My friend has no taste in music. He has very—particular—tastes in other things. But they're not for a lady's ears."

"I'm no lady, as I'm sure you've been told."

"Perhaps his poor temper is the result of my attentions to you."

"How so?"

"He disapproves of my courting you."

How dare he! She turned her gaze to Ravenwell to find his eyes still trained on her.

"Of course," Oakville whispered, "while my behavior is influenced, not always to the good, by my friends, I'm capable of making up my own mind."

He lifted her hand to his mouth. Across the room, Ravenwell's lips pursed, his jaw ticking as if he ground his teeth.

Odious man! If the sight of his friend paying her attention sent him into apoplexy, then it served him right.

"I would like to court you, Miss Claybone," Oakville purred. "May

I call on you tomorrow? Now my coat has been cleaned, I'm anxious to wear it again. What better occasion than to take you for a ride in my barouche?"

"I'd be delighted."

He kissed her hand again, holding it against his lips a little longer than socially acceptable. For a brief moment, his eyes displayed a predatory hunger before their mild expression returned.

Though a little unintelligent, he displayed more gallantry than the rest of them. What harm could arise from receiving his attentions? If she must bear the company of a gentleman, Oakville seemed the least abhorrent.

Unlike his friend.

Ravenwell still watched her, his face glowering with anger.

Why did he hate her so much?

⫸⫷

"THERE HE IS, Jeanie, love. I must say, your young man seems a pleasant chap."

Papa stood at the window, the sunlight catching in his hair which was turning gray. He seemed out of sorts, but whenever Jeanette inquired, he assured her he was well.

"He's more than pleasant," Mama said. "For the past fortnight, he's called almost every day with a poem for Jeanette. Is that not the sign of a man in love?"

The door opened.

"Rupert Beaumont, Viscount Oakville," the footman announced with a bow.

"My Lord!" Mama cried. "Jeanette's been eager to see you. It's so pleasant outside, might I suggest a turn in the garden before tea?"

He held out his hand to Jeanette. "It would be my pleasure."

When they entered the rose garden, he reached into his coat pocket.

"I've another poem for you."

"Lord Oakville," she laughed, "I always thought you a rake, but your poems are so tender. The words you write differ from how you express yourself in person."

"I'm a little shy," he said. "I'm not used to courting ladies."

"I can't believe that."

His cheeks flushed. "I'm well acquainted with the opposite sex, but I've not lived a virtuous life."

"Do all young men behave as you do?"

"To maintain my position in society, I must act in a certain manner."

"You indulge in debauchery to keep pace with your friends?"

"When a man is unmarried, he must display a certain type of behavior to be accepted among his circle," Oakville said. "A married man has less expectations of him. Once I've secured a wife, I intend to settle almost permanently at my country seat."

He kissed her hand. "Let us take tea, Miss Claybone."

"Have you secured him yet?"

Jeanette stood to clear the teacups. "No, Mama, we enjoy conversation, that's all."

"What could you find to talk about?" Mama said. "Good heavens, Jeanette, leave those cups alone! We have servants for that."

"Mariette," Papa said, "perhaps Jeanie prefers to keep the details of her conversations with Oakville to herself."

"Nonsense!" Mama exclaimed. "Has he talked of marriage?"

Jeanette picked up a teacup. "He's spoken of how his behavior will change when he has a wife."

"I knew it!"

"Mama, he's a rake."

"Pshah! All men have their diversions, but a wife will always be treated with respect."

"Mariette, my love…"

"No, Robert! Our family's future rests on Jeanette's shoulders. Oakville is attending Lord Holmestead's house party. That would be a fitting occasion to announce a betrothal. I must prepare, it's only two days away."

Mama flew to the door in a rustle of silk and lace.

Papa shut the door behind her. "It would be a good match, Jeanie, love."

"He's agreeable enough, but I don't love him. Why should I marry him?"

"You could fare worse." He gave a conspiratorial wink. "Come on, love, he tolerates your Mama's company, so he possesses a tenacity others lack. He'd be a good match."

"I want to marry for love!"

"Few can afford that luxury."

He drew her into an embrace. The familiar woody aroma of cigars on his waistcoat transported her to happier times before the baronetcy.

"You don't have to do anything you don't want to, love," he whispered, "but consider your choices. Marriage is your only chance of securing a future and a home, your sisters' future as well as your own."

"Oh, Papa!"

"It's not fair, I know. But whatever you do, you'll always have my love."

CHAPTER FIVE

HENRY LOOKED OUT onto the driveway. The clatter of hooves and the excited chatter of the other houseguests made his stomach clench. Not with the usual boredom. Something else.

Fear. An irrational emotion for a woman unworthy of his notice. Not even the prospect of encounters with Louisa among the grounds of her husband's estate could lift his spirits.

Rupert's attempts to keep pace with him and Dominic had often provided source for amusement, tales of debauchery told over port at White's. But this one was different. Miss Claybone might possess a wit most ladies lacked, but her country upbringing rendered her incapable of navigating the waters of society. Waters infested with predators.

Such as himself. And Oakville.

"Ah, there you are, Dray. Splendid day for a hunt!"

The object of his thoughts joined him at the window.

"And here comes my quarry."

A carriage rolled to a standstill, and Sir Robert Claybone stepped out. He seemed to have aged since Henry had last seen him, his hair a little whiter, body stiff as he helped his wife and daughter out of the carriage. Rumors circulated that his business was experiencing financial difficulties; something Henry knew well enough. Only last week, Barnes had reminded him, yet again, of the Ravenwell estate's lack of funds.

Miss Claybone took her father's arm and he gave her hand a gentle squeeze. Henry's heart somersaulted at the tender gesture. He might feel at ease in the sumptuous surroundings of Holmestead Hall compared to the uncomfortable looking pair below. But he lacked one thing money could never buy: the love between a parent and child.

"She's too intelligent to fall for your wiles, Rupe," Henry said. "The odds are against you."

Rupert snorted. "I stacked the deck in my favor. My beloved Clara's last benefactor was a man of tender words. For a few extra trinkets, I was able to procure a number of poems he'd penned."

"You'll need more trinkets to buy Clara's silence."

"Nonsense! You've always said men like us can do what we like. You can hardly admonish me for following your lead."

Henry sighed. He must make more of an effort to prevent Rupert from ruining her.

⟫⟩⟨⟪

THAT AFTERNOON, HENRY left the main party in search of solitude. Or was it because Miss Claybone was nowhere to be seen and his subconscious had willed his body to search for her? The other guests were content to spend the afternoon in idleness—sipping wine, sleeping off their luncheon, or indulging in facile chatter. No wonder a woman of her intelligence saw fit to distance herself from such insipidity.

A familiar laugh came from ahead, and Henry ventured through an arch which led into the walled area of the gardens where neatly trimmed rose bushes lined the perimeter. Miss Claybone stood beside an armillary sphere in the centre of the garden, holding a stick aloft. A small gundog circled her feet, tail wagging excitedly.

"Off you go!" Laughing, she threw the stick across the garden, and the animal raced after it, disappearing into a bush. Not long after, it emerged with its prize and returned, legs bouncing with the tell-tale gait of an untrained puppy. She crouched beside the dog and threw her arms around it.

"You're such a handsome man!"

In the distance, a man whistled, and the dog disappeared. She turned, and Henry found himself a captive to her green gaze.

"What are you doing here?" she asked.

"Wondering whether your notion of beauty is restricted to dogs."

Her instant smile matched the warmth of the sun.

"How would *you* define beauty, Lord Ravenwell?"

"An object must be aesthetically pleasing to be considered beautiful," he said.

She shook her head as if she were a schoolmistress disappointed with her pupil.

"I beg to differ, sir."

He gestured around him. "Take this garden, for instance. Even I can see the roses are lined in a neat row, trimmed to perfection, forming a pattern of perfect symmetry."

"Then you must look closer."

She moved across the path, and he followed her until she stopped by a rose bush and curled her hand round one of the blooms. "This rose illustrates my point."

"I fail to understand your meaning," he said. "It's flawless."

"That's because you're merely looking at it," she said. "You must *see* it."

He moved closer and bent his head to observe the rose more carefully.

"Can you see it now?" she asked. "At first glance, the rose follows society's rules of perfection, but the more you look at it, the features which lend it individuality become more apparent. Take the color. From a distance, it's a pure pink, but on closer observation, the colors vary from petal to petal."

She ran her fingertips across a petal, stopping where the edge of the bloom had dried in the heat and turned brown and frayed. An insect crawled toward her finger but she made no attempt to flick it away.

"You find beauty in flaws, Miss Claybone?"

"It depends on your meaning of a flaw, Lord Ravenwell. What you might see as a blemish, I see as a definition of character. Nature has given this rose the freedom not to be constrained by society's ideals of aesthetics. The marks on the edges are a sign of life. The insect is proof that another creature not bound by the rules of society has found the flower beautiful."

She cocked her head to one side and gazed at him. His chest tightened at the expression in her eyes.

"It's a sad man who cannot find joy in such observation. But society has deemed it to be so, and is likely to continue to dictate on the definition of beauty and worth."

"Then society is wrong."

Her eyes widened at his words, and he plucked the flower and lifted it to inspect it more closely. He closed his eyes, savoring the delicate scent.

Miss Claybone was right. The flaws she possessed—her intelligence, wit, and courage—set her apart. She lacked the air of brittle elegance men of his rank were supposed to outwardly commend. But rather than conform, she embraced and celebrated the traits which rendered her unique among women.

He exhaled and opened his eyes to find her looking directly at him. But, as she had admonished him earlier, it was no casual glance. The intensity of her scrutiny unnerved him. Such insight on society, as expressed in her opinions on an object as ordinary as a flower, rendered him helpless and very much in danger. She possessed the power to look deep inside his soul, to unearth the creature within who yearned to be loved but protected himself with the armor of the aristocracy, the veneer of disdain he used to ensure no woman could touch his heart.

At length, she nodded toward the rose.

"Lord Holmestead would not thank you for destroying the balance of symmetry in his garden," she said.

"Then I must justify my piracy by offering the spoils to one more deserving than I. Here, take it."

He held out the rose, and she reached for the stem. As their hands touched, a jolt of need shot through his fingers. She caught her breath and looked up, meeting his gaze as an invisible lock slid into place, binding them together. He brushed his thumb against her skin, and her nostrils flared. The floral scent intensified as the July heat curled round them. The sounds of the summer—the bees in the air, the wind in the trees—faded into obscurity against the ripple of understanding.

"Miss Claybone..."

She parted her lips which trembled in recognition of the need in his voice. He had only to lean forward and claim her sweet mouth. One kiss and she would be his...

"Jeanette! *Ma fille!*"

The shrill voice broke the spell, and he drew back.

Miss Claybone's lips tightened into a line of exasperation before she smoothed her expression into that of a dutiful daughter.

Muttering an apology, he excused himself. He passed Lady Claybone under the archway, who gave him a sharp look. When she shifted her gaze to her daughter, her eyes narrowed with the predatory hunger of the ambitious Mama.

"Oh, Lord Ravenwell, how delightful!"

"Excuse me, Madam." He issued her a quick bow, then returned to the house.

He should have cursed Lady Claybone for interrupting him. But it was for the best. Captivating though Jeanette might be, the temptation she presented would soon be too great to resist.

He must avoid her for the rest of the house party, and keep Oakville away from her, too. Not many of Henry's acquaintances could come close to deserving the body—or the heart—of Jeanette Claybone.

⟫⟫⟫⧫⟪⟪⟪

JEANETTE SIGHED WITH relief on entering the dining room. None of the guests were up yet, and her only companions were two silent footmen. Helping herself to eggs, she sat at the table and nodded her thanks to the servant who poured her tea. With luck, none of the other guests would join her, and she could slip into the woods and explore the grounds in peace.

The park stretched beyond the walled garden. She had spotted the line of the trees in Papa's carriage during their journey. Ever the farmer, Papa had pointed out the evidence of deer in the park—the distinctive straight line of the foliage in the trees, as if they'd been severed with a scythe. It was no wonder that venison had graced Lord Holmestead's table during dinner.

Eating a forkful of eggs, she smiled to herself. Lady Holmestead had possessed the grace to merely nod and smile last night when Elizabeth De Witt had complimented her on the quality of the Holmestead beef. Jeanette had stifled a laugh and exchanged a smile with Papa, and Ravenwell had immediately engaged in a conversation with his neighbor on his preference for venison, amusement dancing in his eyes.

Ravenwell…

Jeanette's encounter with Ravenwell that previous afternoon had unsettled her, bringing forth unfamiliar sensations not unlike the uncomfortable heat of the summer or the tightening of her corset when her maid laced it up under Mama's instructions to reduce the appearance of curves.

And now Mama's ambition had been heightened. She had battered

Jeanette with questions and demands. In Mama's eyes, the heir to a dukedom was a better prospect for a baronet's daughter than a mere viscount.

The sneers among the men and women of society told Jeanette such a marriage would never take place. She was too far beneath the suitors Mama aspired to. But if Jeanette were to avoid being paraded in front of every bachelor Mama deemed eligible, she must take action. Simply talking to Mama was not enough. Mama merely redoubled her efforts each time Jeanette voiced her protests. Deeds were needed where words had failed.

And now Mama had set her eyes on Ravenwell, a man so far above Jeanette in station that despite the brief flicker of understanding which had occurred between them in the rose garden, he'd deem her unworthy of even becoming his mistress, let alone his wife, or any of the men of his acquaintance.

His mistress...

Her stomach flipped at the notion of intimacy with such a man. During the night, she had been plagued by dreams of him—brilliant blue eyes watching her while her body yielded to his hands. She had reached for the rose during the night, her fingers caressing the stem where he'd held it. How could the briefest of touches have elicited such sensations in her?

Footsteps approached from the hallway, and the footmen's bodies shifted almost imperceptibly, their backs straightening in unison.

Damn—another early riser. Now she would have to engage in facile talk about the weather or the number of birds the gentlemen expected to kill when the season started. With luck, she'd be able to finish her breakfast and excuse herself without seeming impolite before too many guests joined her.

"Good morning, Miss Claybone."

She looked up to see Lord Ravenwell standing in the doorway, the ghost of a smile on his lips.

➤➤➤❮❮❮

HENRY SAT OPPOSITE Miss Claybone and placed a full plate in front of him. Her demeanor changed from that of a woman eating her breakfast with gusto to a hunted animal, her body stiffening in discomfort or even fear. She placed her fork down and reached for her teacup.

"Are you enjoying your eggs, Miss Claybone?"

"Aside from being a little overcooked?"

"Overcooked?"

"Yes," she said. "Lord Holmestead's funds clearly don't permit his steward to employ a French chef. Last night's cut of meat was in need of a little less salt and substantially fewer minutes in the roasting pan."

"Do you think commerce a suitable topic of conversation for the dining room?"

"Ah," she said, sipping her tea. "I forget, I'm in the presence of an individual who lacks a basic understanding of numeracy. Would the excellence of one's meal be a more appropriate topic?"

"You'll find better quality partners willing to engage in an exchange of words with you, certainly."

"Our understanding of quality differs, Lord Ravenwell."

"Perhaps when it comes to society," he said, "but I'll wager our opinions on the quality of a cut of beef, for example, are more aligned than you think."

"Don't you mean venison? Or have you not woken up sufficiently to notice Miss De Witt is not in the room?"

A ripple of mirth bubbled in his chest, threatening to shatter his composure. He lifted his teacup to hide the smile on his lips. A wave of need threaded through him, tempered by discomfort.

How long had it been since he'd laughed? Not the polite titter issued to satisfy the vanities of ladies in the drawing room, but a genuine expression arising from the joy of an exchange of words with a creature in possession of wit and an unfettered love of life?

Before he could respond, their hostess appeared. After engaging in the exchange of bland pleasantries, she sat at the end of the table, her gaze darting between him and Miss Claybone.

"Henry, darling, I see you're indulging yourself early."

Miss Claybone stiffened at Louisa's familiar address.

"Of course, Lady Holmestead," he said. "I have to admit, your chef possesses an unmatched skill when it comes to cooking eggs."

He ignored the coughing opposite him and focused his attention on his breakfast.

Louisa leaned forward. "Miss Claybone, are you well?"

"Yes, thank you." Miss Claybone cleared her throat and glanced up.

"Perhaps you might indulge in another portion, Henry," Louisa continued. "You've always been in possession of a healthy appetite."

"Maybe later."

"Very well," Louisa said, "but I would counsel you to satisfy your hunger." She lowered her voice to the familiar purr of seduction. "After all, you'll need your strength for this afternoon's—exertions."

He looked up at a clatter of porcelain opposite. With a scrape of wood, Miss Claybone rose from her seat.

"Please, excuse me."

"Is the breakfast not to your satisfaction?" Louisa asked.

"I'm merely finding it somewhat of a challenge." Miss Claybone replied. "But it's nothing a dose of fresh air and good company cannot cure."

A challenge, indeed…

But rather than follow the quarry capable of testing the strength of his resolve and his sanity, Henry resumed eating and turned his attention to the easy prey sitting at the head of the table. A promise was a promise, and he would meet Louisa in secret before dinner, as usual. But as he watched the enthusiasm glittering in Louisa's eyes, he found himself, for the first time, unable to share it.

⋙⋘

CREEPING ALONG A corridor to join Louisa, Henry stopped at the sound of piano music. It could only be Miss Claybone.

During the day, her ill temper had returned and she'd spent the afternoon in Rupert's company, casting acidic glances Henry's way. What was Rupert saying to her?

After dodging Miss De Witt's attentions, he'd stumbled upon Miss Claybone in the woods. It had begun to rain. The ladies had run inside shrieking for their maids while the gentlemen grumbled about the lack of sport, the weather having driven the birds undercover. Henry had sought solitude in the woods surrounding the park.

It had seemed as if all creatures, save the ducks in the lake, were terrified of a little water.

Except one. At first, he'd thought his mind was playing tricks; musical laughter accompanied the patter of rain. Through the trees, a white figure danced in slow circles, and Henry had moved closer to get a better view.

She'd flung her arms out and tipped her head up. Her hair clung to her face, water dripping from the ends. But she'd seemed not to care, twirling round, moving faster and faster until Henry's vision blurred. It was a wonder she hadn't lost her balance.

"Wheeeee!"

She'd stopped moving, bosom heaving with exertion, cheeks aglow with the exercise, her gown soaked. Henry had caught his breath at the vision before him, the outline of her breasts, larger than convention might dictate but all the more tempting for it; soft, luscious flesh, made to fill his hands.

A familiar warmth had ignited in his loins, his manhood hardening with hunger.

What an extraordinary, wild woman she was. What would it be like to tame her?

Where had that notion come from? Shaking his head, he'd taken a step back. A twig had snapped underfoot, and she'd stopped moving.

"Who's there!"

He'd inched further back, concealed by the trees.

"Come out, you coward. Show yourself!"

Coward he was, to be caught peeking at a desirable woman like a teenager not yet awakened to the pleasures of the flesh. Shame burning his cheeks, he'd taken off at a sprint.

His valet, the epitome of discretion, had said nothing. He'd merely dressed Henry, promising to return his clothes cleaned and dried.

Jeanette had been less fortunate. At luncheon, she had sat beside her mother, weathering admonishments with a subdued expression on her face while she'd picked at her food and shivered throughout the meal.

The music increased to a crescendo, returning Henry to the present, then stopped with a cacophony of notes.

"Damn these arpeggios!"

Henry had heard the piece before. A Beethoven Sonata, renowned for the first movement, but she was playing the third movement. Few people of his acquaintance would entertain learning such a complex piece.

The music came from a room halfway along the corridor. Henry drew close and pushed the door ajar. Back facing him, body hunched over the keyboard, her fingers flew across the keys. With a flourish, she repeated the final passage, throwing herself forward at the final chord, and shouted for joy.

Instinctively, he drew his hands together in applause. She slammed the lid down and whirled round.

"Who's there?"

He darted away, resolving to steer clear of her. Miss Claybone was a dangerous woman who made him act contrary to his nature.

Better to spend his time bestowing scraps of attention on his admirers than pay heed to a commoner who despised him.

He climbed a flight of stairs to the floor above where the servants slept. He was unlikely to be disturbed there. The guests kept the household occupied with their needs and whims.

"Henry!"

At the end of the corridor, Lady Holmestead's lithe form emerged from the shadows. The thrill of getting caught accelerated and intensified Louisa's pleasure. In five minutes, she'd be purring with satisfaction under the administrations of his expert fingers.

"Louisa, darling." He pulled her to him and crushed her mouth against his own. He'd taught her well, for she knew how to pleasure him. But this meeting would be all about her. Occasionally a gentleman should see to his lady's pleasure first.

His manhood diminished, no longer eager to enjoy the attentions of such easy prey. What was wrong with him?

As if in answer, his mind conjured soft music, the Scarlatti sonata *she* had played at the Darlington ball.

Louisa broke the kiss. "There she goes again. Why can't Miss Claybone spend her time with the other ladies?"

"She needn't trouble us, darling." Silencing her with his lips, he slipped his hand underneath her petticoats, smiling in triumph as a mew of pleasure erupted from her throat.

"Greedy girl."

Footsteps approached, and her body stiffened with fear.

"Henry…"

"Hush!" He pushed her back into the shadows and spun her around so that she, at least, might not be identified by the passer-by.

"Stay still," he whispered. "With luck, they won't see us."

The footsteps slowed and a figure came into view. The sunlight from a nearby window illuminated a face. Dark green eyes widened for an instant before they blinked. The figure took a step back, then turned around and disappeared, footsteps fading into the distance.

He released Louisa from his grip. With the practiced art of a wayward wife, she smoothed her hair and adjusted her skirts. Within moments, apart from the bright expression in her eyes, she looked every part the virtuous hostess.

"That was close. Do you suppose he saw us?"

Henry adjusted his cravat. "Of course not."

Blowing him a kiss, Louisa skipped away, her enthusiasm for life revitalized. Henry waited the usual two minutes before following at a more measured pace.

With luck, Louisa would not discover his deception. *She* had definitely seen them.

>>><<<

THE DINNER CONCLUDED, and Jeanette followed the ladies into the drawing room to take tea while the gentlemen retired to their brandy.

A hand grasped her arm, and she looked up into the dark eyes of Lord Ravenwell.

"Unhand me, sir."

"Not until I have satisfaction."

"You'll never have satisfaction from any encounter with me."

His nostrils flared. "What were you doing in the servants' quarters?"

"Practicing," she said, "whereas you, I believe, were performing."

His lips parted, the only sign of his composure slipping. "I don't know what you mean."

"Perhaps Lady Holmestead could clarify for me."

"I cannot imagine what tales you seek to spin…"

"You must think me a simpleton!" she hissed. "But don't worry. I'll say nothing of your sordid little encounter."

"How can I trust you?"

"You can't. But as you keep reminding me, I lack the qualities of a lady, a thirst for gossip being one of them." She broke off as a sneeze caught her.

"You should see an apothecary. You don't want to catch a chill."

"A waste of money," she replied. "We farm folk are made of sturdy stock."

He lifted his hand to her chin and tipped it up until his lips almost touched hers. His eyes darkened, a spark of desire glittering in their blue depths. The delicate air of spices lingering on his coat deepened into a musky, woody aroma, the scent of raw male power.

"Are we not the same?" he asked.

She snatched her arm from his grip.

"We are not, and never will be, the same."

Before he could reply, she slipped into the drawing room where he couldn't bully her.

Lady Holmestead advanced on her, brandishing a teacup. Her gown was a deep vibrant red, trimmed with jet beads in an intricate pattern; she looked every part the lady of the estate, her tall, slender frame dwarfing Jeanette's unwieldy form. No wonder men such as Lord Ravenwell were attracted to her. The perfect society beauty.

As Jeanette sipped her tea, a housemaid approached her, holding out a piece of paper.

"Begging your pardon, miss, the gentleman bade me give you this."

Jeanette took the note and opened it. The hand was Oakville's.

Dearest Miss Claybone,

Meet me in the rose garden as soon as you read this. I shall be waiting.

Yours devotedly,

R.

What could he want? Though it defied convention and risked scandal, it would keep her safe from being accosted by Ravenwell when the gentlemen joined the ladies. If Ravenwell disapproved of her acquaintance with Oakville, so much the better. And perhaps a scandal was exactly what she needed to put a stop to Mama's scheming. At all costs, she must be spared the lifeless existence of a society wife.

※※※

THOUGH NIGHT HAD fallen, the air was still warm from the heat of the day. Jeanette's footsteps echoed as she crossed the terrace and slipped through the archway leading to the rose garden.

"Miss Claybone." He stepped into the moonlight.

"Viscount Oakville!"

He placed a finger on his lips. "Hush, my darling."

His body cast a shadow which moved toward her. For a moment, he seemed to grow in size, eyes and teeth glittering with a predatory air before he held out his hand.

"Let us take a moonlit walk."

She hesitated. "I don't want to do anything improper."

"But I've been looking forward to this for so long. And I have another poem for you." He pulled her close and lowered his voice. "My darling." He brushed his lips against her skin. "Let us walk for a while."

He led her deeper into the garden. Squeezing her hand, he caressed her wrist with his thumb, slow, gentle movements, a tender gesture so unlike the baser actions she'd expected of a rake. On reaching the perimeter wall, he took her by the shoulders and turned her to face him. He pushed her back against the wall.

"Miss Claybone—Jeanette—you've no idea how much I've wanted to hold you."

"Lord Oakville…"

"Call me Rupert. Let us dispense with formalities."

"Rupert… I don't think we should…"

He silenced her with his lips. She tried to push him away, but he moved his mouth against hers, and his hot, wet tongue pushed insistently against her lips.

He broke the kiss and took her face in his hands, caressing her cheeks with his thumb. Lust darkened his eyes until they were almost black.

"Oh, Jeanette, you want me, too, don't you?"

He kissed her again, and a deep groan reverberated in his chest, the sound of a male overtaken by the need for a female.

Yet, she felt nothing, no rumble of need shook her. Was there something wrong with her? Or did she have to respond in order to find pleasure?

Tentatively, she touched his tongue with hers.

"That's it, my darling," he said. "Let me give you pleasure. To-night, you'll be mine."

What was she doing?

She broke free from the kiss and pushed against him. "I'm sorry, I cannot do this. It's wrong."

"Would you deny a husband?"

"Rupert…"

"What if we were to marry?" He brought his lips close, his hot breath caressing her skin. "I merely wish to sample the goods first. Wouldn't your father inspect livestock before agreeing to a purchase?"

"Marry? I–I don't know."

"But I do. Trust me, this is what courting couples do. We share pleasures. It's how we get to know one another more—*intimately*. You wouldn't deny me another kiss, would you, darling?"

"One more."

"You're an angel!" He fisted a hand in her hair and pulled her head back to expose her throat.

His breath tickled against her neck. "Such beautiful skin." Wet, open-mouthed kisses traced a line down her throat. Soft fingers fumbled at the lace of her gown. He tugged at the material, and a surge of cold air rushed across her breasts.

"Oh, Jeanette…"

"Rupert, we cannot!"

"Yes, we can, my love. Let your pleasure be my gift."

His fingers reached their destination.

"Good grief, you're as dry as a Muscadet down there!"

"What do you mean?"

He chuckled and his eyes hardened. "You really are as innocent as Dray thought."

She clamped her legs together, hampering the movement of his hand.

"Who's Dray?"

"Drayton. Lord Ravenwell."

He moved to kiss her again, but she turned away. "You've discussed me with *him*?"

"It doesn't matter. Tonight, you're mine, and Dray can go to the devil. He'll have his cash, but I'll have you."

A ball of nausea formed in the pit of her stomach.

"Cash?"

"Hush, my love," he said, lifting her skirt higher.

A scream broke through the air. Voices exclaimed, followed by running footsteps.

"Good God! What's going on here?"

CHAPTER SIX

"*L*OOK AT HER!*"
    A small party of onlookers stood beside the archway.

Oakville turned his head, a triumphant smile spreading across his lips.

Jeanette followed the line of his gaze. Lord Ravenwell stood apart from the group. The shadows obscured his face, but his body stood stiff and erect, fists clenched at his sides.

With luck, she had not been recognized. She shrank back into Oakville's shadow, but her stomach clenched at a familiar voice.

"Jeanette! *Ma fille*! Have you given yourself to this man?"

Mama rushed toward them and slapped Oakville on the arm.

"How dare you? You've not even announced your engagement!"

Oakville shook Mama's hand off. "Engagement? Foolish woman! Your daughter was content to spread her legs for me, married or not."

Jeanette's limbs grew weak. He had tricked her.

"Jeanette!" Mama exclaimed. "Tell everyone he's offered for you. Tell them you're engaged!"

What a fool she'd been, thinking him better than his friend. And Mama expected her to shackle herself to him? *Never!*

She shook her head. "Viscount Oakville never offered for my hand. If he did, I'd refuse him."

Elizabeth De Witt's voice cut through the laughter of the onlookers. "Poor Jeanette! To be ruined on your first season. You have my sympathies."

Jeanette pushed a smiling Oakville aside. As she passed the silent man standing in the archway, she looked up at the hated figure who must have planned her ruination. The usual sneer was missing from his expression. He opened his mouth, but before he could speak, Mama yanked her arm and pulled her away.

Jeanette stumbled into her chamber. She turned to face Mama and a sharp slap exploded in her face.

"How dare you! All my hard work destroyed in a moment of debauchery. Jeanette, you've ruined us!"

"Mama..."

"Don't speak to me! You'll remain here in your room tonight. Do not venture out, do you hear me? I won't have you shaming our family further."

"What is to happen to me?"

"Your Papa and I will decide. Get into bed and don't speak to anyone. With luck, we'll be able to repair the damage you've done."

"And if not?"

"Then our whole family is ruined."

THE FOLLOWING MORNING, Jeanette woke from a fitful sleep. Her dreams had been stained with shrill laughter, ladies' faces twisted with hatred, lips drawn back, teeth bared like savage dogs massing into a pack, eager to rip her apart.

A shadow moved under the doorframe and she sat up, rubbing her eyes.

Something had been slipped under the door. A piece of paper folded, with a single word written on the front, penned in Papa's hand.

Jeanette.

Her hands shook as she opened it and read the words.

My dear daughter.

Forgive me for writing in haste, but I trust you understand the neces-
sity. You have given me no choice. I love you dearly, perhaps the most
of all my children for you bear the closest resemblance to me. I beg you
to understand the consequences of your actions but I have to place the
welfare of my entire family first.

Forgive me, Jeanette, but I must think of your Mama and your
sisters. If I act quickly, they may still have a future.

I ask you not to return home. Go to London. I'll send word to our
lawyers to release funds on my behalf for you. George Stockton will
look after you, Jeanie love. He's a good man.

Papa

"Papa!" Desperation rekindled her strength. She paced along the corridor until she reached the room her parents shared and flung the door open.

The room was empty! Her parents had gone.

HENRY STRETCHED HIS limbs, opening his eyes as his valet scratched around his chamber. His head throbbed, the light burning behind his eyelids.

What had he drunk last night?

After compromising Miss Claybone, Rupert had toasted his triumph, then retired to his room.

The bet was won. Henry's pocket, and conscience, would be heavier after today.

None of them had come out well. Rupert had ruined a respectable young woman. She'd been foolish enough to display her ruination in public. And Henry had done nothing to prevent it.

Though she had been a fool, Henry felt nothing but admiration for her refusal to trap Rupert into matrimony. He could have found himself honor-bound to marry her or exposed to a substantial lawsuit. But she had released him of any obligation.

And in doing so, she had destroyed her future.

Henry sighed. Perhaps he should give her his winnings. Not enough for her to make a living, but it would help assuage his guilt. He waved his valet over. Time to dress and inspect the carnage in the breakfast room.

After a disappointingly quiet breakfast, he went in search of Rupert. The lazy profligate sat reclined on a chaise longue in the morning room, one leg hanging casually over the edge, swinging back and forth. Having helped himself to Lord Holmestead's Cognac, he swirled a balloon glass in his hand, the amber liquid forming a thick film which beaded into fat droplets on the side of the glass.

Rupert raised his glass, then drained it in a single gulp. He let out a cough and a splutter of liquid sprayed from his mouth.

Weak-bellied fool. He never could take his liquor. Unlike…

Unlike *her.* Another image danced across his mind, a young woman pouring her fourth glass of punch, giggling as she issued unladylike curses.

She had plenty to curse about now, the cause of which languished before him.

"Celebrating your conquest, Oakville?"

"You've as much cause to celebrate, Dray. After all, you've made a tidy profit. Not bad considering I did all the work."

Henry curled his index finger into his palm, digging the nail in to control the anger threatening to burst.

"As if you'd understand the concept of work!"

Oakville's smile broadened. "Work is for the lower classes, Dray, and they must occasionally be reminded of their station. Haven't you said that yourself? Why shouldn't I follow in the footsteps of the friend I admire?"

Good heavens! Had Rupert lost all sense of morality in his desperation to compete with Henry's own prowess at seduction?

"I never wanted you to publicly ruin her."

Rupert snorted. "Has your pride suffered a dent because I got there first?"

Henry snatched the decanter and poured himself a brandy, the liquid sloshing over his hand. His senses needed dulling before he planted a shiner on Rupert's grinning face. His Oxford blue at boxing might ensure a sound delivery, but he had no wish to provoke Rupert into challenging him to a duel. Holmestead Hall had seen enough scandal.

He took a gulp, the liquid burning his throat. "Don't you understand what a lucky escape you had? Had Miss Claybone supported her mother's claim, you might have found yourself engaged."

"On what grounds?"

"Honor, Rupert. I suggest you consult Dr. Johnson's dictionary to check the meaning of the word."

Rupert fumbled in his pockets and drew out a wad of notes.

"Speaking of honor, your two hundred guineas."

The door slammed behind them.

"You bastards."

Miss Claybone stood beside the door, fury boiling in her eyes.

"I beg your pardon?" Henry said.

Her gaze fell on the notes in Rupert's hand before she lifted her eyes to stare directly at Henry, the gold flecks in the emerald green irises missing, leaving a dark pool of hatred.

"You heard, you bloody *bastards!*" she cried, the force of her anger propelling him backward. "You've ruined me, and you celebrate it by getting drunk!"

Henry shook his head. "Madam, I'm sorry…"

"Don't insult me!" she cried. "Look at you, grasping your profit with your grubby fingers! Was it worth it?"

"Every penny." Rupert leaned back in his seat, the brandy dulling his words.

She strode toward Rupert and pulled off one of her gloves, then drew her hand back and slapped him on the face.

"What in the name of God are you doing?" Rupert slurred.

She placed her hands on her hips and stood before him, eyes wild with rage, a vengeful, mythological goddess from times past.

"I'm calling you out."

Rupert threw his head back and roared, his laughter turning into hiccoughs.

"I'm serious!"

"Very well, Madam," Rupert said, his laughter subsiding, "I accept your challenge. If you stray onto a man's turf, then you must abide by our rules. What say you to the field by the lake at moonrise?"

"Why not? I've nothing better to do tonight."

Rupert's smile broadened. "Being a gentleman, I should offer the challenger the choice of weapon, but women are weak and swords are heavy. I'd suggest pistols."

"So be it."

"Good. Now run along, there's a good girl. I'll await your company tonight with eager anticipation."

"So will I, Viscount Oakville."

She strode out, slamming the door behind her, the force rattling the glasses on the table. Rupert refilled his glass, but before he could raise it to his lips, Henry snatched it out of his hand.

"Now's not the time for drinking!"

"I suppose not. I should practice my aim."

Henry sighed. "Surely you don't intend to go ahead with a duel with a lady?"

"You said yourself she's no lady."

Why did Rupert act so belligerent when drunk?

"Come on, Dray," Rupert laughed, "she won't turn up. I'll wager that while I stand in the field tonight, she'll be lifting her skirts for the next man. Her mama was sniffing round that fop Hugh Chambers at the Darlington ball."

"Who will you name as your second?" Henry asked.

Rupert raised an eyebrow.

"Come on, Oakville! I've no taste for blood sports."

"It's not as if she'll show up."

"We shall see," Henry said. It was a foolish man who underestimated a woman.

※》》》《《《※

A LAYER OF clouds covered the sky in a thin, wet blanket, moisture thickening the air. Though the moon was almost full, it failed to penetrate the landscape, the shapes of the surrounding trees barely visible.

Rupert stood beside Henry, a wooden box in his arms. "How long do we wait?"

"We both know she'll not come."

Rupert snorted. "She nearly came last night, until her mother interrupted us."

"What a pity she didn't," Henry said. "You could compare notes against your other conquests. That is, of course, assuming you've experienced a woman's pleasure."

Rupert lacked the wit to recognize sarcasm. "Perhaps you fancy a turn with her, Dray. Then *we* can compare notes!" He let out a bark of mirth.

It was a poor man who laughed at his own jokes.

"I'm glad you both continue to find this entertaining."

A stream of diffused light picked out the silhouette of a woman.

Henry recovered his wits first. "Miss Claybone. How long have you been there?"

"Long enough."

"You didn't think to reveal yourself? What an unladylike lack of decorum."

She snorted. "Not something *I'm* likely to be concerned about any more."

"Miss Claybone," Henry said. "There's no need to go through with this."

"Isn't there? Why can't *I* fight for my honor if nobody else will?"

"Let her do what she wishes," Rupert said. "I'll enjoy seeing her lose her nerve."

Curse him! Why did he seek to provoke her? Henry took his friend's arm and whispered harshly in his ear. "Be careful, Oakville. She's courageous, desperate, and angry. A dangerous combination in a woman."

Ignoring him, Rupert lifted the lid of the box. A pair of dueling pistols were nestled together among red velvet folds, dark blue-gray metal barrels enveloped in polished wood.

"Miss Claybone, where's your second?"

"What's a second?"

Rupert gestured toward Henry. "Someone to ensure a fair fight and act on your behalf in case of injury. A friend, if you will."

Her smile disappeared. "What makes you suppose I have any?"

Henry's heart twitched at the undertone of despair in her voice. By all accounts, she must be saved from her own reckless behavior.

"Be sensible while you have a chance, Miss Claybone. You could be killed. Return to your chamber, and Oakville and I will return to our port."

"Do you lack the stomach for it, Lord Ravenwell? What should I care what happens to me now? I have nothing left. Nothing!"

He flinched at the final word, issued in a snarl.

"Oakville has behaved badly, but I'm sure he'd be agreeable to some form of recompense."

"You're worse than your friend." She lifted one of the weapons from the box. Her fingers curled around the handle in an inexpert grip.

Henry gestured to the pistol. "Shall I show you what to do?"

"How difficult can it be?" she scoffed. She waved the pistol at Rupert. "Shall we get on with it?"

"Stand with your back to me." Rupert said. "On my friend's count, you walk forward. On the count of ten, we're at liberty to turn and fire. Come on, Dray! I'm anxious to return inside. It's getting deuce cold out here."

Jeanette approached Oakville, issued him a glare, then turned her back on him.

"Ready?" Henry called. "One. Two. Three..."

Henry's voice cut through the night air as Rupert and the woman he'd debauched moved away from each other.

Rupert's lack of patience would be Miss Claybone's salvation. He wouldn't want the bother of dealing with the aftermath of the duel. Even if shots were fired, they were hardly likely to make a hit. Rupert was a rotten shot when drunk, and Miss Claybone could barely hold her pistol up.

"...Ten!"

The two stopped walking. Henry counted several heartbeats, the dull thump pulsing in his ears, before they turned, almost in slow motion, and faced each other, the barrel of each pistol staring the other down. Rupert's expression held a note of drunken contempt, his hand trembling due to the excesses of port. Miss Claybone's arm shook more violently, but her face bore an expression of grim determination, her body as tense as a coiled spring.

Good God, she was going to shoot!

Rupert laughed. "I'm impressed, Miss Claybone. I never thought you'd come this far. Let's call it a day, shall we? You've had your satisfaction, twice, and I've had mine."

"You think me a fool, Viscount Oakville?"

"Come, Madam, time to admit defeat. Lower your weapon and

we'll come to an arrangement."

"An arrangement?"

Unaware of the danger, Rupert continued to taunt her.

"Let's say five hundred? Not bad for a night's work. It might even buy you a husband. I'm sure there are many who wouldn't mind sullied goods."

"Rupert, that's enough!" Henry sprang forward too late. The spring snapped, and a scream of anger tore from her lips.

An explosive crack echoed into the night, accompanied by a flash of light and a puff of smoke. With a cry, she stumbled backward, her arm jerking with the recoil, and the pistol flew out of her hand.

"You bitch!" Rupert roared. "You could have killed me!"

"Rupert! No!"

Too late. A second explosion tore through the night. Rupert's arm twitched only slightly, the movement of a practiced dueler, and Jeanette collapsed onto the ground.

"Bloody hell, Oakville, what were you thinking?"

"Come on, Dray! You really think I'd shoot a woman? I aimed to the side. She's probably just fainted."

Henry approached her crumpled form. She lay on her back, legs twisted beneath her body. Her eyes were closed, face pale. All Henry need do was rouse her, return her to her chamber, furnish her with a stiff brandy, then forget tonight had happened.

Rupert returned his pistol to the box and searched among the grass for the other, grumbling to himself about having to clean the mud from the chamber.

"I'll leave you to deal with her, Dray, while I take these back."

Rupert really was a selfish animal at times.

"Aren't you going to help her?"

"She turned down my offer of compensation, so I consider myself relieved of any obligation. I'm in need of a warm pair of thighs tonight. I wonder if Lady Holmestead is available."

Henry sighed. "Why do you always seek to keep pace with me when it comes to conquests?"

"Well, tonight it's your turn to keep pace with me." Rupert nodded to the woman on the ground. "Time you sought my leavings rather than the other way round." His footsteps squelched underfoot as he retreated to the hall.

Henry crouched beside her. Time to wake her up.

He circled his hand around her arm and felt warm moisture. A dark patch appeared on her forearm, a blurred imprint of his fingers.

"What the devil..."

The stain began to spread, soaking into the pale muslin, dark red liquid glistening in the moonlight.

Christ. She'd been shot.

CHAPTER SEVEN

J EANETTE'S BODY THROBBED, each pulse sending a bolt of fire through her.

She opened her eyes and the light blinded her, a malevolent flame dancing to the beat of her pain. She tried to move, and an inferno of agony burst in her arm.

"Keep still!"

A shape came into view, blurred edges sharpening to reveal an unfamiliar face. Eyes dark with disapproval, lip curled into a sneer, yellowing teeth which reeked of cheap cigars.

A second, deeper, voice spoke. "Does she need more laudanum?"

Jeanette lifted her head and the world tipped sideways.

"My arm…"

"I *said* keep still! I've not finished binding it."

Jeanette lay back. The sooner she complied, the sooner he'd be finished.

The rim of a glass was forced against her lips. Liquid oozed into her mouth and trickled down her throat.

"Foolish woman. If I'd known…"

"Your bedside manner is sadly lacking, Doctor Lucas." The second voice seemed familiar, but the drug muffled her senses.

"I've no time for this, Lord Ravenwell. This woman has disgraced herself publicly with one rake and now languishes in the bed of a second. I've been dragged from my fireside to tend to a harlot who's been involved in illegal dueling…"

"…you've been well paid for your troubles. Now get out."

"With pleasure."

Warm fingers touched her cheek. Shapes circled before her eyes, an amorphous gray mass sharpened into two pinpoints of clear blue.

A voice whispered her name, and the shapes blurred into darkness, pulling her into oblivion.

➤➤➤◄◄◄

THE NEXT TIME she opened her eyes, it was morning. A shaft of sunlight streaked across the room, picking out the facets of a decanter on a nearby table which winked at her.

"Good morning, miss."

A maid, barely out of childhood, red hair peeking from underneath her servant's cap, drew back the curtains and approached the bed.

Small, thin hands helped her to sit, plumping the cushions behind her and easing her back. Her head no longer ached, but a hot flame burned along her right arm when she tried to move it. Her forearm had been bandaged from wrist to elbow.

"Here you are, miss."

The maid held out a tray on which stood a porcelain bowl, a delicate pattern of roses adorning the rim. Next to it was a silver spoon, its ornate, polished handle gleaming. It sat at a perfect right angle to the linen cloth on the tray, as if someone had taken great pains to place it. A senseless exercise in exactitude, yet society's need for such rituals was very likely the reason why the young woman before her was able to find employment and feed her family.

A veil of steam rose from the bowl, smoke-like patterns dancing in the sunlight before dissipating into the air. The aroma of herbs reached Jeanette's nostrils and her stomach growled in recognition as the maid placed the tray on her lap.

"Are you needing any help, miss?"

"No, thank you."

The maid bobbed a curtsey, "M'lady will be along shortly."

Jeanette reached for the spoon and dipped it into the broth.

Chicken, but more sophisticated than the hearty soups Jeanette had enjoyed as a child. She pushed aside the dainty pieces of vegetable floating on the top. The rose pattern stretched to the bottom of the bowl, visible through the clear liquid. Only the best chefs could refine something as simple as a chicken broth almost out of existence.

The door opened to reveal a woman in a purple gown. Lady Holmestead epitomized the qualities of a lady. Her honey-blonde hair had been fashioned into an elegant coil. She outshone Jeanette as a diamond compared to a lump of coal.

"May I come in?"

Jeanette nodded.

"Clear the tray, Mary, then leave us." With a rustle of heavy silk, Lady Holmestead glided across the room.

"You strike me as a very—frank—young woman, Miss Claybone, so I won't prevaricate with niceties." She turned her gaze to Jeanette, and the sunlight caught her eyes, the pupils contracting to tiny pinpoints.

"You must leave here at once."

Lady Holmestead paused, as if waiting. But for what? Did she expect Jeanette to indulge in hysterics?

Or plead for mercy?

"You ask for no explanation."

"Do I need one?"

"The *incident* of the other night has been mentioned in the papers. You compromised yourself and have been in Lord Ravenwell's bed ever since. Mary has packed your belongings and will help you dress. My carriage is at your disposal."

"Thank you." Jeanette said quietly.

A warm hand covered hers, and Lady Holmestead's expression softened.

"Believe me when I say how sorry I am, my dear. Our society is a delicate organism at the best of times, a fickle friend and a formidable enemy. I have my children to think of. What lies beneath the veneer of respectability of any woman must remain hidden. The sin lies not in giving yourself to a man, but in being discovered."

How could she speak so, when she herself had succumbed to temptation with that rake Ravenwell?

Lady Holmestead held her hand up, stopping the protest before it had formed on Jeanette's lips.

"I make no apology for my own behavior, Miss Claybone. A rake is, by definition, accomplished in the art of lovemaking, but the delights he offers are not worth sampling until one is safely married."

"Where is he?"

"Many women ask that question. He left for London two days ago."

"Two days?"

"You've been unconscious for three nights. You took a chill when you *took the air* the other night."

"Will he return?"

"Forgive me, but that's another question countless women have asked."

She took Jeanette's other hand. "You cannot rely on him, child. I'm told he's a generous patron, but he's never kept a mistress long before replacing her with another."

Hot, salty moisture stung Jeanette's eyes and she blinked, the action causing a tear to spill onto her cheek.

Lady Holmestead averted her gaze and sighed. "I'm sorry for your plight, Miss Claybone. As a lady, I cannot openly condone your behavior, but as a woman, I want to be assured of your safety. Do you have somewhere to go?"

"I'll go to London. Papa said he'd write to his solicitor."

"My carriage can take you to Dorking. From there, you should have no trouble picking up a mail coach. I'll give you sufficient funds to complete your journey."

She patted Jeanette's hand before she rose and returned to the door, turning momentarily to look over her shoulder.

"I'm sorry for what happened to you, Miss Claybone. But for the grace of the Almighty, I might have found myself in your position."

A BALL OF nausea curled in Henry's stomach, exacerbated by the rocking motion of the carriage. He drew down the window and inhaled a lungful of air.

Two days. Two blasted days he'd spent searching for Oakville, but the lazy wastrel had disappeared, most likely to languish in the country until the scandal died down.

And now Henry was on his way back to Holmestead Hall, back to face the consequences of Oakville's antics. And so he should; after all, he'd done nothing to prevent Miss Claybone's ruination, or stop the duel.

His stomach lurched at the image of her broken body as he'd picked her up in the field. Her hair had come loose, hanging limply, mirroring that of the dead woman he'd seen in the arms of the Runners in Hyde Park. Oakville, the bloody idiot! It might have been an accident, but he could have killed her. And what had he done? Left the very next morning without a word, not for his friend, or the woman he'd ruined.

And now Miss Claybone had nobody. Louisa, obliging as she was, would not want her at Holmestead Hall for much longer, not now that the newspapers had got wind of the story.

It was up to him, though what he'd do with her, he didn't know.

With luck, he'd eventually be able to persuade Oakville to offer for her. Rupert would protest, of course, but in time, he might grow to appreciate her worth, that spirited intelligence, the barely-concealed passion, those ripe, round curves, just fashioned for a man to worship.

No cold-blooded society lady was she. Love might be the destroyer of all reason, but imagine what it would be like to be loved by one such as her; to experience that wild abandon in his bed...

Henry's body tightened with a jolt, and he leaned forward to ease the ache in his groin as his manhood surged insistently against his breeches.

Voices called outside, and the carriage drew to a halt. What the devil was the driver playing at? They could only be halfway there, at most. He leaned out of the window and caught sight of the lone figure of a woman sitting on a trunk, shivering under a cloak.

So, Louisa had turned her out. Henry couldn't blame her. Most ladies would have evicted her immediately. He opened the door.

"Get in."

She looked up, fire swirling in the depths of her eyes.

"What are *you* doing here?"

He opened the door wider. "I *said*, get in."

She shook her head. "Leave me alone. Haven't you done enough?"

"You have no choice. Your reputation is in tatters and nobody of any consequence wants anything to do with you." A stab of guilt needled at him as pain flickered across her expression.

"I refuse to tarnish my reputation further by getting into a carriage with you," she said. "I'm going to London, and you're travelling in the wrong direction." She held up a purse. "I've money for my passage and a friend awaiting me. So you're wrong, Lord Ravenwell. Some people are kind enough to admit me. In my mind, if not yours, that gives them consequence."

"Of all the stubborn..." He climbed out of the carriage. "You'd do well to keep your money. Be a good girl and stand up so my man can

71

take your trunk."

"No." she said. "Are all men half-witted brutes, or just you and your friend?"

He pulled her to her feet and she pitched forward with a cry.

"Miss Claybone, are you all right?"

She opened her mouth but no words came, only an airless gasp. She stumbled against him, her body going limp. He wrapped his arms around her, and she gave a soft sigh. Leaning forward, he caught the scent of lavender, and he pressed his lips against her forehead.

"Hush, you're safe now."

He clung to her, savoring the moment of holding this extraordinary woman in his arms.

The driver coughed and broke the spell. Issuing orders to the footman to take her trunk, Henry lifted her up and climbed into the carriage.

CHAPTER EIGHT

ONCE AGAIN JEANETTE found herself in a strange bed. An embroidered canopy hung over her head, suspended from carved wooden pillars. The chamber walls and door consisted of wood paneling. Its rich brown hue was the same as the bedposts, darker and more exotic than the pale oak of her trunk placed near a dressing table. Tall windows stretched from floor to ceiling. Thick, dark red curtains had been partially drawn back to let in the light.

By the window stood a marble figure of a woman, her decadent curves polished into shiny smoothness. One arm barely covered her breasts and a soft mound peeked invitingly over her elbow. A drape fell across her stomach, held by her fingertips. The merest movement and it would fall to expose her nudity. Her sightless, marble eyes bore a soft expression of satisfaction.

A goddess of love, it was the face of a woman who had known limitless pleasures. Jeanette's breath caught in her throat.

A ray of sunlight flickered through the window, a halo, bathing the goddess. Her mouth curled into a secret smile and her eyes seemed to look right at Jeanette. Sightless they may be, but they understood her.

The entire chamber reeked of decadence, an earthy masculine aroma clinging to the air as if the very fabric of the room had been soaked in a fog of passion.

She drew back the coverlet. Someone had replaced her gown with a nightshift. The silky fabric rippled as she moved. The front was cut low enough to reveal the dip between her breasts, the lace trim designed to defy rather than promote modesty. The gown of a harlot.

Had she ended up in a bawdy house?

She swung her legs over the side of the bed and padded to the door.

Opening it, she almost collided into a man standing outside. Though he wore a footman's uniform, his head was bare, hair growing in unruly tufts, defying the rules of convention. He bore the same air as his surroundings.

"Ah, you're awake." He spoke matter-of-factly, as if the sight of a barely-clad woman was a daily occurrence.

It probably was.

"Can you tell me where I am?"

He coughed, an odd, high-pitched little sound. "The master's townhouse. His *second* townhouse."

His tongue slithered around the word, laden with implication. Not a main residence, but a house suited for the pleasures of the flesh. The wealthier men of London set up separate residencies where they could house their mistresses or indulge in more specialized pleasures.

"Where is your—your master?"

"He's left for the day."

"And you are?"

"Sanderson. At your service." He bowed. "Would you like to take tea?"

How very proper! She may be ruined, but society's rituals must always be observed.

Interpreting her silence as assent, he bowed. "I'll let you dress, then show you to the morning room."

JEANETTE LOOKED OUT of the window onto the street below. Her world might have inverted but outside the passers-by conducted their business as if nothing had happened. Couples walked together on the pavement, traders wheeled their carts, shouting their wares. Sanderson had told her they were in Holborn, within walking distance of Papa's lawyers. She dropped a sugar cube into the tea, the brown liquid engulfing the white crystalline shape, dissolving its edges until it no longer existed.

Harsh, female tones echoed outside the morning room door, together with Sanderson's distinctive little cough. The door opened, and a woman walked in; Elizabeth De Witt, dressed in a silk overcoat of a bright poisonous green, her sharp, close-set eyes narrowing into slits. She sat on the chair furthest from Jeanette.

"Fetch me some tea."

Sanderson rolled his eyes and poured her a cup.

"Are you incapable of helping yourself?"

Sanderson's hand shook at Jeanette's words, the crease of a smile playing on his lips before he smoothed his expression and passed the cup to Elizabeth.

"Leave us." The woman waved a dismissive hand at him and waited for the door to close before she focused her spiteful gaze on Jeanette.

"We all wondered where you were," she said. "Out of concern, of course."

Jeanette drained her cup. "I doubt that."

"For your sake, I came to warn you. Henry won't hesitate to discard you once he's had his fill. Is he here now?"

"No."

"It's as I feared." The concern in her voice contrasted with the satisfaction in her eyes.

"If you want him, you're welcome to him," Jeanette said.

"If that's the case, Miss Smith—forgive me—*Claybone*..." Lady Elizabeth's eyes widened in mock innocence "...I wonder at your willingness to remain in London. For the publicity perhaps?"

She drew out a piece of paper, unfolded it, and handed it to Jeanette.

Someone had sketched a parody of a woman. Plump curves had been emphasized, accentuating the thighs and chest. The feet had been replaced by hooves to compliment the tail sprouting from the skirt. Her facial features had been exaggerated, the nose replaced by the bulbous features of a Hereford cow and the mouth magnified with buck teeth poking out from the upper lip. A caption completed the picture.

The Holmestead Heifer.

Beneath the drawing, words nestled into an ugly mass, the letters pulsating on the page as if they, too, laughed at her.

…or the Holmestead Harlot? It has come to the attention of the writer that an incident of some concern has taken place at Holmestead Hall, the seat of Lord William Honeychurch. A Miss C has fallen to temptation though no announcement will be forthcoming. The unfortunate gentleman suffered no ill effects from the escapade, and the writer has it on good authority that he has sought comfort in the arms of the celebrated courtesan, Miss W…

Jeanette crumpled the paper, wanting to crush the words into oblivion. A nasal voice broke through her thoughts, triumph seeping from every word.

"As a friend, I'd suggest you leave London at the earliest opportunity. I'll wager Henry is waiting for you to go before he returns home."

As a friend, indeed! With a rustle of stiff silk, Lady Elizabeth stood. She raised an expectant eyebrow, but Jeanette remained sitting. Decorum be damned. She wasn't going to bestow any civility on someone undeserving of it.

Elizabeth exhaled through her nose. "I pity your education, Miss Claybone, for failing to bestow an understanding of how to behave when a *lady* takes her leave."

"My education has at least enabled me to understand what a lady is."

Confusion clouded Elizabeth's eyes, and she shook her head as if to dissipate her stupidity. She turned her back and swept out of the room. Shortly afterward, Sanderson reappeared, but Jeanette waved him away. More tea wouldn't alleviate her predicament. Elizabeth De Witt was right; Ravenwell wouldn't hesitate to turn her out. Jeanette might have lost her reputation, but she still had her dignity. She must leave before he ejected her.

⟫⟫⟫⟪⟪⟪

THE SOLID BLACK door stood like a barrier shutting her out of society. Jeanette traced the names etched into the brass nameplate, her fingerprints leaving a stain as ugly as her reputation.

Allardice, Allardice, and Stockton.

She pushed the door and stepped inside. The last time she'd come here she'd been a hopeful young girl entering womanhood, accompanying Papa on a business trip. Uncle George had lifted her onto his knee and patted her head affectionately while he talked with Papa.

Papa. His last words formed an imprint in her mind.

George Stockton will look after you, Jeanie love. He's a good man.

Would she ever see Papa again?

Sunlight filtered through the window in the roof, casting sharp shadows across the walls from the chandelier, the occasional burst of color diffracting through the crystal.

"Ahem."

A single word, but the contempt echoed thickly across the hall. A clerk, dressed in black, approached her as a crow might circle carrion.

Her reputation had preceded her.

"Do you have an appointment, *miss?*"

"Please tell Mr. Stockton he has a visitor."

The clerk's face twisted into a sneer. "And you are?"

"Miss Claybone."

"There are no appointments for a—*Miss Claybone.*"

"Would you be so kind as to tell Mr. Stockton I'm here?"

"That won't be necessary. Let me escort you out."

"But…"

He took her arm, and she suppressed a cry at the sting of pain from the bullet wound.

"Tell him the Holmestead Harlot wishes to see him!"

"Really! I must protest…"

A soft, deep voice interrupted the clerk. "Unhand the lady, Wilkes."

"Lady, indeed!"

"That's enough! Return to your office. I'll deal with this."

"But Messrs. Allardice…"

"…need not be troubled. Miss Claybone is *my* client."

The newcomer stood halfway up the staircase. He gestured to Jeanette. "Come with me."

Freeing herself from the clerk's grip, she followed the man. His cane tapped against the marble stairs, the echo changing as it met the wooden floor of the corridor on the top floor. He stopped beside a half open door.

"In here."

He gestured toward a chair in front of a desk. Instead of sitting behind the desk, he chose the chair beside her and took her hand. Only then did she look into his eyes.

Her godfather had changed over the years. The smooth skin was now puckered and wrinkled, the shock of blond hair a pale gray, but the kindness in his mahogany eyes was as she remembered.

"What on earth have you been doing, my dear?"

Having withstood derision and ridicule, these few words of kindness were her undoing. Hot, fat tears spilled onto her cheeks. She reached up to wipe them away, and he took her hands and gave them a gentle squeeze.

"Jeanette…"

"Mr. Stockton…"

Tutting, he shook his head. "You know me better than that."

"Uncle George."

His cane clattered to the floor as he pulled her into an embrace. Unable to stifle the sobs, she cried into his waistcoat while he stroked her head as if she were a child again until she grew quiet, comforted by the aroma of parchment and cologne.

"I was so worried, Jeanette! I'd expected you sooner."

"But the clerk…"

"Never mind Wilkes. Your father wrote to me three days ago."

Shame heated her face, and he gave her another squeeze.

"We shan't discuss the past. Let us look to your future."

"Do I have one?"

"Not what you'd originally hoped for, but your papa's done his best to help. He's settled a sum of one thousand on you. Not much, but it should secure a husband."

"A husband?"

"We must wait until the scandal dies down, but I can make inquiries once the season is over and London is less hungry for gossip."

"I've no wish for a husband. Can't you find me employment? I could help you with your ledgers."

"I'm afraid that's out of the question."

"Because I'm a woman?"

"Partly, but the other partners wouldn't permit it. You saw how Wilkes treated you."

"A governess, then?"

"Could you see yourself in such a position?" He tipped her face up until their eyes met, his glistening with compassion.

"A governess is nothing. She's too far above the servants yet beneath the members of the household, subject to the constraints of the upper classes with none of the freedom of the lower. You'd be miserable."

"Are there no other professions?"

"There's only one profession for a ruined woman, and it would break my heart to see you enter into it. Marriage is your only choice. It'll secure you a home, children of your own. A man willing to take you for one thousand with the history of scandal would be a good man."

"Does such a man exist?"

"Of course. Not all men are like…" He sighed. "Never mind, we shan't speak of him. Many young men in trade, eager to prosper, would appreciate a little financial support and an intelligent helpmate. But your chances of a match with a gentleman are limited."

"From what I've experienced, Uncle George, I've no wish to marry a gentleman."

He nodded and placed a fatherly kiss on her head.

"I'll secure lodgings for you in the interim, and when society has turned its ugly attention toward another poor soul, we'll plan for your future. Where are you staying?"

Jeanette shook her head. At all costs, he mustn't know she'd been residing in a rake's love nest.

"No matter. I made inquiries as soon as I heard from your father."

"Is he well? And Mama, my sisters?"

"Aye, they're well, but do not write to them."

"Why not?"

"Your father bestowed the money on one condition. No contact until you are respectably married."

Papa…

He'd disowned her. But had she expected better news, that she'd find him in Uncle George's office, waiting to take her in his arms and tell her to come home?

No. She was alone in the world with nothing but one thousand pounds and a ruined woman's reputation. What did society care that her virtue was intact?

"I'm sorry, Jeanette."

"It's not your fault."

"I know, but it breaks my heart to be the one to tell you."

Jeanette nodded, the action releasing another droplet which rolled down her face.

Uncle George drew her to him again.

"Your father would want me to take care of you," he whispered.

His heartbeat echoed against her ear, the deep, slow pulse of the lifeblood of her only friend in the world.

The pulse quickened, an echo growing louder. No, not an echo. It came from outside, together with voices; one, loud and authoritative, overpowering the other.

Quick, angry footsteps approached and the door flew open.

"What in God's name are you doing here, woman?"

Ravenwell stood in the doorframe, hair unkempt, jaw squared, eyes dark with rage.

"You should be in your bedchamber!"

A squat, balding man stood behind him, back hunched in servitude, his voice an obsequious nasal whine.

"Lord Ravenwell, I must apologize…"

Ravenwell raised his hand. Abruptly, the man bowed and stepped back.

Uncle George stood, facing the marquis as an equal, even though the younger man towered over him.

"I believe it's customary for visitors to knock."

The balding man cringed. "Stockton, don't you know to whom

you're addressing such discourteous remarks?"

"I'm addressing someone who entered my office unannounced, Mr. Allardice."

Allardice turned his attention to Ravenwell.

"Forgive my partner's lack of civility, my Lord. Rest assured, I'll admonish him."

Ravenwell snorted. His disdain for those who made a living from trade exuded from him in a cloud of contempt.

Hateful man! Though she shared Ravenwell's dislike of the toad-like Allardice, Jeanette could not forgive his dismissive manner toward others purely because of their birth.

"No matter, Mr...."

"Allardice, my lord, at your service."

"Mr. Allardice." Ravenwell nodded to Jeanette. "But she must come with me now."

"I must protest." Uncle George placed himself in front of Jeanette as if to shield her from Ravenwell's formidable gaze. "My goddaughter is under my protection. Her already fragile reputation will be ruined irrevocably by an association with you. Do you want that on your conscience?"

"Mr. Stockton!" Allardice exclaimed. "That's precisely why you must turn her out. We're a respectable business, and our clients value our discretion. If you defy me, I'll have to call a meeting of the partners to discuss your future."

Uncle George bristled with anger. How Jeanette loved him at that moment! To stand up to a marquis, a bully who'd led a privileged and pampered life, whom nobody dared speak against. What a contrast to the simpering Mr. Allardice. But she couldn't allow Uncle George to suffer for her folly.

She kissed her godfather's hand.

"No, Uncle George," she said softly, keeping her eyes on Raven-well. "I love you for defending me, but I cannot let you harm your livelihood by an association with me. You have your family to consider."

"You're like a daughter to me, Jeanette. How do you know this man won't harm you?"

"I don't, but I have no choice."

Ravenwell's eyes hardened at her words. "Then do as I say, madam. Go to my carriage and wait there while I speak with Mr. Stockton." He gestured behind him. "Allardice, please escort Miss Claybone out."

"Of course, Lord Ravenwell, sir. I must say what a pleasure it is to be of service…"

"Yes, yes," Ravenwell sighed irritably before stepping aside to let Jeanette through.

The last thing she heard was Uncle George's words as she was led out of the office.

"Take care, my dear."

CHAPTER NINE

H ENRY APPROACHED THE carriage. The unsavory Allardice had
done as he'd asked, for Miss Claybone was sitting inside. Henry
sat beside her, and she immediately moved to the opposite seat and
turned her head to stare out the window. Though she appeared calm,
her hands were curled into fists.

Good. Her spirit still remained, that flame which had first drawn
him to her.

His anger subsided now he was assured of her safety. Having returned to his Holborn townhouse to find her gone, he'd been
consumed by panic. Another prostitute's body had been found, the
wounds on her neck suggesting foul play. Two more had disappeared.
Sanderson had told him of a tradesman's daughter who'd gone for an
evening stroll on the banks of the Thames and never returned home;
tales exchanged over sour ale in the taverns of London's underbelly.
Visions of Jeanette's lifeless form floating on the water had crushed the
air from his lungs while he'd stared at her empty chamber before
admonishing Sanderson for not keeping her contained.

From their first encounter, she had captivated him. Her artless
manners, the natural laugh borne from a life of love, freedom, and
laughter—a life he'd never experienced—had drawn him to her as a
ship to a lighthouse.

Would she ever laugh again?

He sat back and closed his eyes. In a few moments they'd reach his townhouse and battle would recommence. Until then, he could relax knowing, she was safe.

At least Stockton recognized her worth. In better circumstances, Henry might have taken pleasure entering into business with him. Few men had the courage to stand up to him, but George Stockton, a mere trader, had done just that, a man of principle, fervent in his defense of Jeanette. Stockton's love for his goddaughter shone through every word he'd uttered as he'd demanded she be treated well.

The carriage drew to a halt, and Henry offered his hand to Jeanette. Sighing, she took it. Ignoring the surge in his body, he helped her out. She snatched her hand away as soon as her feet touched the ground.

"Am I to be your prisoner?"

"Come inside and we'll discuss it."

She snorted, turned her back on him, and strode toward the door. It swung inside to reveal a shamefaced Sanderson. Pushing past the servant, she strode inside and flung open the door to the morning room.

"I'd thank you, madam, to show more respect in my home."

"Respect!" she scoffed. "I've no wish to be here!"

"I don't care," he replied. "You can't wander about on your own. You're still recovering from your wound…"

"…which your friend inflicted."

"For heaven's sake, woman!" he roared. "Have you no sense?"

She opened her mouth to respond, but he stepped toward her, forcing her back against the wall. He gripped her chin and tipped her head up until their eyes met.

"It's immaterial how you came to be injured. What matters is that you need to recover. Walking the streets is bad for your health, not to mention your reputation."

"My reputation! You've already destroyed that. You and your friend conspired to ruin me, then tossed me aside."

Moisture glistened in her eyes, and she wiped it with an angry hand.

"My family has disowned me. I have nothing, no means of earning a living. I'll forever be known as the Holmestead Harlot, to be parodied and ridiculed in the papers. You are to be congratulated on your handiwork."

Henry gritted his teeth. Who had shown her the newspapers?

"You're overreacting."

"How would you know? You live life with no thought for how it affects the lives of others. The women you seek to seduce? Do you know what happens after they're discarded?"

Visions of the whore flashed across his mind, her corpse face down in the river.

"Yes, I do."

"You know nothing!" Miss Claybone raised a fist. Were it not for his boxing training, he might have missed the move which was driven by anger rather than skill. He parried the blow just before her fist connected with his jaw.

"Damn you!" she cried. "Damn you and all your like!"

She raised her other fist. He caught her wrist and pushed his body against hers. She struggled, but he pinned her to the wall.

"Let me go!"

"Only when you cease prattling and listen to reason."

"I shall not…"

He crushed his mouth against hers. Curse the woman, there was no other method of silencing her.

He'd gone beyond the point of no return. The urgent need simmering inside his body burst forth, and he thrust his tongue into her mouth. Good God, she tasted so sweet! Like a courtesan, rich honey with a hint of fire and an undercurrent of innocence.

She circled his tongue with her own, but he was knowledgeable enough in the ways of women to know the difference between an innocent and a woman learned in the arts of seduction.

Now that Oakville had taken her maidenhead, she had little to recommend her. Despite Stockton's assurances, no man in possession of his wits would take her for one thousand. Her best option was as a courtesan but, unlike Charlotte, she knew nothing of seduction.

His blood warmed at the notion of teaching her, and he pulled her head back to expose her throat, moving his mouth from her lips to forge a trail of open-mouthed kisses toward her collarbone.

A groan escaped her lips, a sign of her hunger for him, and his own body tightened in recognition.

Ye Gods—no wonder Oakville had not been able to resist her!

He lifted his head and met her gaze. Her eyes were filled with need, face flushed with desire.

"Miss Claybone," he whispered, "I must stop while I still can."

⇶⫷

HER BODY HAD come to life the moment he'd kissed her. Rather than battle against the arms holding her, she drew strength from Ravenwell. Unlike the men of society who assumed supremacy over the souls within their influence, he had given her a choice—and in doing so, surrendered the power to her.

In a small morning room, tucked away behind closed doors, the world shifted around her. The grief which had sprouted from the seed of her ruination nurtured a bud of hope. She might be able to seek comfort in the arms of another, to forget the consequences which had been thrust upon her. If only for a moment, she might find solace in the act of passion which the outside world already assumed she had indulged in. Not only did he yield to her, but she faced the choice of submitting to him. The prospect of this mutual act appealed to her in every way.

In a world where few women were granted such a thing, it was the greatest gift he could offer her.

Sealing her fate, she nodded and pressed her lips against his. He recognized it for what it was. Capable hands clawed at the hem of her gown, and suppressing a whimper at his touch, she shifted her legs apart.

He thrust eagerly into her, and she cried out at the sharp sting. His breathing hitched and he stopped moving, as if to withdraw, but she curled her fingers round his arms and parted her legs further, encouraging him to keep going.

He withdrew slowly, then plunged into her again. His breathing grew more ragged with each thrust, then he let out a cry and pulled her close, his hot breath in her ear.

Her legs eventually gave way, and she sank to the floor in wonder and bewilderment. What had she done! Was this the lovemaking women gossiped about? How could a man show affection for a woman with such an act?

The source of her initial pain became apparent as she spotted a patch of blood between her thighs.

"Shit!" Ravenwell muttered.

The tips of his boots appeared in front of her. Unwilling to face him, she closed her eyes.

"Why didn't you tell me?" he said.

"Tell you what?"

"That you are—*were*—a virgin? Foolish girl!" He raked a hand through his hair. "Do you realize what you've done? I've been wasting my time trying to persuade Oakville to stand by you, thinking the worst of my friend, yet he left you untouched!"

She bit her lip to stop it from trembling.

"Have you nothing to say? Don't you understand you've just thrown away your virtue? Christ, woman, I gave you a chance!"

She tried to look away, but he gripped her chin and she winced. He relaxed his hold and coaxed her with gentle pressure to look at him.

"Jeanette," he said quietly, "tell me why."

"I had nothing left to lose," she whispered. "They say a fallen woman suffers a lifetime of regret in exchange for a moment's pleasure. I have endured all the pain and censure associated with the act of—of love. Why should I deny myself the pleasure?" Her eyes misted at the memory of him inside her, which still burned between her thighs. "But there was little pleasure. Why would a woman risk her reputation for an act which hurts so much?"

"It doesn't always hurt," he sighed, "except perhaps the first time."

"Don't you know for certain?"

"No, Miss Claybone. I've never—enjoyed—the body of a maiden. I'm not in the habit of taking women who don't understand the rules."

He moved to the door and called for Sanderson, who arrived suspiciously fast, his face reddening as he met Jeanette's gaze, the first sign of discomfort in the stoic servant who'd not turned a hair at the sight of her scantily-clad form only that morning.

"Sanderson, return Miss Claybone to her chamber. Make sure she stays there."

"Yes, my lord."

Jeanette straightened. "You intend to incarcerate me?"

"No," Lord Ravenwell sighed. "I intend to marry you."

She scrambled to her feet. "No, you can't! I want my freedom!"

He took her shoulders, his grip sending a pulse of pain through her wounded arm.

"You fool! You think a woman can be free? You have two choices. Find a husband to restore what little respectability you still possess, or sell yourself on the streets where goodness knows what dangers may befall you. With the first choice, you'd be ruled by the man who owns you. But it's a better prospect than the alternative where you'd be subjected to the laws of the beast. You wouldn't survive."

She struggled to step back, but he was too strong.

"You can't force me to marry you," she said. "You can drag me to the altar, but you cannot speak the vows for me."

His lip curled into a grim smile. "I wouldn't be too sure of that."

"You're despicable!" she cried, "worse than your friend. You masterminded my ruination, placing a wager on it as if I were a horse. You should have left me to die in that field! I hate the ton and everything it stands for, but I hate you most of all!"

"I see no point in continuing this conversation until you're disposed to listen to reason. Until then, you're not to leave this house."

"You can't make me stay."

"Madam, with your behavior, you've relinquished all rights to be treated like a rational adult," he said. "Sanderson, take her to her chamber." His eyes darkened with menace. "Use force if necessary. My pistol is at your disposal."

Defeated, Jeanette let the servant usher her upstairs and into the chamber with its decadent furnishings and odor of debauchery. She sank onto the bed as a key turned in the lock. The statue stared at her, the smile lending an air of malevolence to the room. Shadows fell across the statue's face, giving the eyes a dark gray hue.

Eyes as soulless as the man who held her prisoner.

CHAPTER TEN

HENRY CLIMBED INTO the carriage and slammed the door.

What had he done? He'd lost control of his body, and his senses had promptly followed. What on earth had possessed him to offer for her? Imagine the ridicule he'd earn from his friends, Oakville for a start, not to mention the censure from Grandmamma. Her strict morals and codes of decency and proprietary would be offended.

To say nothing of the danger he might subject Miss Claybone to if he continued to investigate the abductions and murders. True, Sanderson was the one who prowled the streets at night, but Sanderson was *his* servant. Those involved in the ruthless and lucrative business of slavery wouldn't hesitate to stop anyone in their path be it Sanderson, Henry himself, or anyone associated with him. Such as a wife.

He could always renege on his offer. Who would believe her if she claimed foul play, pleading abandonment with those soulful, passionate eyes?

His manhood surged in his breeches, either from the aftershocks of his explosive climax or in its eagerness to be buried once more inside her heat.

He took a deep breath as the carriage drew to a halt outside White's. A few hours in male company plus a stiff brandy would ease the stiffness elsewhere.

He wouldn't be in this predicament if it hadn't been for Oakville.

Neither would he have experienced such pleasure.

Was it because she'd been a virgin? No, it had been something else, her artless, natural invitation, her body's awakening to pleasure under *his* hands.

Her angry little face overtook him, their duel of words almost as exciting as the duel of their bodies. She could master him with words, but with his superior experience, he'd always emerge victorious. He would win his campaign by weakening her defenses. Starting with her godfather.

"Are you getting out, sir?"

"No." Henry gestured to the driver. "Take me to the offices of Allardice, Allardice, and Stockton."

⋙⋘

"AH, DRAY, HOW pleasant! Do join me."

Entering the drawing room at White's later that afternoon, Henry gritted his teeth to stem the tide of anger. The prodigal had returned at last.

Oakville stubbed his cigar out on the tray and deposited his empty glass next to it.

"Fetch me another."

"Don't you think you've had enough?" Ravenwell asked.

"I've only had two."

Two brandies and already inebriated. Had Oakville's weapon of choice been liquor rather than pistols, Miss Claybone would have won hands down. She'd drink him under the table.

"I've been looking for you, Oakville."

"Now you've found me."

"Too bloody late."

The footman reappeared with two glasses. Rupert reached for his. "Don't tell me, she's disappeared, married, or fallen into the Serpentine to join the other prostitutes."

Drink never improved a man, but with Rupert, the effect was more savage.

"It's no laughing matter."

A spark of fear ignited in Rupert's eyes, albeit dulled by the brandy. "Is she hurt?"

"You shot her, Oakville. But she's recovering. She's with me."

"*With* you?"

"I've offered her marriage."

Rupert gave an explosive snort. "Don't tell me you shagged her."

"*You* never did."

"She told you that?"

Henry sighed, swirling the brandy round his glass. In this very same spot he'd done the same, perhaps with this very same glass, just before he'd signed that ridiculous bet.

"I discovered it myself this afternoon."

Oakville looked up, eyes sharpening with understanding. He threw his head back and laughed. The other gentlemen in the room rustled their newspapers in annoyance, tutting amongst themselves.

"You fool; you poor, bloody ass!"

"Drink your brandy, Oakville."

"What, toast the fact that the cleverest one of us has been snared by a farmer's daughter? Conniving little thing. Don't you see she must've planned it, along with that mother of hers?"

"What do you mean?"

Rupert choked down the rest of his brandy. "She made a great show of denouncing me publicly, then threw herself at your mercy, seeking the greater prize."

"Nonsense! To risk her reputation on the chance I'd be tempted? No woman of her intelligence would play such a game."

"She's cleverer than you think, Dray. You know how desperate single ladies and their mamas are when they catch a whiff of you." He spluttered a laugh. "Then again, she's no lady. After all, it was straightforward whoring that hooked the fish in the end. I congratulate myself on a lucky escape."

Rupert didn't even bother to rise when Henry took his leave.

He must confront her. She only need refuse him one more time and he could withdraw his offer with his integrity intact and accept Oakville's congratulations on his own lucky escape.

Time to go home and solve the problem.

⫸⫷

JEANETTE WOKE TO a knock on the door. She sat up, wincing as pain scraped across her forearm. Red patches had begun to peek through the bandages.

The key rattled in the lock, and Sanderson appeared in the doorway.

"You have a visitor."

Who was it now? More ladies come to vent their spite at her expense? Perhaps she could test the strength of their stomachs by describing the act of losing her innocence in detail...

"Miss Claybone?"

Sanderson's voice interrupted her thoughts. "He's in the drawing room."

Jeanette's insides fluttered with a wave of nausea. Had Oakville come to taunt her, or worse, ask for her hand?

Very well. She'd give him her hand. In the shape of a fist.

Her mind rehearsed the action; a swing of her arm, the pleasant crack of bone as her fist met Oakville's nose, a like-for-like payment for the injury he'd inflicted on her. Perhaps Sanderson might lend her his pistol.

She strode into the room and addressed the shadow standing beside the window.

"Do you continue to offer money for my services, or are you anxious to know whether your friend elicited greater moans of pleasure from my lips?"

"Lord Ravenwell was right. You *are* staying here."

As he stepped into the candlelight, Jeanette realized her mistake. Shame slithered over her skin; her only friend in the world, witness to how far she had fallen.

"Uncle George!"

He narrowed his eyes and nodded to Sanderson. "Unhand the lady."

"My orders are to ensure she remains in the house."

"I know what your orders are. Now leave us."

"The master told me not to let her out of my sight."

"I've no intention of helping her escape out of the window." Uncle George moved closer, his soft voice holding an undercurrent of iron. "You have my word as a man of honor, assuming your master understands the concept."

Sanderson loosened his grip.

"Very well, Mister Stockton, but I'll be right outside this door."

Uncle George waited until the door clicked shut, then held his arms out.

She moved into his embrace. "Why are you here?"

"To tell you to accept Ravenwell's hand." Uncle George had never believed in prevaricating. "It's the best offer you're likely to get, my dear."

"But he hates me! Or at best, sees me as something to be pitied and ridiculed. He must only wish to marry me to avoid being tainted by scandal."

"A marquis who stands to inherit a dukedom? He can do what he pleases and society will let him. He's not offered his hand because he has to, but because he *wants* to."

"Uncle George, I can't…"

"He'll give you a home, Jeanette! Respectability, safety, comfort."

"What about love?"

He sighed as if placating a petulant child. "Wait for love and you'll be disappointed. Women of your class marry for more rational reasons. Call it convenience if you will."

"Women of my class? I don't belong here!"

"You cannot return to what you were before your papa was elevated to the baronetcy, no matter how much you wish it. We move forward, not back. It's time you lost the sensibilities of the schoolroom and saw the world through the eyes of a grown woman."

Tears stung her eyes. He sighed and spoke more kindly.

"Forgive me, my dear. The world is harsh, and that little corner occupied by the aristocracy is harsher still. But despite appearances, I believe Lord Ravenwell is a good man. I won't insult your intelligence by pretending he lives a virtuous life, but your body, at least, will be safe."

His soft hands engulfed her own, the skin of a scholar, so smooth compared to Papa's palms which would always carry the callouses from farm life.

"Guard your heart, my child, and seek solace in your occupation. You'll be too busy for melancholy when you're a marchioness."

"I have no wish to be a marchioness. I want to be happy."

"And you will. Utilize your talents. You'll have a household to manage, staff and tenants to care for."

He kissed her hand. "I'm sorry your papa isn't here to counsel you, but let me give you a father's advice. Marry him. You'll find happiness if you look for it, in your home and your children."

"Children…"

"Of course. He'll be anxious for an heir."

The memory of her body's unfathomable need which went unsatisfied, the pain and embarrassment and the anger in Ravenwell's eyes when he couldn't withdraw quickly enough once he'd finished inside her. The bull had serviced the cow before leaving to conduct more pleasurable business elsewhere.

But how many other bulls would take what they wanted from her if she refused his offer? What had Theodore O'Reilly spoken of that day in the park? Women, stolen and sold, spirited across the ocean, never to be seen again.

"You really think I should accept him?"

"Yes." Uncle George kissed her hand. "I must leave, my family is expecting me. But think on what I've said."

The door opened and Sanderson appeared, discomfort lingering in his expression. At least he took no pleasure from eavesdropping.

"Wait here, madam, while I show Mister Stockton out."

She sank into a chair, succumbing to her body's weakness, and closed her eyes as the murmur of their voices receded into the distance.

Dear Uncle George, the only soul she could trust when all others had abandoned her. Perhaps he was right. A woman's choices were limited. If she couldn't choose the best path, she must follow the least abhorrent.

Her body gave an involuntary shiver; fear of placing herself in *his* hands coupled with a forbidden thrill which nestled in a dark corner of her mind, whispering of unnamed pleasures, accentuated by the faint masculine aroma, the heady potion compelling her mind and body to submit.

The door flew open to reveal the subject of her thoughts. His hair hung on either side of his face, framing it with a thick, dark pelt. Mouth set in a hard line, his eyes glittered with frost. Broad-shouldered and masculine, he dominated the room. A man who had never been denied anything in his life.

"Your time has run out, madam."

HENRY ALMOST COLLIDED with Stockton in the entrance hall. The lawyer looked a pale shadow of the steadfast man he'd spoken to not two hours ago, the man who'd vigorously defended his goddaughter's honor. Now he seemed to have shrunk into himself, a resigned look of despair etched into his features. Henry had placed his age at around forty, but the gray pallor was that of a man in his sixties.

"Mister Stockton. Let me show you out if you've finished your visit."

He held out his hand, but Stockton merely stared at it before lifting his eyes to meet Henry's gaze. They were the eyes of a seasoned lawyer, a man capable of penetrating the innermost thoughts of others.

"Won't you shake my hand like a gentleman?"

"*Gentleman!*" Stockton scoffed. "I warn you, break that child's heart and you'll regret it."

"Are you threatening me?"

"Bully me all you like, Ravenwell, but I've known Jeanette since she was a child. She's worth more than all the ladies of your acquaintance put together. She's bright, intelligent, and caring and utterly wasted on someone like you. I've just lied to her saying I believe you to be a good man who won't harm her. I pray my words to her will not be disproved."

Stockton gave a mock bow. "I'll see myself out."

Heavens above! It was not worth the trouble. Henry sighed. He should withdraw his offer. Let Stockton take her in if he cared so much about her.

He leapt up the stairs, taking them two at a time and flung open the drawing room door.

Miss Claybone sat demurely on an armchair as if she were an innocent who'd planned nothing.

"Your time has run out, madam."

She looked up, her expression resigned.

"Miss Claybone," he said. "I've come to a decision…"

"So have I," she interrupted, stumbling over the words as if eager to release them as quickly as possible. "I've decided to accept your offer."

"You've *what?*"

"I will marry you, and I'd ask that we become man and wife as quickly and as quietly as possible."

A sharp intake of breath hissed behind Henry. Sanderson had followed him into the room. There was no reneging. He had a witness.

The skin on his neck grew cold as if the chains of matrimony secured themselves around him. She may have won the battle, but in a marriage, the man had the upper hand. Victory in the war would be his.

CHAPTER ELEVEN

"**T**HERE'S A LADY to see you, miss."

Sanderson led Jeanette to the morning room. Her betrothal to Lord Ravenwell made no difference to her captivity. The servant insisted on accompanying her everywhere as if he expected her to run at any time.

The familiar figure of Elizabeth De Witt rose to acknowledge her, this time accompanied by her friend, Caroline Sandton. Two against one.

Jeanette gestured to the door. "I suggest you leave, for I've nothing to say to you."

The ladies shifted positions, chests heaving audibly at her lack of civility. But what did she care?

"I wonder why you're still here," Caroline said, her thin nose wrinkling at her words. "Wouldn't you feel more at home in a bawdy house?"

"Caroline, my dear, you're being unfair to poor Miss Claybone," Lady Elizabeth said, her voice reeking of false compassion. "We should be more charitable toward a former member of our social circle. I'm sure she has no wish to visit a brothel, not even the one Henry visits. Though we could always give you the address, Miss Smith, sorry, *Claybone*."

"For shame, Lizzie!" Caroline said, getting into her stride like a horse several furlongs into a race. "I couldn't possibly imagine what

Miss Claybone could find to occupy herself with in such an establishment, unless she wishes to compare notes."

The door opened, cutting them short, and a deep voice spoke from behind Jeanette.

"I'd thank you not to insult the woman who's to become my wife."

Caroline colored and looked away, but Elizabeth stood her ground.

"Have you lost your senses, Henry? She's not even wearing your ring."

Jeanette's skin prickled at his proximity, a visceral reaction as his masculine aroma caressed her senses. Her needy body tightened in anticipation of his touch. But when he placed his hand on her shoulder, her body relaxed. She dipped her head until her chin touched the back of his hand, and he drew in a sharp breath.

"You're wrong, Lady Elizabeth." He took Jeanette's hand and deftly lifted one of her fingers, slipping a cool metal band over it. She looked down and gasped.

A huge emerald winked at her. A rich, imperial green that had been cut into multiple facets, each one reflecting the light as she moved her hand.

Lady Elizabeth leaned forward. "Surely that's not…"

"My grandmother's ring."

"Good heavens!"

Elizabeth's brow furrowed, etched with acidic lines, her down-turned mouth rendering her features quite ugly.

"I'm sure you wish to give my betrothed the honor to which she is due," Henry said.

He drew Jeanette's hand to his mouth and brushed his lips against her skin. She turned to face him, but he was watching the two women, his smile widening as they lowered into a curtsey, muttering their congratulations.

"Sanderson, please see the ladies out."

"With pleasure."

After the door shut behind them, Henry dropped Jeanette's hand as if it burned him and moved to the door.

"Lord Ravenwell?"

He stopped, his back to her, and his shoulders rose and fell in a sigh.

"Henry?"

He turned to face her. "What do you want?"

"To thank you."

His eyes hardened. "For what? The jewelry?"

"No. For standing up for me."

"You gave me no choice."

"Why? Because you were the first to … to take me?"

"No, madam. As I'm sure you're aware, your family have already capitalized on the situation and issued the announcement."

He drew a sheaf of paper from his jacket and thrust it toward her. She unfolded it and read the words written under *notice of births, marriages, and deaths.*

Sir Robert and Lady Mariette Claybone are delighted to announce the engagement of their eldest daughter, Jeanette Frances, to Henry Philip Edward John Drayton, Lord Ravenwell, heir to the dukedom of Westbury.

A bitter laugh burst from her lips. "I should rejoice that Mama and Papa recognize me again now their prize cow has been auctioned off to the most sought-after bull in London."

"Prize cow indeed. You're to be congratulated on your success. I could never have parried so swift a blow."

"But…"

He held his hand up. "I'd advise you to speak no more on the matter."

Turning his back once more, he left the room. Shortly afterward, she heard him speaking to Sanderson before the main door opened and shut.

Her blood turned to ice. He thought she'd deliberately set out to ensnare him. His eyes which had burned with passion for a fleeting moment when he'd taken her against the wall in this very room now only burned with hatred.

>>><<<

HENRY WAVED AWAY the carriage and strode along the street. Fresh air and exercise might not remedy his predicament, but at least they were good for the body.

How could he have been so foolish! He must be the laughing stock of his friends, having handed himself on a platter to the daughter of a farmer and his overbearing wife.

Life at the top end of society afforded no pleasures for him.

But it was at least safer than the bottom end. Yet more women had gone missing. The authorities showed little interest, declaring that fewer whores in London meant less disease on the streets. Didn't they realize, or care, that the sustained increase in abductions displayed a distinct pattern?

And now he had this cursed marriage to contend with which would divert his energies away from hunting the perpetrators. Only that morning, Sanderson had gleaned fresh information. A sailor he'd bribed with too much ale had spoken of a woman's involvement in the abductions. It only confirmed his suspicions that women possessed a deviousness surpassing that of the worst men.

Last night Betty had greeted him unenthusiastically. The women she employed were terrified, unwilling to engage with anyone other than established clients. Perhaps it was time he took Edward into his care. He was no longer safe there. Unlike others of his rank, Henry didn't view his son solely as the product of a mistake, even if his unfortunate mother had been careless.

Poor Jenny. At least she'd died of natural causes, giving birth to the child. Her beauty, once so clear in his mind, was a distant memory; the unremarkable face of one of the many women he'd enjoyed. Lately, when he tried to recall her features, they'd been replaced by those of another. A lovely face but with sharp, clear eyes, deep green with flecks of gold pulsing in their depths.

Curse her!

A smile crept across his mind. If Jeanette had trapped him into marriage, then he must show her the duties he expected of her. Rather than idle her way through life at his expense, let her care for the unwanted son of a prostitute, the lowest possible class of human being. Perhaps then she might regret this marriage as much as he.

With renewed vigor, he strode toward his lawyer's offices. Time to secure the special license and get this marriage over and done with.

The light was fading on his return to his townhouse. Usually quiet, unless he was in residence hosting one of his infamous parties, the house was alive with activity. The upstairs drawing room windows blazed with light. What was she up to now?

Sighing, he entered the hall.

"I said get out!" a voice screamed, the country accent rendering it unmistakable. Good heavens, must he endure that for the rest of his days?

A man emerged at the top of the stairs and scuttled down like a beetle fleeing a predator. He almost collided with Henry before stopping short and offering a simpering bow.

"Lord Ravenwell! Sir, I must say how obliged..."

A curse rang out upstairs. The trader's ears, already pink at the tips, turned a bright shade of red. As if the papers didn't have enough material to keep their readers entertained!

"Leave us." Henry growled.

"Of course, sir, how kind…"

Henry ignored him and headed up the stairs.

Jeanette stood in center of the drawing room, hair unkempt, face flushed, glaring at the man bowing before her. Another fawning tradesman.

"But, Miss Claybone, I was sent to offer my services. I can assure you, I'm the epitome of discretion and capable of making the arrangements for your hasty marriage."

Who on earth had sent him? A shame-faced Sanderson appeared in the doorway. *Of course.* The man was capable of procuring anything, day or night. He'd even made the arrangements for Edward's needs, intuitively knowing that Henry could not be openly associated with his son.

Now, however, Sanderson's intuition had served him ill. *Hasty marriage* indeed! By this time tomorrow, every trader in London would be discussing how Lord Ravenwell had sired a child with a farmer's daughter out of wedlock.

She might be carrying his child, even now…

His stomach clenched at the notion, and she lifted her eyes to his. A spark ignited in their depths before she resumed her attention on the trader.

"I don't care for your tone," she said, her voice laced with ice. "The length of an engagement bears no reflection on the circumstances of the betrothal. If you discuss the matter outside this room, my solicitor shall hear of it. You are *not* to cast aspersions on the respectability of Lord Ravenwell. Do I make myself clear?"

"Of course, madam, I'm sorry, I meant no disrespect…"

"Yes, yes…" In a perfect imitation of Henry's own gesture, she flicked her hand. "…now leave."

"But Mister Sanderson…"

"…made a mistake, which I shall discuss with him later. Now please go."

Beating a hasty retreat, the trader barely acknowledged Henry at the door. Sanderson shifted uncomfortably, but rather than admonish him, Jeanette slumped in a chair. The actress, having finished her performance, had returned to her natural state.

"Will that be all, madam?" Sanderson said.

"Yes," she said quietly. Rubbing her forehead, she leaned forward and sighed. "Except, perhaps, a glass of water?"

"Very good, madam." Sanderson left the room almost as quickly as the trader.

Henry closed the door and leaned against it, watching the woman who had duped him.

"What do you think you were doing?"

Her body stiffened. "I see no reason why I should be forced to make an exhibition of myself at a society wedding. It's a waste of time, effort, and resources which could be better spent elsewhere."

"Don't all ladies want lavish weddings to display themselves in all their finery?"

"I want a quiet wedding."

"Unfortunately, you can't always have what you want. Neither can I."

His conscience flared as she flinched. She looked away, but not before he caught a glimpse of moisture on her eyelashes. Her body began to shake before she composed herself, the steel backbone seeming to strengthen under his scrutiny.

"All my life I wanted to marry for love, a private union between two people, not a public exhibition."

She turned her gaze on him, a note of fear in her expression. "I've been denied the former, but it's within your power to grant me the latter. I'll hold my head high and do my utmost not to disgrace you in front of your peers. But if you want me on parade with half of London willing me to make a fool of myself, then you're not a good man."

Stockton's words jabbed his conscience.

I've just lied to her by telling her I believe you to be a good man.

"Please," she whispered.

"Very well, a quiet wedding it is. I've managed to secure a special license. We can be married within the week."

She visibly relaxed, her lips lifting into a smile, but before her wiles could tempt him again, he retreated out of the room.

Henry didn't see her during the evening. Sanderson informed him that she'd asked to dine alone in her room. Before he retired, he could swear he heard crying from behind her door, but when he called out, he was met with silence. What did he care if she was unhappy? She had what she wanted, the hand of a marquis, and must now reap the rewards.

CHAPTER TWELVE

"E VERYTHING TURNED OUT for the best, didn't it, love?"

"I wouldn't count your ledger just yet, Papa. The cow may be here but the bull is not."

Jeanette's wedding day had dawned damp and cold, the streets covered in a thick cloud of mist as if Mother Nature wished to hide her embarrassment and see Jeanette married under a veil of obscurity.

Female whispers echoed in the church, spiraling up into the roof, forming a cacophony of hisses, Mama's voice overpowering those of Jeanette's sisters. Were they discussing her disgrace, or perhaps the groom's failure to appear?

The church door rattled. Two pairs of footsteps, the groom and his best man, echoed along the aisle. They grew closer with each step until they stopped beside her.

The parson cleared his throat. "Shall we proceed, my Lord?"

Henry didn't answer, but the heat from his body prickled her skin. Her arm itched, still sore from the bullet wound.

"Ahem."

She turned her head in the direction of the cough. Henry's best man. Cold amusement danced in his eyes. Henry might have given her the private ceremony she wanted, but he had other weapons to sting her with.

Oakville.

"What a pleasure to see you again, Miss Claybone. May I congratulate you on a successful hunt."

⨠⨠⨠⫸⫷⫷⫷

As soon as Jeanette's new husband spoke the vows, he dropped her hand, his body vibrating with barely suppressed tension as if this was the last place he wanted to be.

The party attending the wedding breakfast numbered less than ten, almost all of them from Jeanette's side. Henry's parents had been killed in a coaching accident when he was a child. His grandmother had either not been invited to the wedding or, most likely, had declined to attend.

After the lackluster toasts, Uncle George sidled over to her.

"Try to be happy, my dear."

Her reply was cut short by Mama's enthusiasms.

"Jeanette! *Ma fille!*"

Papa trailed behind, his face pink. Most proud fathers of brides would be inebriated by now, but Papa rarely drank. His color matched the shame in his eyes.

"Daughter, there's so much to say…"

"No there isn't, Papa." She'd intended to be angry, but it was society's fault he'd been forced to disown her.

Jane and Susan stood awkwardly at the edge of the room, overwhelmed by the surroundings. Why should Jeanette expect Papa to sacrifice their futures by tainting them with her scandal? By marrying Ravenwell, she had restored her family's honor, or at least the appearance of it.

"If there's anything I can do to make amends, Jeanie love, please let me."

She nodded toward her sisters. "My future is secured, Papa. See to theirs."

"Of course. I was intending to speak to Lord Ravenwell about it."

Mama took Papa's arm and ushered him toward her new son-in-law who stood by the door talking to the parson. Papa said something to Henry who cast a glance at Jeanette, his expression thunderous. Her bridal gown grew tight, restricting her movements as if to confirm she'd just placed herself irrevocably in a cage.

She moved toward the window, barely registering the footsteps behind her.

"So now you've secured your prey, Miss Claybone, sorry, *Lady Ravenwell*, do you now seek suitable quarry for your sisters so they may enjoy similar good fortune?"

Oakville smirked and raised his glass.

How had she ever found him agreeable?

"I wouldn't call it good fortune, Lord Oakville," she said. "A society I never wanted to be part of will be forced to welcome me. They'll view me as a fortune hunter when I'd prefer them never to have noticed me at all."

"Why should you care? A marchioness, with the prospect of being a duchess in the future, will be admired by everyone."

"For what? A title?"

"Of course. My friend has been the premier catch for several seasons."

"Is that how people in your world value each other? What about kindness? Compassion? How can anyone in command of their senses be content to spend their days sipping brandy in gentlemen's clubs or taking tea with the worst snobs in London? Is that how you value your friend, and he you? Has he nothing to recommend him other than his title, wealth, and accomplishments in the bedchamber?"

Oakville choked on his champagne, his face turning pink.

"Don't tell me you're squeamish," Jeanette said, "but I see you're incapable of understanding me, so there's no point explaining why I see today as a defeat, not a victory."

He wiped his mouth, frowning. "You're unhappy?"

"What's this?" Mama's voice made him jump, almost sending him into another fit of coughing. "My daughter's unhappy because you plague her with your presence. Be off with you!"

He headed toward the footman brandishing a replenished tray of champagne glasses.

"At last," Mama said. "I've wanted to speak to you all day."

"Now you can."

Mama's brow creased into a disapproving frown. "You should have involved me in your wedding arrangements. People will think Lord Ravenwell's too mean with his funds to give you the wedding you deserve."

"I didn't want a big wedding…"

"…and your dress, look at it! A complete absence of lace! You should have let me take you to my modiste. Today is partly my victory, too. We must celebrate our family's new status. Jeanette, I'm so proud of you."

"Why? Because I'm no longer a disgrace now I've married a title?"

Mama's chest wobbled with a sigh, "It cannot harm us, Jeanette. Think of your sisters. Their station in society has increased." She leaned close and lowered her voice. "Your papa's business has been suffering. Only part of it is due to the scandal. It seems as if the clerk he appointed two years ago was less than honest."

The clerk who'd replaced Jeanette when she'd been turned out of Papa's offices to learn how to be the daughter of a baronet.

"He must restore their dowries, Jeanette. They have nothing. He's speaking to your husband even now."

"I hope he won't be too greedy, for their sake," Jeanette said. "Large dowries attract fortune hunters. I want Jane and Susan, at least, to find husbands who value something other than their ability to fund a lavish lifestyle."

She lifted her left hand, fingering the gold band on the third finger, the symbol of her enslavement.

"It's too much to hope my sisters could embark on a marriage built on love. I doubt such marriages exist."

A thin hand took hers, interlacing her fingers in a gesture Mama rarely performed.

"Jeanette, despite what you think, I love you dearly. You may laugh at me, but I've only ever wanted to see you happy. For a woman, her only choice is to marry well. I've known fear, and poverty, and would rather see myself dead than have you endure either."

"But..."

"...I know what we did to you, Jeanette. My conscience has plagued me ever since. We would have taken care of you when the tongues of society found other poor souls to carve into pieces with their spite, whether you had married or not. We did what we thought was right, and you're in the best possible situation we could have hoped for you."

How could Mama understand so little? Tears burned behind Jeanette's eyes, but her resolve battled to stem the tears. She would not give anyone the satisfaction, least of all the man she'd married who stood in the corner engaged in conversation with Papa, body vibrating with barely suppressed fury.

"I never wanted to marry a title, Mama. I wanted a kind, honorable, hard-working man. Like Papa."

"That would have been impossible, *ma fille*."

Bile rose in her throat and she took a gulp of champagne to obliterate the taste. "Why? Because Papa is too far below the situation you aspire to?"

Mama's shoulders slumped, making her shrink in stature. She shook her head. "No, *cherie*. It's because another such man does not exist. I've seen much of the world, from the highest end of French society to the lowest. I've yet to meet a single man who could even begin to measure up to your papa."

She lowered her voice. "Ma *chere* Jeanette, your chances of marrying a man who'd cherish you as you deserve were always small. Do not fall in love with Lord Ravenwell or he'll break your heart. Hateful though society may be, we are part of it. Though I may reveal my feelings to you, I must conceal them from the world for your sisters' sake. We must all make the best of what we have."

"Then what can I do to be happy, Mama?"

"Take solace in the comfort your husband's money and position can afford. And take care never to give him your heart."

"I could never love him, Mama. Men like him prey on the less fortunate and frown upon those who seek an honest living. They live an idle life, displaying a carefully staged indifference to everything around them. They waste opportunities and privileges others could make such better use of. Just think what this country could achieve in the hands of honest, hard-working men!"

A shard of pain crossed Mama's expression. The memory of the Terrors in France still pained her.

Jeanette took her hand. "Forgive me, I'd never support a cause of bloodshed. But I wish men like Papa were given the regard they deserve. Society cannot evolve through revolutions from the outside, but by stealthy progress from within." She forced a smile. "Let me further the cause of equity by putting to use the resources of the marquis I snared. Come, Mama, we must toast my success!"

Mama's face brightened before her smile dropped as if a seizure had taken her. Clamping her lips together, her eyes widened and she stepped back.

"Mama?"

A prickle of apprehension crawled over Jeanette's skin. The scent of musk and spices overcame her senses, and the air thickened as if heralding an impending thunderstorm.

She turned and saw the source of the storm. Her new husband's body cast a shadow which almost completely engulfed her. Nostrils flaring, he took in a slow, measured breath, but beneath the veneer of calm, his mouth, set in a hard line, quivered. Dark blue eyes bore into her, burning with rage.

Without a word, he turned and crossed the room in quick, angry footsteps.

CHAPTER THIRTEEN

RUPERT'S LAUGHTER ECHOED in Henry's mind as he stepped outside, followed by the rest of the wedding party. A whip cracked, and the carriage bearing his family crest rolled up and came to a halt beside him.

Oakville approached, hand outstretched.

"Surely you're not congratulating me, Oakville?"

"No." His friend shook his head. "I'm wishing you luck. Take consolation, my friend, from the fact that your bride seems as miserable about the union as you."

"If anyone deserves compassion, it's me, Oakville, not the scheming creature I've just married."

What a damned fool he'd been, believing Jeanette stood apart from the soulless women who prowled society ballrooms hunting titles and fortunes. That she'd proven herself to be the same as the rest of them was perhaps no surprise. But the fact he'd been duped cut him deep. Having resolved never to make the same mistake as Father, Henry had failed at every turn.

Save one.

Love.

He'd not fail there. He would never be so foolish as to love his wife.

A footman opened the carriage door, but Henry remained still. Sir Robert Claybone gave an embarrassed cough, then helped his daughter inside. Henry climbed in after her. Ignoring her inquiry, he sat opposite her and stared out the window, his anger warring with the flood of heat in his blood at the prospect of claiming her body tonight.

The carriage set off with a lurch. Jeanette pitched forward and almost lost her seat, but suppressing his sense of gallantry, he sat unmoving while out of the corner of his eye he saw her resume her position and smooth down her skirt.

When the carriage arrived at their destination, Henry's Mayfair residence, he pushed the door open and climbed out. After an awkward pause, his new wife followed.

Her foot slipped, and he grasped her arm as she winced. When she regained her balance, he released her and wiped his hand on his jacket.

A row of servants stood in a line leading to the main door.

Jeanette moved toward the door. If she didn't learn how to behave properly, Henry would be a laughing stock. He snatched her wrist and hissed in her ear.

"What do you think you're doing?"

"Going inside."

"The staff are waiting to give you the respect my title affords you," he said. "The least you can do is show them similar courtesy and greet them."

He tightened his grip. "I won't have my servants gossiping about my wife's lack of decorum and her low birth."

She met his gaze, face flushed, eyes defiant. "I'm not ashamed of my background."

"I wouldn't expect *you* to be."

Ignoring the flare of guilt, he pushed her toward the servants. She showed no sign of the anger she must be feeling. Instead, she smiled and held her hand out to greet them, addressing each with a few words; first the butler and housekeeper, followed by the rest in descending order of rank.

At a word from Henry, they scuttled inside, disappearing behind different doors until one maid remained.

Jeanette crossed the hall floor, then stopped in the center, a lost expression on her face.

"Is there a problem?" he said.

"I don't know where to go."

Henry gestured to the maid. "Show *my wife* to her room."

"This way, m'lady." The maid bobbed a curtsey.

Henry called after her. "I'll expect you in the library at seven o'clock."

"What for?"

"It's not your place to ask questions," he replied. "I expect my household to do as they're bid."

"Very well," she said quietly. She inclined her head, then followed the maid up the main staircase. He'd expected a retort, but she had merely obeyed him. Wasn't that what he wanted? A biddable wife who understood her place?

But it was a hollow victory. Where had her spirit gone?

⋙⋘

As JEANETTE'S FEET touched the elegantly tiled hall floor, tiny bells chimed a waterfall of tones which descended before a single note rang out, seven times.

Any one of the doors lining the walls could lead to the library. How was she expected to know which was which?

The butler appeared in a doorway and bowed.

"Lady Ravenwell."

His face, though smoothed into the expressionless visage charac-teristic of the upper servants, bore accents of kindness. Together with his air of calm, he resembled Uncle George.

"Let me show you to the library."

"Thank you. I don't know where to go."

Or what to do.

He issued a quick smile before smoothing his face again. "It's always difficult at first for those unused to the customs of the aristocracy."

"Therein lies the problem," she muttered to herself. "I don't belong."

He turned and raised his eyebrows. Did all butlers undergo specialist training to ensure their ears registered every whispered word?

"My lady," he said, "should you need help adjusting to your new position, I'd consider it my honor."

He knocked on one of the doors, and a deep baritone answered.

"Enter."

Jeanette stepped into the room. From floor to ceiling, every wall was covered in books. Sets of volumes formed regular patterns, gold leaf embossing winking in the light of the chandelier. The occasional spine of dark green or blood red lent accents of color to the shades of brown.

Did her new husband appreciate the books in his collection? Or did they gather dust quicker than the bookshelves gathered new volumes?

Henry sat at a large desk. He drew out his pocket watch and opened it. Frowning, he clicked it shut with a snap and motioned to Jeanette to stand in front of the desk.

"Is it your intention to interview me as you would a servant, sir, or do I have permission to sit in your presence?"

He nodded toward a chair. Very well, if he refused to speak, so would she. Many bullies used silence to intimidate their victims into saying more than they wished. But she wouldn't give him the satisfaction. Levelling her gaze, she looked him directly in the eyes.

He blinked and broke eye contact.

"I summoned you here..."

"How dare..."

"Very well, I *asked* you here so I could explain what I expect of you, now you are my *wife*." He curled his lip at the final word. "Your position as a marchioness makes it all the more imperative that you abide by the vows of obedience and fidelity you made today."

He continued to lecture her on the behavior of a lady, who she could and could not fraternize with, and which servants would help her in her role.

"They're busy with their own tasks and cannot be expected to spare too much of their time teaching you how to behave appropriately. I don't wish to find their regular duties have been neglected due to this unexpected burden on their time."

He cocked his head to one side, eyes narrowing, goading her to respond.

I won't give him the satisfaction.

"Will that be all, husband?"

He paused, tapping his fingers on the desk, then nodded.

"Good," she said. "May I explain what I expect of you?"

His cheek twitched. "I'm your husband. There's nothing for you to expect. I see no reason why my lifestyle should be affected by the *inconvenience* of a wife."

"May I inquire what you mean by inconvenience? Do you refer to your vow to honor and protect me? Or the vow of fidelity?"

He leaned forward, the coiled spring of anger snapping, a cold blue flame in his eyes. "I've paid for my mistake by marrying you. What I do is no concern of yours."

Pain burst into her palm as she dug her fingernails into the flesh. "Thank you for explaining my situation so clearly."

"I'm glad we understand one another," he replied. "Now let us dine together. I'm anxious to see how you behave in private before I present you in public as my wife."

A knock on the door interrupted her response, and the butler appeared. His eye twitched, and she could swear he winked at her before he bestowed a solemn butler-like expression on his master.

"Dinner is served."

JEANETTE PUSHED THE piece of meat to the side of the plate. Her stomach already threatened to expel the previous course. Each time she'd placed the fork into her mouth, the cold watchful eyes of the man at the far end of the table had taken in every movement.

Four footmen accompanied them, two standing at the door and one at either end of the table. She pushed her plate away, and a liveried arm appeared on her left to remove it.

"Thank you."

Henry slammed his glass on the table.

"We don't thank the staff."

"I thought civility was the mark of a lady," she said, "and a gentleman."

"To our equals, yes, but not our inferiors."

She picked up her wineglass. "I was brought up to judge superiority and inferiority by a man's treatment of others, not by his rank."

Waving a dismissive hand, he stood and moved toward the door, not acknowledging the footman who rushed forward to take his chair.

"Where are you going?"

"To enjoy my port in peace."

"Isn't this our wedding night?"

"Eager for me already?" He cast her a dark glance. "Wait for me in your chamber."

Before she could reply, he left the room. The footman behind her pulled back her chair as she moved to stand.

"Thank you."

"You're welcome, my lady."

At least someone appreciated a little humanity.

➤➤➤◀◀◀

JEANETTE SECURED THE lace at the front of her nightgown and sat on the chair beside the fireplace, curling her legs beneath her. The sputtering logs took her back to her childhood at Papa's farmhouse, poking at the log fire, blowing at the embers until they burst into life with a warm orange flame. Her wound still ached, and she adjusted the bandage on her arm and waited.

The door flew open, and Henry strode in. He'd already removed his jacket, and his shirt lay open, revealing his chest. Muscles nestled together in pairs, covered with a dusting of dark hair which grew denser as her eyes travelled lower and her body began to pulse thickly with desire.

He swirled a brandy glass in his hand.

"Get on the bed, wife."

"Can I have a brandy first?" Jeanette asked. Her body may have come alive at the sight of his hard, virile form ready to claim her, but her mind cried out with shame at her wantonness. Perhaps a brandy might muffle the voice in her head.

"No," he growled. "Do as you're told."

He placed the glass down and tugged at the laces of his shirt and wrenched it over his head. Tossing it behind him, he moved toward her.

A knot formed in her stomach. "Will it hurt this time?"

He laughed softly. "You impugn my talents, Jeanette. I'll make your body hum with pleasure and have you begging me to take you."

He moved to the bed and gestured to her nightgown. "Do as I say and take that off."

A surge of need coursed through her at his gruff command, and she drew a sharp breath to dissipate the fog of lust swirling in her mind. She lifted her nightgown, grimacing as it brushed against her bandage.

His potent masculine aroma thickened in the air, and he moved closer. He touched her shoulder and ran his fingertips across her throat until he reached the top of her breasts.

Her skin tightened as he traced a circle around her breast, moving inward until he reached her nipple, which sprang forward in a painful little point. His breath caught in his throat and a low moan escaped her lips as he pinched her nipple.

"Lie back."

She shook her head.

"It wasn't a request."

"Please..."

"Please, what?" he asked. "Take you to the heights of pleasure beyond your wildest dreams? You may think me a fool, Jeanette, but I know a willing woman when I see one."

How could he read her mind so easily? She closed her eyes and turned her head away. His fingers continued to caress her breasts before a burning heat claimed her nipple and she cried out with the sweet agony of it. He had taken her breast into his mouth. His teeth grazed her flesh, and her body quivered at the sweet, exquisite torture. His throat rumbled in a deep growl, and a surge of heat rippled through her limbs before settling between her legs. The very place where she'd felt pain when he'd first taken her now pulsed to a different rhythm, a tempo of need.

He covered her body with his own and brushed his lips against her throat. He moved his mouth lower, and her breasts ached with longing. His lips drew closer, tantalizingly closer.

"Henry..."

He lifted his head at her soft whisper and blinked; then he lowered his head again, his mouth almost touching her breast while his breath cooled the moisture on her skin, tightening it once more.

The longing grew unbearable, and she arched her back, offering her breast to him, willing him to ease the ache inside her.

He sat up, and a low chuckle bubbled in his throat.

"Not as reluctant as we said, are we?"

He raised his arms, stretching them with an air of nonchalance, then unfastened his breeches. He brushed his hand across the growing bulge at his groin and closed his eyes, jaw tightening as he inhaled sharply.

"I can smell your need for me..."

He stepped out of his breeches and crawled toward her. She had never seen a man completely naked before. His thick, hard member jutted toward her, shifting with each movement of his body. His size and confidence intimidated her.

"Open for me," he urged gently.

"Henry, please, you're so—so..."

"Big?" A dark smile crossed his lips. "Many women have said as much, but a woman's body is made to accommodate a man's, even one of my size. You'll soon learn, particularly with your mathematical brain, that the size of the man inside you bears a direct proportion to the pleasure you'll experience."

He dipped his head to claim her breast again and delivered hungry kisses across her skin, insistent little nips to brand her as his own. The pulsing between her thighs grew stronger, and a wicked heat radiated through her limbs. Soft, expert fingers caressed her stomach, massaging her flesh in slow, sweeping circles before moving lower, toward the center of her need.

"Let me show you," he whispered, his throat rumbling against her chest, "let me show you the pleasures I can give you."

"Henry..." She reached up to him.

"No," he growled. "Hands by your sides."

Her body obeyed, compelled into submission, and she surrendered to his exquisite touch.

A slow heartbeat of need grew stronger with each movement of his fingers. She gave a low mewing cry as he dipped a finger between her thighs.

"So wet for me."

He eased the tip of his finger inside her, and a rush of air filled her lungs as her body contracted.

"Only for me…"

A second finger joined the first, and a jolt of pleasure shuddered inside her.

His nostrils flared. "Ah, the sweet scent of a woman's need."

He withdrew his fingers, and the sensation of pleasure diminished. She pushed her hips toward him, and a low chuckle of triumph rumbled in his chest.

"I said you would beg for me. Shall I satisfy that greedy body of yours?"

How could he have known the craving inside her body which had lain dormant until he touched her?

Something hard and hot nudged insistently where her sensitive flesh quivered with need. He placed his hands on either side of her and straightened his arms, lifting his body while he looked down, his face framed by his dark hair.

He moved against her, his manhood rubbing against her in a slick, smooth motion. Pleasure reignited inside her.

"Are you ready, Jeanette?"

"Yes."

In a swift, forceful movement, he thrust inside her. The sharp sting of pain she'd expected did not come, only a feeling of fullness as her body stretched around him. A wave of heat pulsed inside her but faded. Opening her legs to chase the heat, she moved against him, and he whispered her name before withdrawing and plunging inside her once more. The wave surged higher before receding, but before it disappeared completely, he thrust into her again, increasing in speed until the wave swelled to a crest and spilled over.

She screamed as ripple after ripple of pure sensation shattered her body. Her mind burst with color until she dissolved onto the bed, her bones melting into the heat.

"Jeanette…" a soft whisper rumbled in her mind, and she floated back to consciousness, muted aftershocks trembling through her sated body. A delicious weight pressed against her, claiming her as they fused into a single creature.

Still inside her, Henry continued to move, his soft undulating motion a pale echo of the earlier frenzied thrusts which had sealed his ownership of her.

His head moved against her chest, lips searching until they found their prize. His tongue teased her nipple until it hardened once more, then he covered her breast with his mouth and sighed.

"Jeanette…"

The soft whisper ignited a memory, blue eyes dark with concern, strong yet gentle arms lifting her up from the mud-ridden field, carrying her to safety before placing her in a bed as delicately as if she were a bird's egg. A deep voice of concern berating the surgeon for his harsh words while he bandaged her wound.

He could have abandoned her after Oakville had shot her. But he didn't. He'd taken her from the brink of death when everyone else had forsaken her.

"Henry."

She drew her arms around him and his body relaxed. His breathing steadied and his heartbeat slowed to a deep pulse which echoed in her chest.

Take care never to give him your heart.

Jeanette squeezed her eyes shut to force Mama's warning from her mind. However badly Henry had treated her today, she'd caught glimpses of compassion in the man who now lay content in her arms. The law dictated that he owned her body, and she'd given it to him as willingly as he'd said she would. But tonight, he'd unconsciously taken a piece of her heart. She would have to take care to prevent the rest from following.

A rush of cold air pricked her skin and the bed moved beneath her. She sat up, rubbing her eyes. Her nightgown landed on her legs, and she looked up to see her husband pulling his breeches back on.

"Where are you going?"

"That's no concern of yours."

"Are you not staying here tonight?"

His eyes turned to glaciers. "That's not a question a wife should ask her husband."

"Why? Because you intend to visit your mistress or a bawdy house?"

His cheek twitched and he glanced sideways. Her remark, meant to insult, must be close to the truth.

"May I remind you, my dear, this is a marriage of convenience. Though perhaps more your convenience than mine."

"How can you say that?"

"When you offered yourself to me, you rendered me in danger of having another illegitimate child. You gambled your reputation to secure a marquis and entered this marriage knowing what you were about. So, you of all people should understand society marriages are never built on love."

"Aye," she said bitterly. "Men of the ton breed with their wives but love their mistresses."

"And I, madam," he said, his voice rising with anger, "can most certainly be described as a *man of the ton.*"

After the door shut behind him, she sank onto the bed, releasing the tears which stung her eyes.

Not once had he kissed her on the lips.

CHAPTER FOURTEEN

H ENRY LEANED AGAINST the bedchamber door. How would she react? Would she throw the tantrum of a scorned woman?

At length, a small sound penetrated the quiet. Muffled sobs, the kind uttered in desolation, kept quiet to prevent discovery rather than exaggerated to incite sympathy.

Each cry sent a needle of guilt through his heart. But *she* was the one at fault. She still brandished that bandage on her arm though the bullet wound must have healed. Did she think to fool him into feeling sorry for her?

But in one aspect, she'd guessed the truth. He was going to Betty's. The woman had been living in fear this past fortnight. Another one of her girls had disappeared, and nobody gave a damn about their welfare.

Or the welfare of their children. It was time Henry sent Edward to Sussex; removed the boy from the bawdy house he'd been raised in. Sanderson could take care of it. A sense of duty to his son pricked Henry's conscience; or was it compassion for the boy who'd never known his mother?

Edward would soon have another mother, the grasping woman Henry had married. He smiled at the idea of the look on Jeanette's face when she learned of her new duty. It would do her good to know he'd fathered a child with another, and to think he visited other women. The best way to control a shrewish wife was to convince her she had rivals.

"Sir."

Henry turned and drew a sharp breath. Sanderson stood before him, his features distorted, a split lip, scratches across his cheeks, dark where the blood had dried, one eye so swollen it was almost closed. A purple bruise adorned one side of his face.

"Good Lord, Sanderson!"

"Shh!" The servant lifted a finger to his lips, inclining his head to the chamber door. Grazes covered his knuckles, the skin missing in places.

"Where have you been?" Henry hissed.

"Betty's. I was on my way back from the docks. My contact had further news of this mysterious woman who'd been sighted in the area. But he never showed." He gestured to his injuries. "Someone must have made him a better offer."

"Betty's isn't on the way back."

"I know," Sanderson said, "but Hyde Park is. That's where I saw her body."

"Good God, not Betty?"

"No. Lydia."

Lydia. The woman Sanderson had tasked to care for Edward. An unremarkable creature, but willing to take the child under her wing for a regular stipend.

Sanderson's eyes glistened. Lydia had been his favorite, and she'd often admitted him for the night at no extra cost.

"Sanderson, I'm sorry," Henry said, the inadequacy of his words thinning his voice. "I know you were fond of her."

The servant shook his head. "There are whores enough." His expression belied his words and he wiped his eyes. "What concerns me is that she offered to help me, to make inquiries among her clients and the girls she knew from other houses. I don't think she was killed at random."

"You think she found something?"

"Or someone," Sanderson said. "You must be careful, sir. If Lydia was killed because of you, then you may also be in danger."

He gestured toward Jeanette's chamber.

"And those close to you."

⋙⋘

THE CARRIAGE DREW to a halt, and Jeanette's skin tightened with apprehension. Tonight was her first ball as Lady Ravenwell, and the weight of expectation, her husband's and society's, bore down on her.

Henry, who had spent the journey brooding, broke the silence.

"It's best I say this before we go inside."

Her heart withered under his ice-cold stare. A week had passed since her marriage, and he'd grown colder with each day. He had visited her every night and made her body sing with pleasure, only to leave as soon as he'd finished.

Her cheeks burned with shame every morning she joined him for breakfast while the servants attended them in silence. Did they hear her cries at night, when she begged him to take her, then screamed his name as he burst with life inside her willing body?

Did they whisper 'harlot' behind her back?

Henry cleared his throat. "I expect you not to disgrace the Ravenwell name tonight."

She gritted her teeth and smoothed her face into a bland expression. She wouldn't give him the satisfaction of seeing her distress.

He leaned forward. "Have I made myself clear?"

"Perfectly," she said. "But as you're ashamed of my very existence, I'm likely to fail before I set foot in the house."

After leading her inside, he introduced her to one or two people, then escorted her to a seat. After bringing her a glass of punch, he crossed the floor to join Oakville. The two immediately engaged in conversation. Oakville glanced in her direction and frowned.

The chatter of the guests merged into a cacophony, low murmurings of the men topped by the shrill notes of women. Harsh, glacial whispers joined the chorus.

There she is…

The Holmestead Harlot…

Strains of music cut across the voices as the violinists tuned their instruments. Henry walked past her, Felicia Long on his arm, as the couples formed a line. Oakville joined the dancers, his partner all vapid smiles while his face glowered with ill humor.

"Would you care to partner me for the next dance?

Jeanette looked up. A thick-set man in his thirties held a fleshy hand out to her.

"Forgive me, but no. My husband…"

"…is neglecting his delectable wife."

As if on cue, Henry's laugh filtered across the room. If he intended to torture her by flaunting his attentions to others, why shouldn't she do likewise?

"Very well."

The man bowed. "Viscount De Blanchard at your service."

THE SATISFACTION JEANETTE gained from the sour look on Henry's face couldn't offset her disgust at her dance partner. De Blanchard stepped on her foot twice. His breath, which reeked of sour brandy and stale cigar smoke, made her stomach churn each time he drew her close. He was only able to wheeze out a few words, his face growing a deeper shade of puce with each step. At least it spared her from his conversation.

The dance concluded, and a wave of nausea overcame her. She bent forward as the room began to swirl around her.

"Are you all right, Lady Ravenwell?"

"I need air."

He took her elbow and propelled her across the room and out onto the terrace where she drew in a lungful of cool, night air.

"Is that better?"

"Yes, thank you, it's…"

A hand grasped her shoulder and he thrust his face close. Greasy lips parted with greedy anticipation as red-rimmed eyes glittered with drunken lust.

"My lord, I must protest!"

"Come, come," he slurred, "isn't that why you asked me to take you outside? To let the stallion service the mare?"

"No! I was unwell."

His hand grasped at her breast, and she pushed him away. "Get off me!"

"Don't be coy, my dear. We all know what a harlot you are. You need a real man between your legs while your husband's busy bedding every woman in town."

"How dare you!"

Balling her free hand, she swung at him and connected with his nose.

He lifted his hands to his face and staggered back. Red liquid oozed between his fingers.

"You've broken my nose!"

He advanced on her, hands outstretched. Grasping his wrists, she thrust her knee into his groin. A strangled cry burst from his lips as he doubled up and fell to his knees.

"You're no lady!" he spluttered.

"I'm the daughter of a farmer, Lord De Blanchard. Consider yourself fortunate I'm not in possession of two bricks or the stallion might have turned into a gelding."

She slipped back inside. The next dance had already begun. Couples moved across the floor, the ladies' headdresses nodding in unison with the music. All simpering smiles and petty conversation, the couples had eyes only for each other.

Except one. Two cold blue sapphires followed her progress, lowering the temperature of the room. Waving aside a gentleman offering to partner her for the next dance, she took a seat apart from the rest. Solitude was infinitely preferable over the company of these people.

"My dear Lady Ravenwell." The familiar nasal voice grated on her senses as a woman sat beside her. "What an unexpected pleasure to see you here! Of course, we all expected Henry, but I'd have thought you'd find the society here rather *unexciting* for your taste."

Elizabeth De Witt wafted her fan from side to side in an exaggeratedly elegant fashion. "It is a little hot this evening. You were right to venture outside, though perhaps you had motives other than temperature?"

"I've no idea what you're talking about."

Elizabeth tutted. "Your husband is no fool, my dear. Ah! Here he comes now."

She closed her fan with a snap and held out her hand to the man approaching them. The anger in his stance seemed to absorb the light in the room. He cast a swift, cold glance at Jeanette before turning his attention to Elizabeth.

"Lady Elizabeth, I believe you're mine. For the next dance, at least."

Elizabeth rose and took Henry's hand, and he led her into the center of the room.

Fury boiled in Jeanette's gut, mixed with despair. Did he intend to humiliate her publicly as well as at home? Pain throbbed behind her eyes. She pinched the bridge of her nose to ease the headache. The floor tilted beneath her. On no account must she attract further attention by fainting.

"You look like you need this."

A hand held a glass of punch in front of her. She lifted her head. *Oakville.*

She pushed the glass away. "I want nothing from you."

He took the seat Elizabeth had vacated. "Would you honor me with the next dance?"

"Why do you persist in forcing your company on me, Lord Oakville?"

"There was a time when you took pleasure from my company."

"Not a day goes by when I don't regret setting eyes on you."

He leaned back and smiled. "You came off rather well though, didn't you?"

"Only a half-wit would say that," she snarled. "What woman in possession of her senses would scheme to place herself in such a miserable position?"

"Many society women would snare a marquis if they could."

Arrogant, ignorant fool! Jeanette didn't know who was worse, the man who'd ruined her, or the one who'd married her.

"Might I remind you, as everyone is so fond of telling me, I don't belong in your society. I possess none of the qualities, and my values are diametrically opposed to yours."

He opened his mouth to respond, but she leapt to her feet.

"Leave me alone. You're my husband's friend, but that doesn't give you the right to plague me with your presence."

He caught her hand, and she squealed as pain shot through her fingers. Dark spots stained her glove above the knuckles, and his eyes widened. She snatched her hand free and strode to the main doors.

A hand grasped her arm.

"Oakville," she sighed, "why do you…"

"Be quiet!"

Henry had followed her. Lady Elizabeth stood, un-partnered, in the center of the room as the couples continued to dance, maneuvering their steps around her.

"What in the name of God are you doing?" Henry pulled her toward him until she had to crane her neck back to look at him. "Do you seek to cuckold me with another?"

"What about *you*?" she hissed. "I'm not the one displaying my prowess at seduction. I danced only once tonight, yet you've secured a different partner for every dance. Was it your wish for me to sit near the door with the lower classes for the entire evening?"

"My wish is that you do as you're told and not disgrace me any further. I can do what I like, but you must abide by my rules."

"Why?"

"Because you're the one with the fragile reputation. And because I refuse to raise another man's child."

A cold hand clutched at her insides. Did he really have such a low opinion of her?

"You're the one betraying our marriage vows," she said.

"You shouldn't have trapped me into marrying you."

"I didn't! Do you think this…" she gestured between them "…is what I dreamed of? I wanted to marry a man who would make me happy. You, sir, have but one merit, the only trait this wretched society uses to measure a man's worth. Your title."

"And you, madam, have no worth at all."

She closed her mouth, swallowing the bitter taste of rejection. A small flicker of emotion clouded his gaze before his eyes hardened.

"You need to grow up, my dear. Any notion of love must be left behind in the schoolroom. Don't expect love from marriage."

"Yet you'll indulge in it with your mistresses, will you not?"

"You will cease speaking," he said, his jaw trembling, "before you disgrace yourself further. You are my wife and will act accordingly. Do I make myself clear?"

A low growl rumbled in his throat, the sound of an animal with its prey in its grasp. Behind him, the chattering of the company morphed into cackles, the cawing of crows circling in the air, waiting for their chance to pick at her carcass.

He tightened his grip. "Well?"

She nodded, keeping her voice steady. "I'll not bring further shame on you tonight."

If anything, his eyes showed a hint of disappointment before he relaxed his grip and stepped back. She gestured toward Lady Elizabeth.

"Go and join your partner. You wouldn't want to disappoint *her*, would you?"

He sighed and turned his back on her, resuming his place in the dance. What did she care? Let him dally with the premier bitch of the season and secure his reputation with his own behavior. But he couldn't force her to watch.

She slipped into the main hall. A faint rustle of fabric whispered an echo as the servants straightened their postures and stood to attention. One stepped forward and bowed.

"May I be of service?"

"Would you ring for Lord Ravenwell's carriage?"

"Is his Lordship leaving?"

"No, but I am."

The servant's face colored. "Forgive me, but I can only order the carriage at his lordship's request."

"Then I'll walk. Fetch my cloak."

"But my lady, the streets aren't safe..."

"Now!"

He gestured to another servant, barely older than a boy, who scuttled off and returned with her cloak.

"What shall I tell his lordship?"

"That his wife has gone home. But don't disturb him now. I have no wish to spoil his enjoyment while he's so pleasantly occupied."

The rush of cold air tightened her skin as the door opened and she drew her cloak around her. A fog had descended, the damp air beading against the woolen weave.

Not safe, indeed! If Henry thought to contain her through fear, she'd relish the opportunity to disappoint him. Unlike the fragile ladies of his class, she wouldn't be cowed by the dark. The only hazard she might encounter on her way home was an angry husband, and she wasn't afraid of *him*.

⟫⟫⟩⟨⟨⟨⟨

"RAVENWELL, YOU'RE A damned fool!"

Having deposited the odious Lady Elizabeth with her mother, Henry found himself intercepted by Oakville, his friend's usually jovial face pale with anger.

"What are you prattling about, Rupe?"

"Whatever you think of your wife, should you display your cruelty so publicly? Flaunting your seductions in front of the whole room?"

"She's hardly innocent. I saw her scurrying outside for a tryst with De Blanchard."

Rupert made an explosive sound of outrage through his nose. "That old lecher? You should give your wife more credit. If you'd taken the trouble to observe them more closely, you'd have seen his nose was swollen and her gloves were stained with blood."

"What are you implying?"

"Must I spell it out? You abandoned your wife, leaving her prey to men such as De Blanchard. And for what? To enable her to earn the title society has bestowed upon her?"

Was Oakville delivering a lecture?

"Oakville, you're quick to forget that were it not for your plot to seduce her, she'd never have set her cap at me."

Oakville shook his head. "We're a merry pair, are we not? You regret having offered for her hand. I'm beginning to regret that I didn't."

"If you think so highly of her, why aren't you by her side?"

"She refuses to have anything to do with me. Besides, she's disappeared."

136

"Indulging in another liaison on the terrace."

Oakville held up his hand. "That's enough! She left by the main entrance, not the terrace doors. If you will continue to insult her, find another audience." He creased his mouth into a sneer. "Perhaps Lady Elizabeth would be more obliging. Her behavior toward your wife is matched only by your own."

Who'd have thought Oakville would find some moral compass at last? What had Jeanette done to convince him to be her champion?

Henry pushed through the door to the main hall. The servants stood to attention and Henry addressed the older of the two.

"Have you seen Lady Ravenwell?"

"She's gone."

"You sent for my carriage without my permission?"

"No, my lord," the younger of the two interjected. "She left on foot."

"She *what*?"

"When she realized we couldn't send for your carriage, she asked for her cloak. She told us to tell you she had no wish to spoil your enjoyment..."

"...while you were so pleasantly occupied," his companion added.

"How long ago was this?"

"About an hour."

Rather than seek him out, she'd ventured into the night.

Good heavens! Had he humiliated her to the point where she'd thought it better to risk her life wandering about the streets of London? Didn't she know what happened to women alone on the streets? Women disappeared or worse, were murdered, their bodies tossed aside as if they were worthless.

Worthless. Wasn't that how he'd described her? His Jeanette, outside in the cold. *Alone. Defenseless.*

Prey for murderers.

"Fetch my carriage! Immediately!"

CHAPTER FIFTEEN

THE FRONT DOOR swung open before Henry had even stepped out of the carriage. Jenkins waited in the hall, his face smoothed into the expressionless mask he wore so well.

"Her ladyship is in her chamber."

An undercurrent of disapproval resonated in the butler's words. Henry almost missed it as his lungs deflated at the news she was safe. The fear which had almost paralyzed him in the carriage dissipated, causing pinpricks to break out all over his skin.

Jenkins's eyes narrowed. Ever perceptive, he'd caught Henry's reaction.

"She looked unwell, sir. I took the liberty of sending one of the chambermaids up with some tea. But that was an hour ago. I believe she'll be more *receptive to an audience* in the morning." He delivered a stiff bow. "Will that be all?"

So, beneath the stoic servant, who in five years had never displayed anything but bland respect for his master, was a human being. Was he as smitten with her as Oakville?

What did Henry care for a servant's opinion? They answered to *him*.

As did she.

"Jenkins, bring me a candle."

HENRY PUSHED THE door open, wincing as the hinges creaked. The candle threw a soft, yellow glow across the bedchamber, highlighting the gold thread in the embroidered coverlet which rose and fell in a gentle, rhythmic motion.

His wife's face seemed almost childlike in sleep. Her eyes were closed, thick lashes almost brushing her cheeks, yet furrows strained across her forehead.

Setting the candle down, he sat beside her. The bed dipped under his weight, and her body shifted toward him. He brushed his knuckles over her cheeks. When he'd first touched his wife, her skin was smoother than he'd expected. Her country upbringing had led him to believe it would be as coarse as her unbridled laugh. Yet his fingers glided across the contours of her face from her eyelids to her nose and finally those plump, lush lips. Lips he had kissed the day he'd sealed his fate but had not ventured to claim since he'd married her.

She parted her lips and a rush of warm breath tightened the skin of his fingers. Her mouth creased into a smile. Who did she dream of?

"Henry…"

The creases in her brow disappeared and her chest expanded in a deep sigh. The smile on her lips broadened, tempting, inviting…

He bent down, his mouth almost touching hers, and she opened her eyes. She stared, pupils dilated so they were almost black.

His loins flooded with heat and he caught his breath. Her eyes narrowed, and she flinched as a new expression formed on her face.

Fear.

Oakville was right. Henry had demanded she not dishonor him at the ball, but it was his behavior which had been lacking.

She drew out a hand to ward him off, and he caught it. Dark bruises marred her knuckles, the skin broken, adorned with brown patches where the blood had dried. Blood to match that on De Blanchard's nose. It mirrored Sanderson's hand, the marks of one who lived in the world of brutality and savagery. Jeanette had no place in such a world.

At all costs, she must be kept safe from it.

She tried to sit, but he pushed her back.

"No, don't get up."

She pulled her hand under the covers. "What do you want of me?"

"Nothing."

The candlelight picked up a bead of moisture in her eyes. He placed his palm on her cheek again. "I only mean that you need to rest."

Images invaded his mind, bodies floating in the Serpentine, women torn to pieces, abducted, never to be seen again. He forced his voice to become harsh to disguise the fear which Jenkins had spotted underneath his veneer of aristocratic indifference.

"You were a fool to leave the ball unattended."

"I had no wish to trouble you for the carriage."

"Don't you know how dangerous it was?"

A spark of flame pulsed in her eyes. "I'm no weak-bellied lady."

"Lady or pauper, you endanger your life, not to mention your reputation, wandering the streets unescorted."

Her lips thinned into a hard line.

Stubborn fool!

"London isn't the countryside, Jeanette. It's a dangerous place for a woman on her own."

"Aye." Her eyes dulled over. "I am on my own."

He curled a finger under her chin. "You're not alone. For all that our marriage is one of circumstances and convenience, I have no wish to place you in danger. But you're a marchioness now. Appropriate behavior is expected of you."

She blinked, and the bead of moisture swelled into a tear and fell onto her cheek.

"I can't help not knowing what you expect of me."

"You'll learn."

She turned her head away. "I'll never learn, never belong."

Guilt prodded at the back of his mind. Wasn't that what he'd said to her?

"Society will always accept a woman of rank."

She fixed her gaze on the wall. "Like they and you did tonight?"

He wiped away the tear but she remained still, her attention focused on anything but him.

"Get some sleep," he sighed. "Matters will improve in time."

She closed her eyes, not even reacting when he stood and moved to the door.

What was happening to him? Women, wives in particular, were supposed to be obedient. Why had he succumbed to an irrational sense of guilt? Was it the doe-like eyes she'd flashed at him or the hand she'd injured defending her honor when no one else was there to defend it for her?

Why should he, Lord Ravenwell, feel guilty for behaving in the manner to which he'd been born? Heaven above, he'd even turned down Lady Darlington's offer of a tryst tonight. Though he relished the idea of keeping his wife in line by making her believe he turned his attention elsewhere, his conscience forbade him. A stoic little angel had sat on his shoulder, wearing Grandmamma's face and speaking in her voice.

Henry, my boy, a young man might sow his wild oats across every patch of arable land he can lay his hands on, but the time must come for him to settle upon a single estate and confine himself to it.

Grandmamma—dear Lord! Only that morning her letter had arrived, her clear bold hand and frank words expressing her disapproval of his choice of wife. He'd been a coward, only informing her of his hasty marriage after the event. The woman was over eighty, by God, and he was bloody terrified of her.

As for his wife, curse the woman! What possessed her to make him feel such guilt? He'd already drawn attention to himself by marrying so far beneath him. He couldn't afford to attract further notice. He placed himself in danger with each prostitute he questioned and each tavern he visited. But society would never suspect they were being spied on by a man incapable of civility toward his wife. An arrogant soulless rake would not possess the compassion to help the less fortunate.

A man who was *not* in love with his wife…

Dear God, where had that notion come from? He didn't love her and never would.

Are you certain?

To keep Jeanette away from danger, he would have to curtail the treacherous voices in his head and tighten her reins.

Tomorrow he would begin again.

MATTERS WILL IMPROVE in time.

Henry's words echoed in Jeanette's ears as she approached the breakfast room where he sat at one end of the table. He stood and gave her a stiff bow before resuming his seat.

She helped herself to a plateful of devilled kidneys and sat at the opposite end of the table, nodding to the footman who approached with the tea. Brown liquid splashed up to the rim of her cup, obscuring the floral pattern inside.

The silence extended into discomfort, the only sound the scraping of cutlery on the plates. At length, Henry pushed his plate forward, ignoring the footman who plucked it from the table.

Jeanette set her teacup down with a clatter, and he looked up, frost in his eyes.

"Ought we to talk, husband?"

"About what?"

"Last night. If matters are to improve, perhaps we should discuss it."

"Very well," he sighed. "I suggest we start with your behavior. I'm not minded to grant you freedom if you're disposed to roam the streets unaccompanied. But when you have fulfilled your primary duty, I may reconsider."

"My primary duty?"

He narrowed his eyes and leaned back in his chair. "To beget an heir. Once you've performed satisfactorily in that respect, I may give you some concessions depending on how you've been conducting yourself."

Cheeks flaming, she turned her attention to the plate in front of her.

"You must furnish me with an heir as soon as possible. Given my efforts since the day we married, I expect my labors to bear fruit soon."

Choking on the mouthful of food which had turned to dust on her tongue, she gestured toward the footmen.

Henry gave a scornful laugh. "My servants act with discretion. Perhaps they could teach you a thing or two, for your class is lacking in that particular quality."

She slammed her fork on the table. "At least we have compassion! We possess the ability to consider the feelings of others. At least *we* are capable of love."

"And that is your greatest weakness. Where would your compassion have got you wandering around the streets of London with a ruined reputation? No protector of courtesans or patron of bawdy houses wants *compassion*, I can assure you of that."

"And you, my lord, are the authority on such matters."

"*My* behavior is not under discussion."

"But..."

He raised his hand. "I've heard enough! Like it or not, the rules apply differently to women because they bear the fruits of any liaison. I have no intention of being saddled with an unwanted child, particularly when I have been saddled with..."

"What?" she cried, fury bursting into a flame. "An unwanted bitch? Is that what you were going to say? Rest assured, husband, my ears aren't as delicate as those of a *lady*. An upbringing in the farmyard has rendered me immune to the language of the gutter."

Her body jerked with fright as he slammed his hand on the table. He stood, his chair scraping against the wooden floor.

"This conversation is over."

He pushed the chair aside and moved to the door.

"Where are you going?"

He turned, the slow, deliberate movement contrasting with the earlier flash of anger. Fury flared in his eyes as he spoke through gritted teeth, emphasizing every word.

"I'm *not* answerable to you."

The door slammed behind him, and his quick, sharp footsteps faded into the distance. After she could no longer hear them, she stood, holding the table for support. Looking anywhere but at the servants who'd witnessed her humiliation, she followed him out of the breakfast room, seeking the solitude of her bedchamber.

»»»«««

"YOU HAVE A visitor, my lady. Shall I show him in?"

Jeanette turned her attention from the view outside to the butler standing before her, one hand outstretched, a silver salver balanced on his fingers. She plucked the card from the tray and read the inscription.

Rupert Beaumont, Viscount Oakville.

"Are you sure he's not here to see Lord Ravenwell?"

"He asked particularly that he might be granted an audience with you. Shall I fetch some tea?"

"Yes, thank you."

Her guest bowed as soon as he entered the room.

"Lady Ravenwell, what a pleasure…"

"Sit down, Lord Oakville."

He moved to the chair she'd indicated and waited for her to sit, a ridiculous ritual where a man must never sit if ladies present were standing. What a pity such proprietary didn't extend to seducing women in public. He perched himself on the edge of the seat, stretching his legs in front of him.

Jeanette poured the tea and handed him a cup. Thanking her in a soft voice, he took it. His fingertips brushed against hers, and she snatched her hand away.

"To what do I owe the *honor* of this visit, Lord Oakville? You must have better things to do, people to see who are more suited to your tastes."

The charming, confident exterior seemed to have dissolved. Crossing and uncrossing his ankles, his gaze shifted to the floor, then darted around the room until they settled on her.

"I'll come straight to the point..."

"Yes," she said, "you seem to prefer the direct approach."

"I want to apologize for Dray, Lord Ravenwell. A husband should treat his wife better. *You* deserve better."

She raised a hand. "Stop. Who are you to discuss my marriage after your behavior? You've no right to speak badly of my husband."

"Even if what I say is true?"

"I won't tolerate rudeness."

He nodded toward her hand where bruises adorned her knuckles.

"I've seen how you treat men who behave poorly. I, for one, am delighted De Blanchard has been given a lesson on how to behave appropriately toward a lady." His mouth curled into a lopsided grin. "You've done your sex a service. If we lived in a fair world, you'd be revered for your courage."

How different his manner was compared to the smooth demeanor of a practiced seducer. She could almost believe a different man sat before her to the one who'd ruined her.

The bullet wound in her arm itched, the flare of pain reminding her of the role Oakville had played in her downfall, and she suppressed the involuntary smile which had formed on hearing his words of praise.

Why could *he* not find reason to admire her?

Thoughts of Henry cast a spell in her mind and his footsteps echoed in her ears.

"You flatter me," she said, "but that won't exonerate you from showing disrespect toward a man you profess to be your friend."

"Oakville, what are you doing here?"

Jeanette's body jerked at the deep voice. Her teacup rattled in its saucer, almost toppling off before she caught it.

Henry stood in the doorway. Jeanette's body hummed to life at his voice. The familiar scent of him, which always intensified when he visited her at night, penetrated her senses as he claimed her body, her cries of pleasure uniting with his roar of finality as he poured his life into her. Afterward, for a brief moment, he would hold her as if he cherished her before he pulled away, the cold seeping into her body even before he left her to sleep alone.

Shameful heat lingered between her thighs as he moved into the center of the room.

"W-would you like some tea, husband?"

Not responding, he sat beside his friend. Ignoring the slight, she reached for a cup and poured the tea, the crockery rattling as she fought to steady her hands.

"That's not your job."

Her fingers slipped at his sharp tones and hot liquid splashed onto her hand.

Oakville cleared his throat. "Dray..."

"My wife should understand that's a job for servants."

"I have arms and legs the same as the next person," she retorted. "Why put our servants to the bother of walking up two flights of stairs to perform a task I can do before they've even placed a foot on the first step?"

"You see, Rupe," Henry said, "servants grow lazy unless they stay active. In my opinion, those from the lower classes must be kept occupied. It prevents a descent into idleness and ensures they know their place."

"Then applying your logic, husband, I should continue to pour the tea."

Henry's jaw twitched, and Oakville suppressed a snort.

"Admit it, Dray, you've been bested."

Jeanette handed Henry the teacup, but he sat unmoving. A dull ache spread through her arm, the teacup rattling against the saucer as her hand shook.

Oakville cleared his throat. "For heaven's sake, Dray."

Henry took the teacup. Oakville nudged him and he sighed.

"Thank you."

"Oh, you're *very* welcome, husband."

His expression hardened, but she refused to break eye contact. Why should she be embarrassed by his lack of civility?

He opened his mouth to respond, but Oakville interrupted him.

"Oh, Dray! You wouldn't believe who I saw today."

Henry focused his attention once more on his friend who continued to fill the silence with hurried words.

"I saw Sir Daniel Winters and his wife."

"How is Lady Charlotte?"

"Looking well. Business is prospering. Sir Daniel told me almost all of the premier modistes of London actively seek him out every time one of his ships docks."

"I'm astonished by his success. He never struck me as particularly shrewd. Charlotte, on the other hand, is the most intelligent woman of my acquaintance. I wouldn't be surprised if she instructs him on how to manage his business."

Oakville chuckled. "I suspect she instructs him on everything. She's often seen at the docks, conducting his business for him. Sir

Daniel's too smitten to attempt to control her behavior. There's an inappropriate balance of power in that relationship."

"She's too strong a woman for a man such as him to control."

"And you'd know. Why you and she…" Color rose in Oakville's face and he cast a sidelong glance at Jeanette. "They asked me to give you their congratulations, Dray, and said they hope to see you and Lady Ravenwell at their country seat before the winter."

"I thought they had only a modest house in town."

Oakville shook his head. "He acquired Firbridge Park last month. Clearly he aspires to join the landed gentry."

Henry snorted. "He'll never secure his position in society through trade. Birth is what matters, my friend. Birth is everything. It cannot be bought…" He looked at Jeanette before continuing, "…or married into. The stain of the shop can never be scrubbed clean."

Jeanette could bear it no longer and she stood, her cheeks flaming. "It's time I spoke to Jenkins about supper. Will Lord Oakville be joining us?"

"No," Henry replied. "We're dining out."

"Then please excuse me."

Before she reached the door, Henry called out. "Do you not ask when I shall return?"

"No, Henry," she said. "I know better than to ask you such a question."

Oakville rose to his feet. "I must thank you for the pleasure of your company, Lady Ravenwell."

She nodded at him before leaving the room, not glancing at her husband.

AFTER HIS WIFE left the room, Henry snorted. "I must thank you for the pleasure of your company, indeed! Rupe, are you trying to seduce my wife?"

Oakville's face darkened, his normally mild eyes glittering with anger. "What if I was trying to seduce her? You care less than nothing for her. For once I must say I'm utterly ashamed to be your friend."

"My wife is a fortune hunter. She'll taint my family's heritage with her blood…"

"…blood which includes that of the French aristocracy. On her mother's side, she's as much a lady as you are a gentleman."

"She'll never be a lady."

"Good God, man, didn't you see her just now? Despite your attempts to humiliate her in front of company, she acted every part the lady. Whereas you were far from acting the gentleman. Birth may define a gentleman, but so does behavior."

Rupert's words couldn't attack Henry any more than his own conscience, which had begun to war with his suspicions that she'd tricked him into marrying her.

Rupert snorted. "You don't fool me. I see the way you look at her."

"How do I look at her?"

"Like a toper trying to convince himself he doesn't crave the brandy."

"Don't be a simpleton."

"She's your wife, Dray. Why deny your craving? It's in your eyes. I can hear it in your voice, and I definitely see it in your breeches."

Since when had Oakville found such powers of observation?

Henry's groin had tightened as soon as he'd heard her voice. The faint scent of her lingered in the house, heating his blood. Blood which had surged through him at the sight of her leaning forward to pour the tea, her cleavage spilling over the lace of her gown. Her creamy flesh formed two smooth curves, the valley between promising a land of pleasure. Below her lace tuck, two little dents poked at the silk of her gown—delectable flower buds which only last night he'd devoured, his body wild with need.

Each night he pushed his conscience aside as he thrust into her tight, welcoming body. Each time she drew him to her more powerfully than the last. The deep green of her eyes, which promised such earthly pleasures, was beginning to capture his soul.

What the devil was she doing to him? Unless he continued to force the invisible barrier between them to stay thick and strong, he'd find himself succumbing to her spell.

CHAPTER SIXTEEN

"W HEN WILL YOUR ladyship require dinner?"
Jenkins had the uncanny ability to be everywhere at all times. But his omnipresence, rather than lending an air of oppression, gave Jeanette comfort.

"Tell the cook to take the rest of the day off," she said. "I'll see to my own supper."

The sharp intake of breath betrayed the dent she had inflicted on the butler's sensibilities.

"My lady, that's not how things are done. We run the household properly."

"I'm sure my husband has told you, Jenkins, I've no understanding of propriety."

He raised an eyebrow at her bitter words. Unlike Henry, Jenkins had tried to make her feel at ease. The least she could do was repay him with respect.

"Forgive me, Jenkins. When I'm—tired—I cannot guard my tongue. I'm afraid it'll be some time before I understand what's expected of me."

"I'd be honored if you'd let me help you, my lady."

"You're too kind."

"And I'll send word to Mr. and Mrs. Barnes."

"Mr. and Mrs. Barnes?"

"The steward and the housekeeper at the Ravenwell Hall, the

master's country seat. Mrs. Barnes will be delighted it's finally in possession of a lady."

"I'm no…"

"Yes, you are." He spoke sternly. "Doubt yourself and others will also. Mrs. Barnes will help you. She's a kind-hearted woman and, if you don't mind me being so bold, she will cure your loneliness."

"I'm not lonely."

"Your eyes say otherwise. But occupation is the best cure. A lady is expected to entertain. Why not host a supper party to establish your position in society?"

"I couldn't imagine a more miserable way to spend an evening. Besides, there's too much to learn."

"Then we'll start now, beginning with the cook, Mrs. Pratt. I'll summon her now to discuss menus with you. She's one of the best cooks in London. I daresay she could rival the chefs of France. She'll accompany you to Sussex and would relish the chance to demonstrate her skills."

≫≫⊱⊰≪≪

AFTER AN HOUR'S discussion with Mrs. Pratt, Jeanette sank back into her chair and closed her eyes. The cook was well versed in many of the French dishes Jeanette had enjoyed at home under Mama's direction. Like Jenkins, Mrs. Pratt had at first seemed overly formal, but she'd soon warmed to Jeanette and had been eager to help her new mistress.

The rattle of porcelain interrupted her thoughts.

"Your tea, my lady." Jenkins stood over her, his eyes twinkling with pleasure.

"Is everything all right, Jenkins?"

"Couldn't be more so, my lady. You've given Mrs. Pratt a purpose. Lord Ravenwell has in his possession the finest cook in England but doesn't value her as she deserves."

"Hush, Jenkins. I won't hear a word against my husband."

The butler's eyes widened a fraction, then he nodded.

"Of course. But if I may take one more opportunity to speak boldly, I'd venture to note that the same could be said for his wife."

He tilted his head to one side, the almost imperceptible movement so like Papa in those quiet moments when he used to tell Jeanette how much he loved her.

"You're very sweet, Jenkins."

He bowed and withdrew to the door. "Dinner will be ready at eight."

<hr />

HENRY RAPPED ON the bawdyhouse door. It opened a fraction, and a face appeared. Eyes glittered with seduction, red lips parted, showing the pink tip of a tongue. The woman smiled.

"Lord Ravenwell! I thought you'd abandoned us after your marriage."

Despite her age, Betty still possessed that unknown factor seen in few women. A woman might have perfectly proportioned features and a body trained for seduction, and she might be experienced in the arts of pleasure, of taking a man into her mouth or her body until he burst with life, but without that missing piece, the mysterious allure which cannot be defined, her appeal wouldn't last forever.

Betty had made a fine enough living from her talents, tutoring her protégées in the arts of seduction. She had put her allure to good use and earned enough as a courtesan to establish one of the finest bawdyhouses in London. She had no need to work herself, but occasionally serviced a small number of her favorite clients, Henry included.

Had Charlotte Winters not secured the heart, and hand, of Sir Daniel, it might have been her opening the door tonight. But Charlotte, now respectably married, preferred to pretend the past did not exist. Sadly, society had a long memory.

"Don't stand there in the cold," Betty purred. "Come inside and we'll warm you up."

The timbre of her voice had always set his body on fire, but tonight, there was no telltale twitch in his breeches, and Betty was experienced enough to notice. His body no longer desired her. She wasn't the only woman of his acquaintance who possessed that indefinable magnetism. Another existed.

Jeanette.

Since encountering his wife taking tea with Oakville, Henry had dined out each night. But absence from her company had only heightened his need for her. She'd seemed indifferent to his neglect. Last night he'd returned early while she was still dining. After issuing a cool greeting, she had resumed her meal as if he were merely a casual visitor. She'd mentioned something about dinner guests at which point he'd nodded and retired to his study.

He should have rejoiced at her behavior, but her indifference pierced his heart. Where had her passion gone?

Betty opened the door more fully. Her smile disappeared as he slipped inside.

"Betty, what's wrong?"

"Mary's missing. That's six girls I've lost now."

"Do you suspect anyone?"

"I trust my patrons."

"Perhaps a spurned client?"

"I've never had to send a client away, not even that lecher de Blanchard."

"Is he here tonight?"

"Yes, in the scarlet room."

The venue for Betty's orgies, where Henry had enjoyed many a party, often sharing Betty with Rupert and Dominic, her legendary stamina able to satisfy all three at once.

"I must pay it a visit."

She held out her hand. "You're overdressed. Let me help. I found a replacement for Lydia yesterday. Rosaline. A sweet little thing. You'll like her."

⟫⟫⟫⟪⟪⟪

TEN MINUTES LATER, Henry stood on the threshold of the scarlet room. The party was in full swing. But Betty's services and those of her employees no longer held any interest for him. Not only was his wife's body the only physical pleasure he craved, but he yearned for something else—a connection of mind and soul.

What the devil was happening to him?

A bony hand curled around his wrist and a voice purred in his ear.

"A new god to worship!"

A young woman stood before him. Thin for a prostitute, her voice still held that lightness of youth. The image of Jeanette's face burned into his mind's eye, and he pushed the woman away.

"Ah, there you are. Delectable goddess!"

The slurred words could not disguise the voice, boorish, pompous, and accompanied by the stench of sweat and tobacco.

A pale body stumbled toward him, folds of white flesh dusted with black hair. The mask obscured his eyes, but Henry knew them to be pale brown, set close together, surrounded by fleshy features reminiscent of an over-fed hog. The bulbous nose, reddened through too much port, bore a slight kink and a bruise which had yet to fade.

De Blanchard.

"Come here, delightful creature," De Blanchard said. "Let me show you the god between my legs."

Her fingers tightened on Henry's wrist and she whispered in his ear. "Please..."

155

Henry pulled her to him and crushed his mouth against hers.

"I say old chap, that one's mine!"

Pushing the woman behind him, Henry drew himself to full height. Though drunk, De Blanchard had the wit to recognize the challenge. Cursing, he retreated.

Henry released the girl's hand and moved toward the door.

"Don't leave me! He'll only find me again!"

"Then deny him."

"What doxy can say no? Someone must service him. The other girls said it's my turn unless another patron takes me for the night."

Visions of dead women crossed his mind. What if it was De Blanchard? This thin, naïve little creature would be easy prey for one such as him. But tonight, Henry could ensure she remained safe.

"Very well," he said. "I'll keep you safe for the night. Come, let's find a private room for you to stay in."

CHAPTER SEVENTEEN

"**I** TRUST YOU'VE not forgotten we're attending the opera next week."

Other than the occasional remark, they were the first words Henry had spoken to Jeanette for two days. She had begun to crave him, the air thickening with her desire whenever he entered the room, but his desire for her must have cooled. Two nights ago, he'd not returned until the morning, slamming the door on his arrival as if he wanted to wake her and let her know he'd been enjoying the pleasures of another.

Jeanette lifted her eyes and met his gaze. He blinked, and the faint sheen of concern in his expression disappeared. A figment of her imagination, a product of hope.

She forced a smile. "I'm fond of the opera."

He lifted an eyebrow.

"Even commoners visit the opera," she said. "One can enjoy music from any social position, and The Marriage of Figaro is one of my favorites. I know the story well."

His eyes darkened. "Enlighten me."

"A young couple of low station, very much in love, want to marry. An aristocratic lecher wants the woman for himself but his plans are thwarted. The story is about fidelity, a subject which I know is of particular interest to you."

"How do you know so much?"

"It's called an education," she said crisply.

"Education alone cannot atone for poor breeding," he replied. "And I have made a start on addressing that. You are to attend Madame Dupont today. She's expecting you."

"And who is she?"

"The premier modiste in London. You need to be dressed in a manner which befits someone of my station."

"As opposed to someone of mine?"

His lip twitched at her response, but he left the room without a word.

MADAME DUPONT'S ESTABLISHMENT was situated on Bond Street. Ribbons decorated the window in a minimalist fashion, as if the proprietress wanted to discourage patronage.

The shop was empty save for two women at the back who looked up as Jeanette stepped inside. They stood beside a cabinet piled with rolls of material. One was dressed in bright, fashionable colors. The second, taller and older and dressed in a more somber black, broke away from her companion and approached Jeanette.

"Lady Ravenwell!"

"Madame Dupont?"

"*Oui, c'est vrais*, your ladyship. I was delighted when Lord Henry asked me to receive you. He's a valued patron, but I didn't expect him to send his *wife* here." She shifted her gaze to the other woman in the shop. "No matter. I'll make you the finest gowns in London. I've recently taken a delivery of the most delightful silks. The merchant gives me first refusal."

The other woman stepped closer, moving into the ray of sunlight from the window. Jeanette's breath caught in her throat. She had never seen anyone so exquisitely beautiful. Clear blue eyes, slanted in an exotic fashion, gave her an air of mystery. Her skin glowed with health and vitality. Rich amber-colored hair completed her beauty, and a soft cascade of curls framed her face which bore an expression of overt astonishment.

"*You're* Lady Ravenwell?"

Was there nowhere Jeanette could go without being insulted? Jeanette set her mouth into a hard smile and addressed the stranger.

"Perhaps you'd rather address me as the Holmestead Harlot, like the other ladies."

The woman laughed. "Society ladies always direct their venom to anyone they deem a threat." She dropped a curtsey. "Forgive me, you must think me dreadfully rude. My name is Charlotte Winters and I'm delighted to meet you. My husband has been generous enough to indulge me with yet another set of Madame Dupont's delectable gowns."

"It's the least I can do, *Madame*," the modiste said, "given the beautiful silks he supplies me with."

Charlotte linked her arm with Jeanette's. "Madame Dupont is right. The silks are exquisite. I'm sure there'll be something to emphasize the color of your eyes. Such an interesting shade of green!"

"I must protest!" the modiste cried. "I'm sure Lady Ravenwell has no wish to indulge in such a level of familiarity with a woman of your background."

"Her background?"

Charlotte sighed. "I'm surprised Henry hasn't told you. Before I married Daniel, I was a courtesan."

"Which is why you must leave," Madame Dupont said.

"No, let her stay," Jeanette said. Charlotte's easy smile outshone the harsh, polite masks most ladies wore, and Jeanette sorely needed to see a friendly face.

"Good. Then let me show you the silks. There's a red which would suit you perfectly."

"Wouldn't green be more befitting?" Jeanette asked.

"Nonsense! Henry won't want you hidden away in dreary colors. The red will contrast with your eyes. Better still, if we find you some green trimming, the effect will be stunning. You'll be the talk of London."

As if she wanted *them* to gossip about her!

Charlotte's smile faded. "Forgive me, I always rattle on when I'm nervous. I've been anxious to meet the woman who finally snared Henry. The man no courtesan could keep longer than a few months. You're nothing like I expected."

Jeanette withdrew her arm. *This was intolerable!* Had Henry sent his mistress to humiliate her?

"No, no!" Charlotte cried, "I meant it as a good thing! I assumed he'd fall victim to someone like Elizabeth De Witt or that horse-faced Felicia Long, some insipid creature with all the character bred out of her. It warms my heart to see he's not thrown himself away."

"Were you his mistress?"

Charlotte had the grace to blush. "He was my protector when I was younger. But I'm happily married now. My beloved Daniel is one of the few men in society capable of ignoring my past and loving me for who I am. I count myself extremely fortunate."

But the look of unfulfillment in her eyes was not that of a happy woman.

"I'm sorry," she said, "you must think me terribly insensitive. Madame is right. I should leave. Daniel may be a knight, but his title can never remove the stain of my past."

Jeanette took Charlotte's hand. "Please stay. Why should I blame you for the circumstances you once found yourself in, circumstances I was myself placed in? The men of this world have much to be responsible for."

Charlotte cast Jeanette a sharp look, her eyes radiating intelligence. Her eyes hardened momentarily before she smiled. She squeezed

Jeanette's hand, and Jeanette flinched at the spike of pain.

"Oh, forgive me! I'd forgotten," Charlotte said. "News travels fast, you know. I hear Viscount De Blanchard treads more carefully now his nose has been bloodied. You're to be commended for showing him the error of his ways. He offered to set me up not long after I entered into the life of a courtesan. But I refused. I'd rather starve."

"Was starvation an option for you?"

Charlotte's smile slipped. "My energies always had to be focused on keeping my patrons interested in my body. And, of course, I was shunned by decent society."

"That depends on your definition of *decent society*."

"You're too kind. Of them all, save Daniel of course, Henry was the only one who would acknowledge me publicly. In the eyes of the others, especially the ladies, I didn't, and often still don't, exist."

"From what I've seen, their attention is nothing to crave. But I'm glad my husband was kind to you."

"He's a good man, Lady Ravenwell, and I'm convinced he'll be a faithful husband now he's settled. I know you'll make him happy, and he you, of course."

How was it that Lady Winters, a woman with her understanding of human behavior, could be so wrong? Henry despised her! If this vivacious beauty could not have secured his interest for longer than a few weeks, what hope did Jeanette have?

She swallowed her desire to set her companion straight. "I hope we can be friends, Lady Winters."

"Then you must let me show you the red silk. And please, call me Charlotte."

As the morning drew to a close, Jeanette completed her order—three evening gowns and two day dresses. At Charlotte's insistence, one of the evening gowns was to be made in the bright red silk with green trimmings. A second would be fashioned in a rich imperial green, the third a more muted shade of blue.

"I don't know if I'd dare wear the red."

"Nonsense, your ladyship," Madame Dupont said. "That will be the best of the three. I'll venture to say it will be my finest creation, and I've been in business many years, had many customers."

Charlotte let out a laugh. "Many ladies accompanied by their patrons, or should I say, their uncles? Almost every unmarried lady who arrives on the arm of a man is his *niece*."

Madame Dupont looked up from writing Jeanette's measurements on her ledger. "One of my customers has more than twenty uncles."

"My, my," Jeanette said. "Her grandparents must have been busy."

Charlotte snorted. "As is she!"

Bidding the modiste farewell, the two women stepped out into the street together and embraced. Charlotte squeezed Jeanette's arm and she flinched at the sharp spike of pain.

"What's wrong?"

Jeanette pulled her arm free. "Nothing."

"No, I insist."

Undeterred, Charlotte pushed up Jeanette's sleeve to reveal the bandage covering the bullet wound. Brown and red patches adorned the clumsily wound strips of linen. Defeated, Jeanette stood still while her new friend unwound the bandage.

"My God!"

Though the bullet had been removed weeks ago, the flesh still glistened an angry red.

"What caused this?"

"I was shot."

"*Shot*? Has Henry seen this?"

"He mustn't." Jeanette said. "It was a duel at Holmestead Hall. I've no wish to remind my husband of the events which led to my ruination. It'll heal eventually."

"Even I can tell that wound's festered," Charlotte said. "You need to be seen, and soon, unless you wish to lose your arm. Henry would understand."

The memory of his cold eyes froze Jeanette's blood. He would not forgive a reminder of the scandal which had thrown her into his path.

Charlotte took her hand. "I have a solution if you have no wish to trouble your husband. I know a very discreet surgeon. I can send him to you."

"Was he one of your protectors?"

"No, he's a respectable family man. But he dealt with all my little *accidents.*"

Little accidents, good lord! Is that how courtesans viewed the unborn children they were forced to dispose of to enable them to continue their livelihoods?

Though Charlotte smiled, the little creases in her eyes betrayed her. In their blue depths lay dark tones of grief. She might never admit it, but her expression bore the loss of each unborn child.

Had Henry fathered one of them?

"No," Charlotte said, her perceptive eyes understanding where Jeanette's thoughts had taken her. "Henry was always careful."

"Do you have any children?" Jeanette asked.

A sad expression clouded Charlotte's eyes. "It was not to be. But I must make the most of the life I have. I'm fortunate to have Daniel's love. Husbands in society are not known for loving their wives." Her hand flew to her mouth. "Oh, forgive me!"

"What for?" Jeanette said. "You speak the truth."

"Please permit me to send Doctor Hill to you."

"Very well. Send him tonight. My husband has dined out every night this week. I'm sure tonight will be no different."

HENRY GESTURED TO his front door. "Coming in for a brandy, Oakville?"

"I don't know…"

"My wife will have retired."

"You'll have to speak to her at some point, Dray. A woman as stunning as your wife will attract predators if it's widely known you abandon her every evening."

"As soon as I know she's carrying my child, I'll send her to Sussex. The young bucks hereabouts won't bother her in the country when there's sweeter meat to sniff around in London."

Oakville's tone hardened. "Such as Rosaline?"

"Rosaline?"

"Betty's new girl," Oakville said. "You were seen with her at Betty's last masquerade party. I heard tell you spirited yourself away for a whole night with her and weren't seen leaving Betty's till after sunrise." He folded his arms. "I'm not adverse to a little variety after marriage, but it's poor form to return to your wife *after* daybreak."

"Your new-found conscience is becoming a bore," Henry said. "Nothing happened."

Oakville snorted. "The champion rake holes himself up with the prettiest doxy in town for an entire night and nothing happened? Have you lost your mind, or perhaps your cock has fallen off?"

"I merely removed her from the scarlet room. De Blanchard had been sniffing round her. For a mere ten guineas, I purchased her safety for the night."

"And nothing else?"

Heat warmed Henry's cheeks at the memory of the grateful girl's administrations, the shame in her eyes when he'd rejected her.

"Dray?" Oakville nudged him. "Are you all right?"

He nodded, and they approached the front door.

A shrill cry rang out.

Oakville chuckled. "That's the sound of a woman being pleasured."

Henry's stomach tightened. The cry had come from inside the house. He looked up at his wife's window. Two shapes moved, silhouetted against the light. A man and a woman. They drew close, merging into a single shape, then parted. Moments later, a man emerged from the side of the house and disappeared down the street.

"I'll have that drink another night," Rupert said. "I have no wish to witness the cuckolded husband confronting his wife's infidelity." He lifted his lapels and thrust his hands into his pockets and set off in the stranger's wake.

Once inside the house, Henry went straight to his study and poured a brandy. His fingers itched to curl around his wife's throat. *How could she!* Thoughts of her had invaded his dreams, driving out the images of the other women he'd enjoyed over the years. Each morning he woke with a cockstand which ached to be inside her. She even penetrated his waking thoughts. Rosaline's offer to pleasure herself for him had awakened a primal appetite; the need to see his wife, his Jeanette, bringing herself to pleasure at her own hands, readying her body for him until he buried himself inside her, claiming the moment of completion for himself.

Yet she had turned her attentions elsewhere.

He tightened his grip on the glass, then hurled it at the door. It burst into splinters on impact, pinpricks of light shattering in the air before dissolving onto the floor.

"Damn her!"

CHAPTER EIGHTEEN

"CHARLOTTE!"

Jeanette's heart leapt with joy at the sight of her new friend in Hyde Park.

"Lady Ravenwell, should you greet me so openly? Aren't you concerned what people might say?"

"Let them say what they will. And please, call me Jeanette."

"What about Henry?"

An invisible fist clenched her heart at the mention of his name, and Charlotte's familiar use of it.

"We barely speak," she sighed. "He's gone by the time I take my breakfast and at night…"

Heat rose in her face, her body burning with need and loss.

"Has Doctor Hill visited you yet?"

"Yes." Jeanette nodded. "He warned me of the dangers of leaving the wound untreated but assured me it should heal cleanly now. I cannot thank you enough.

"I'm so glad," Charlotte said. "Will you be wearing your red dress to the opera tonight? Madame Dupont showed it to me before she packed it to send to you."

"It's a little daring. Perhaps the green…"

"Nonsense! If Henry doesn't already love you, he will once he sees you in that red silk."

Charlotte was right. Henry couldn't maintain the wall of hostility forever. The loving tender man who caressed her to pleasure at night would emerge once more. Perhaps he only needed a little encouragement.

When hope returned to her, hope that he might grow fond of her, then she'd dare to wear the red dress.

⇥⟫⟪⇤

JENKINS ADDRESSED HER as soon as she returned home.

"His lordship awaits you in the library."

Mirroring the interview on the day of her marriage, Jeanette found herself standing before her husband while he sat at his desk. He gestured to the chair in front of him.

As soon as she sat, he held up a letter between thumb and forefinger, distaste on his lips as if the paper burned his skin.

"Doctor Hill is a most anxious correspondent," he said. "You should tell him it's not seemly for husbands to pay him for his services. I rather think *he* should be paying *you*."

"I–I'm sorry…"

He raised a hand, cutting off her apology. "Isn't it a little late for that?"

"I'd asked Doctor Hill to send the account directly to me. Let me settle it myself. I have money of my own."

"Money which I provide." His expression hardened. "Whichever method is used to settle the account, I'm the one who ultimately pays, am I not?"

He crumpled the piece of paper in his hand, then tossed it behind him.

"I've already settled the account. Now go."

He bent his head down, dipped his pen into the inkpot in front of him, and began to write, seemingly ignoring her.

Her legs wobbled as she stood. Before she reached the door, he called out.

"You're not to receive visitors without my permission. Do I make myself clear?"

"Yes," she said quietly.

"...and I trust you appreciate why I must leave you alone until the fruits of your disgrace are revealed or not." He set his pen down and turned his gaze on her, his eyes glacial. "Do you understand?"

Her heart screamed at her to admit she didn't, but his narrowed eyes and dark anger forced her to nod.

"Good. Now get dressed. We leave for Covent Garden in an hour."

Jeanette wouldn't be wearing the red dress tonight.

⫸⫷

BY THE MIDDLE of the third act, the music had driven away Jeanette's melancholy. Her heart lifted as the principal sopranos sang her favorite passage, a duet where the voices soared into the sky like songbirds circling in the warm summer air, higher and higher until they touched the heavens.

Such pure voices! Music had always been a kingdom she could dwell in, away from harsh realities of the world.

She leaned over the edge of the private box Henry had secured to get a better view.

A warm hand touched hers.

"What are they singing?" he whispered in her ear, the soft timbre she thought she'd imagined when he'd carried her from the field, his embrace strong and protecting.

"*Che soave zeffiretto*" she breathed. "What a gentle little zephyr."

"What's the song about?"

"Infidelity. The countess and her servant are seeking to entrap the count, to expose his infidelity."

The hand withdrew, shattering the fragile bond between them.

"Herr Mozart understands the wiles of women almost as well as I."

At the end of the act, he leapt to his feet even before the host announced the interval.

"Stay here," he commanded. "I'll fetch you a drink. Don't speak to anyone."

He disappeared as if he couldn't remove himself from her presence quickly enough.

Moments later, the door opened and a thin, blond man in his forties slipped into the seat beside her, concern on his face.

"Lady Ravenwell, I told you to rest."

"Doctor Hill! I hadn't thought to see you here."

"My wife permits me to indulge in my love of Mozart."

"She must be very accommodating."

"As is your husband. I've never had an account settled so quickly."

Panic tightened her skin. "Doctor Hill, you should leave. My husband mustn't know we've spoken."

"He won't hear it from me."

"Won't hear what?" Henry stood in the doorway, body shaking with anger.

"Have you no shame, woman? I leave you five minutes and this is how you behave!"

"Husband, I…"

"No, your ladyship," Doctor Hill interrupted. "My lord, let me explain…"

"How dare you address me!" In one stride, Henry was upon him and grasped his lapels.

"Come outside."

"Lord Ravenwell, there's been a mistake."

"Be quiet!" Henry pulled him to his feet.

"Can't we discuss this like gentlemen?"

"Gentlemen? Ha!" Henry scoffed "We'll settle this outside. Now."

A handful of onlookers had gathered at the door. By the time Henry manhandled the doctor out of the box, it had turned into a small crowd.

"Henry, no!" Jeanette cried, but he ignored her, dragging the doctor along the corridor. Pushing past the tittering ladies in the crowd, she followed the two men outside. Doctor Hill's protests echoed in the night air as Henry pushed him to the ground.

Ripping off his jacket, Henry drew his hands into fists and adopted a boxing stance.

"Come on, you coward, fight me like a man!"

Whispers rippled through the onlookers, mirroring the shame rippling through Jeanette's body.

"Henry, please…"

"Be quiet, woman!"

The doctor struggled to his feet "Let her explain…"

"There's nothing to explain," Henry snarled. "You've made a cuckold of me. Clearly children of trade flock together."

"Don't be a fool!" the doctor cried. He gestured toward Jeanette. "Show him, for God's sake, woman! Show him what I've been doing."

Henry rushed toward the doctor, fists raised.

"Henry!"

He froze at her scream. For a moment, concern flickered across his face before the fury returned.

"Stop! I'll show you!" She tugged at the fingers of her glove.

"What are you doing?" Henry roared. "Good God, does the Holmestead Harlot seek gratification from giving public displays?"

The nickname cut deep, but she continued to pull her glove off to reveal the bandage on her arm. A dark red stain ran along its length where the wound was, at last, healing cleanly where Doctor Hill had cauterized it with a hot knife.

HENRY STARED AT his wife as she held out her arm. Pain glistened in her eyes. And humiliation to match his own. How could he have thought the worst of her, that she had lain with another? Was it because he'd wanted it to be true in the hope it might extinguish any feelings he harbored for her?

Ugly bloodstains marked the bandage on her arm. Henry ached to ease the pain she must be feeling and he reached out to her.

She flinched from his touch. "Please don't. It's still sore."

"Of course it is," the doctor said crisply.

"What is it?" Henry whispered.

Jeanette looked away. "My bullet wound. From the duel."

Doctor Hill straightened his cravat and issued Henry a hard stare. "It festered. Your wife was lucky not to lose her arm."

While Henry had neglected his wife, she'd had to turn to a stranger, even though Henry had vowed to honor and protect her.

His anger deflated. Henry rubbed his forehead, then addressed the onlookers.

"You've had enough entertainment for tonight. Go back inside."

A few of the ladies disappeared, the rest murmuring to each other.

"Now!"

At his roar, the rest dispersed.

Doctor Hill took Jeanette's hand, and a stab of jealousy tore through Henry. "Have you been taking the draught I prepared for you, Lady Ravenwell?"

She cast a swift glance toward Henry, then nodded.

"And bathing it twice a day as I instructed?"

"Yes."

Henry took her other hand. Her fingers were cold. She tried to pull free, but he held her firm. "Why didn't you tell me, Jeanette? Why were you so damned secretive, letting me think the worst of you?"

"I wanted to spare you further embarrassment and expense," she said. "As for why you thought the worst of me, only you can answer that question."

The light in her eyes had gone.

"Doctor Hill," he said. "I'll send you something in recognition of the care you've taken of my wife thus far, but I'll employ my own physician from now on."

"But…"

"I'm sure you're very capable," Henry interrupted, "but my wife is *my* responsibility."

The doctor's stance changed as he read the challenge in Henry's tone. "Very well," he said. "I'll leave your wife in your care."

Henry took Jeanette's arm, careful to avoid the wound. "It's time we returned home. You've had enough excitement for one evening."

"Henry, I'm sorry…"

"Don't speak of it."

He continued to hold her while they waited for the carriage. Not trusting himself to speak lest he reveal the fear for her which had almost crushed him, he remained silent on the journey home.

CHAPTER NINETEEN

A
LMOST A FORTNIGHT after the altercation at the opera, Jeanette stood alone in the hallway, waiting to greet her guests. Henry was nowhere to be seen, having left the house soon after breakfast. Other than providing the guestlist and giving permission that Sir Daniel and Lady Charlotte be included, he'd shown little interest in Jeanette's dinner party.

Armed with a new haircut and her red silk dress, she greeted her guests cheerfully as if an absent husband was an everyday occurrence.

Jenkins, the model of discretion, had already cleared away Henry's place by the time they entered the dining room. When Jeanette sat at one end, the guests settled in their places along the table, politely ignoring the blank space at the opposite end. To her left sat two members of parliament—Tories Benjamin Green, with his wife Annabel, and Guy Chantry, with his wife Roseanna, together with the Earl of Strathdean. To Jeanette's right sat Sir Daniel and Charlotte. Oakville sat next to Charlotte, and beyond him, the Countess of Strathdean. Dominic Hartford completed the party.

Conscious of several pairs of eyes watching her, Jeanette signaled for dinner to begin and the guests began to eat. The complex palette of flavors burst on her tongue with every bite. Mrs. Pratt was indeed a genius in the kitchen.

"I must congratulate you on your new cook, Lady Ravenwell."

She turned to the gentleman on her left. "My cook has been in my husband's employ for several years, Mister Green."

"Then I must commend you, madam, on your choice of menu. I have never tasted a meal at your husband's table as enjoyable as this."

"You flatter me."

The politician's fleshy face puckered into a leer, and he moved his hand toward hers. His gaze drifted over her gown, settling on the green trim at the top of her bodice. "Perhaps I should make him an offer."

Jeanette picked up her wine glass, the action pushing the unwelcome hand aside. "I'll pass your compliments to Mrs. Pratt, but neither she nor I are open to any offer you might make. I'm taking her to Sussex with me when the season is over."

"*Mrs.* Pratt? A woman?"

"A woman of talent is not such a remote possibility, surely?"

"We live in a world of men, Lady Ravenwell. Our finest monarchs have been men."

"Only because the law, written by men, dictates in favor of male supremacy," she said. "And I beg to differ. The greatest monarch to rule this country was a woman."

"Do you insult the present king, madam, or the Regent?" Wounded male pride rendered his voice thin and reedy.

"Not at all," Jeanette laughed. "I'm saying that given the same opportunities as a man, a woman may show merit in equal measure."

"Good lord, woman, if I were your husband…"

"…you'd be ruled by her, and rightly so," Charlotte interrupted, leaning forward into the candlelight. Her expressive blue eyes sparkled with wit and intelligence. No wonder Henry had once been captivated by her.

"A man may appear robust," Charlotte said, "but even the mightiest fortress relies on the foundations upon which it has been built, even if those foundations are overlooked."

Charlotte raised her glass and gestured toward Jeanette. "A clever woman is the foundation of a successful marriage," she continued. "An individual's quality is not a function of their sex, yet the recognition they achieve is wholly dependent upon it."

"Indeed," Sir Daniel interjected, "and I count myself the most fortunate of husbands."

"As is Lord Ravenwell," Charlotte replied. "Let us toast Lady Ravenwell on what promises to be an excellent evening."

The meal concluded and the men disappeared to enjoy their port while Jeanette ushered the ladies into the drawing room. The politicians' wives, clearly old friends, paired up and moved toward the window, casting furtive glances at Charlotte.

"How tedious!" Charlotte sat beside Jeanette and sighed. "If my life were forever confined to drawing room gossip, I'd pray for death. I'm glad to have you as a friend. Women who wish to elevate themselves above the status of biddable slaves are rare indeed."

Jeanette took a sip of her coffee. "Sir Daniel permits you to speak so freely?"

"I temper my speech to suit his tastes," Charlotte said. "The trick to ruling your man is to make him believe he's in command of the ship and the business."

"How do you achieve that?"

"By steering his mind and ideas in the right direction," Charlotte said. "Of course, a woman must never be obvious. Her methods should be indirect."

"Underhanded?"

"If you like. A wife can ensure her own ideas are carried out if she's capable of persuading her husband they're of his own making. One only need to sow a few seeds, watch them grow in his mind, and nurture them as necessary."

Charlotte drained her cup. "Sir Daniel is not without wits, but he sometimes requires a little *direction*." Her mouth curled into a smile. "All men can be ruled if the hand on the tiller is skilled enough."

"Does that include my husband? Can you rule him?"

Charlotte's smile slipped. "Nobody can persuade Henry to do anything he doesn't want to." She placed a hand on Jeanette's arm. "And that includes his decision to marry you. You're an intelligent woman, Jeanette. I'm sure you'll learn to rule Henry as effortlessly as I rule Daniel. Ah, here he is!"

Jeanette's heart leapt at Charlotte's exclamation before it deflated just as rapidly as Sir Daniel entered the room with the other gentlemen. The men helped themselves to coffee and distributed themselves among the ladies.

Sir Daniel joined his wife, and Jeanette rose to leave them, unwilling to look any longer at the devotion in his eyes. *Some* men loved their wives.

But not all. Guy Chantry rolled his eyes while he watched his wife tittering with laughter before he joined Jeanette by the fireplace, Oakville in his wake.

"I must thank you, Lady Ravenwell, for a most interesting evening. I'm sorry your husband was unable to attend."

Was he taunting her with Henry's absence? Did he know Henry was pleasuring another woman?

"Not at all," she replied, "given the enormity of my husband's *business,* I didn't expect him until late."

Chantry fixed her with a hard stare. "So you know? About all the-the..."

"All the women?" she said bitterly. "Of course."

Chantry shook his head. "Hardly a topic for conversation with one's wife, murdered whores."

Murder? What was he speaking of? Had her idle words, spoken in anger, revealed something more sinister than mere debauchery? Chantry glanced at Oakville.

Jeanette drained her coffee in an attempt to regain composure. "Whether the victim is a prostitute doesn't render the crime any less severe. Or do you think such a woman has no worth?"

"A whore is a whore, Lady Ravenwell."

"She serves a purpose, and a man's needs, Mister Chantry. If some poor soul is willing or desperate enough to service those needs, who are we to judge?"

Oakville's mouth twitched into a smile as Chantry's expression grew uncomfortable.

"May I ask you a direct question, Mister Chantry?" she asked.

"Of course." His expression contradicted his words.

"Have you partaken of a courtesan's services?"

Oakville snorted, and Chantry choked on his coffee.

"Forgive me," Jeanette said, "I'm asking for academic reasons. I'm not interested in gossip. It's my belief that men who enjoy those services have a responsibility to help those who provide them."

"Madam, I beg you to be discreet..."

"Help can be given discreetly," she interrupted. "These women are human beings, victims of circumstance or birth. Mister Chantry, had God chosen differently I, even you, might have found ourselves in a similar position."

"But we're not," Oakville interjected.

"That's your good fortune, Viscount Oakville. Fate placed you into a life of idle luxury, but you could have been born into poverty, even slavery."

"That, as you say, is my good fortune," Oakville said.

"Why not put that good fortune to better use? We shouldn't judge a person by the circumstances of their birth, but what they do with the hand fate dealt them."

"If I may be excused," Chantry said. "I believe my wife wants a word."

He scuttled off, a look of nausea on his face.

Oakville smiled. "You never cease to amaze me, Lady Ravenwell. I'm beginning to understand the enormity of what I lost when I abandoned you."

How dare he continue to taunt her with what he'd done!

"Don't be friendly toward me, sir. I tolerate your company tonight as my husband's friend and nothing more."

Before he could reply, she clapped her hands and addressed her guests.

"Time for a little music?"

Amid murmurs of assent, Oakville led her toward the pianoforte and helped her to sit. He leafed through the sheet music and selected a piece.

"I haven't forgotten what you said to me about music. I often think of it."

Ignorant fool! As if he'd listened to anything she'd said!

His smile wavered. "I see you're skeptical. But you've taught me to view the world differently. I remember everything we talked about."

"Oh, really?"

"You prefer music to the written word. You said a musician can put her soul into a recital. And I agree. Depending on how she articulates herself, the same piece of music can be happy and merry, or tragic and melancholy."

"Some pieces are meant to be played tragically," she said, lifting the sheet music he'd selected. Beethoven's Sonata number fourteen in C-sharp minor.

She began to play, and the guests murmured among themselves as they recognized the melody. A well-known piece, nevertheless, Oakville's ability to turn the pages at the right moment was unexpected.

His proximity grew unsettling. As Jeanette let the music overtake her, the sense of abandonment coursed through her body. Her fingers expressed her desolation at the prospect of a life without love. Oakville's silent, watchful aid only increased her distress.

As the first movement drew to a close, his fingers brushed her shoulder, a gesture of recognition and consolation.

"Bravo."

Strength flowed from her heart and soul into her fingers. She cut her guests' applause short by continuing with the second movement, a brighter, happier piece, before pausing for breath on the final chord.

Melancholy morphed into fury. Henry had abandoned her, such that she found herself unwillingly drawing comfort from a man she had determined to hate. Turning the pages with a sharp snap, she threw herself into the final movement. Her fingers flew across the keyboard as months of practice and weeks of neglect forged a union in the fires of her anger.

Only through music could she withdraw from a world where women were slighted, abandoned, and murdered, and the men ignored it. Henry might despise her, he might have abandoned her to failure and humiliation, but with music, she could express her disgust while these ignorant fools around her listened, oblivious to her emotions.

Not all. After she played the final chord, Oakville whispered in her ear, "That was exquisite. Tonight, you've shown us what true beauty is."

CHAPTER TWENTY

A S HENRY ENTERED the hallway, music filtered into his mind. A passionate run of notes swelled into a crescendo before the flourish of arpeggios, ending with the final chord as the footman opened the drawing room door.

He didn't need to look to identify the pianist. Since he'd first heard her practicing that Beethoven piece, she'd grown in accomplishment.

He held his hand up to silence the footman who was about to announce him. Transfixed by the music, the guests had not noticed his arrival.

The woman at the piano was barely recognizable. Since he'd left her that morning, she'd had her hair cut, the sleeker style becoming her. Her gown radiated confidence, the red silk resonating against the color of her eyes. The shockingly low cut of the gown revealed the swell of her breasts. Madame Dupont had surpassed herself. Just the right side of decency the style would likely grace most of London's ballrooms before the end of the Season.

Oakville stood behind her. From his vantage point, he'd be able to view much more of her flesh than was acceptable, yet he seemed too spellbound by the music to notice.

Henry's groin hardened with exquisite agony at the sight of her. Falling in love with her was out of the question, but his body, and latterly his heart, had other ideas. If he didn't take care, his soul would follow.

Oakville bent forward and whispered in her ear. She turned her head toward him and a smile played on her lips. What had he said to her?

He looked up, and his eyes met Henry's, and their shared expressions hardened.

"My lord!" Jeanette rose to greet him, hurt and hope in her eyes.

Henry took her hand and kissed it before acknowledging the guests, the odious Green and the slightly more appealing Chantry, who at least recognized that whores were being murdered, even if he didn't care enough to spur the Runners into a more active investigation. Sir Daniel approached him, his wife on his arm. Lady Charlotte blushed and glanced at Jeanette.

Oakville drew him aside.

"You've finally graced us with your presence. How long do you intend to continue your disgraceful behavior toward your wife?"

"Save your breath, Oakville, I'm not in the mood."

"The least you can do is apologize. You abandoned her to the mercy of these people, yet she's coped admirably considering how she must be feeling."

Fueled by guilt, Henry lashed out. "*You're* the villain, Oakville. You compromised her and left me to pick up the tatters and shackle myself to her."

"Shackle yourself!" Oakville scoffed. "I'd give anything to be in your position. You don't deserve her."

"Stay away from her," Henry growled, "she's mine."

"You don't want her! Or is it that you don't want anybody else to have her?" He gestured to the other guests. "Look around, Dray. Right now, you're the only man in the room who's not utterly, completely in love with her!"

Henry pushed past his friend and addressed the guests.

"Forgive my late appearance, but I trust you understand, I'm a little tired."

"Of course." Ever the diplomat, the Earl of Strathdean took the lead. "Come, my dear," he said to his wife, "it's time we left. I hadn't realized how late it was."

The Earl bowed over Jeanette's hand and kissed it. "I hope to enjoy the pleasure of your company, and Lord Ravenwell's, at our ball later this week. Having enjoyed your accomplishments at the pianoforte, I'm anxious to see you dance."

Jeanette lifted her eyes in question, but Henry shook his head.

"My wife leaves for Sussex tomorrow."

The Earl frowned, but his expression did not match the hurt and confusion in Jeanette's eyes.

"Perhaps another time," she said quietly, giving the earl a tight smile.

Like a receding tide, the rest of the party followed the earl's lead, each taking Jeanette's hand to bid her goodnight. Oakville, however, remained, puffing out his chest in a gesture of challenge. Henry ignored him and ushered the other guests out.

When he returned to the drawing room, Jeanette was busying herself tidying the coffee cups. He opened his mouth to admonish her, but when she lifted her gaze to him, his conscience silenced his tongue. He'd hurt her enough for one evening.

In that, at least, one person agreed. Oakville slid across the room, his eyes narrowed into slits.

"I've never been so ashamed to call you my friend."

Porcelain clattered in the far end of the room. Jeanette moved about, seemingly absorbed in her task, but her spine had stiffened.

"Where would you be, Oakville, if it weren't for my friendship?"

"On a more virtuous and prosperous path."

"Nonsense! You've relished the chance to play the rake. How many mistresses have you serviced this season?"

"At least I have the tenacity not to grow bored after only a few fucks."

"Why you…"

"Stop!" a female voice cried. Jeanette stood before him, body heaving, face flushed a distressed shade of red.

"Get out," Henry snarled. "This is no place for you."

"Do you mean I have no place in a dogfight between two foolish men or that I have no place in society?"

"Let your conscience decide."

"Oh, that's enough!" Oakville cried. He pushed Henry against the door, forcing the air from his lungs as his back met the solid wood.

"I'm calling you out."

"Don't be a fool."

Oakville thrust his face close, his eyes dark with rage. "You think I jest?"

"Very well," Henry snarled. "Choose your weapon."

"No!" A high scream pierced the air. "Please!"

Why did she insist on remaining? A duel was a matter of honor between men, not women.

"This is no place for you, woman. You don't understand."

"Yes, I do." Her quiet words cut into his heart more deeply than her scream. "Henry, please. A bullet wound is nothing I wish to see inflicted on anyone."

For a moment, her eyes mirrored the image which seared through his mind; the flash of an explosion, the sting in his ears at the sound of the shot, blood spreading across white muslin, and finally her inert body, crumpled and broken in the middle of the field, the culmination of her ruination which his friend had plotted. And Henry had encouraged and profited from.

"Very well," he said, "no pistols. But Oakville and I must settle this."

"No…" Jeanette protested.

"Silence!" he roared. "You pledged to obey me. Do as I say and remain where you are while we finish this."

"Come on then." Oakville pulled Henry into the hall. He peeled his jacket off and threw it onto the floor.

Jerking loose from Oakville's grip, Henry removed his own jacket and fisted his hands. Anger and frustration boiled within him, a coiled spring waiting to release. His superior boxing skills would flatten Oakville at the first strike.

"Do your worst," Henry said.

Oakville circled him with the controlled motion of a predator, waiting for the moment to strike. *Foolish man!* Henry was ready for him, superior in everything—looks, wealth, and prowess. He even possessed the woman Oakville wanted.

"I need do very little to expose you for what you really are, Dray."

"Words?" Henry laughed. "Is that all you have, the weapons of a woman?"

"All you have are your cock and your fists, the weapons of a savage," Oakville replied. "It may have escaped your notice that society has evolved since the dark ages. This has been well overdue."

"What has?"

"The opportunity to educate you." Oakville's mouth curled into a smile. "Time you learned how to be a man."

The spring snapped. With a roar, Henry lunged forward and landed a punch on Oakville's shoulder.

Oakville skipped to one side. "Is that all you can do, besides humiliate your wife in public?"

Henry threw his body at Oakville again, and the two men toppled to the floor, arms and legs thrashing against each other. He threw punch after punch, many of them striking the floor with a burst of pain in his fingers, but the occasional blow met its target. Oakville's grunts of pain accentuated the pounding of bloodlust in Henry's ears.

"Stop! Please!"

Oakville's body stiffened at the sound of female distress. Curse the man, had he grown to care for her as well as lust after her? Henry scrambled to his feet, wiping his mouth while Oakville struggled to rise more slowly. A red mark just below his left eye was already beginning to swell.

"That's enough, both of you!" Jeanette's voice had the angry tone of a schoolmistress. "What are you thinking, brawling on the floor while you accuse me of being unfit for society? Is this how men settle their differences, using their bodies because their minds are too weak?"

Oakville brandished his fists, and she stepped between them.

"Stop! If you can't respect my husband, try to respect yourself. I won't have bloodshed in my home."

"Does the lady waver at the sight of blood?" Henry sneered, the invisible little devil lurking inside his brain willing him to taunt her for forcing him to lose self-control.

She turned to face him, defeat in her eyes. Behind her, Oakville tensed, his visceral reaction more vivid than Jeanette's quiet sigh. He lunged toward Henry, drawing his arm back to deal the final blow.

But Jeanette was in the way.

"Jeanette!"

Henry pushed her aside just in time. Oakville's blow connected with Henry's jaw, and he staggered back as pain exploded in his head.

"Stop! I insist!" Jeanette cried. "I've had enough of this. I want you to leave. You've disgraced yourself and me more than enough for a lifetime."

Her voice hardened. "I said *leave*. Now!"

Finally, the devil within Henry had succeeded. He'd lost her regard. Wiping his eyes to clear them, he nodded. It was better this way, to not to let himself fall in love with her.

But Jeanette wasn't addressing Henry. She prodded Oakville in the chest.

"Go."

Oakville cast Henry a look of disgust, picked up his jacket, and limped out of the hall.

Soft, warm fingers curled around Henry's hand.

"Let me take you to the kitchen."

The heat from Mrs. Pratt's cooking had yet to disperse. Henry sat at the kitchen table while Jeanette peeled off his shirt, tutting at the marks on his skin where Oakville's punches had hit home. His chin throbbed, each heartbeat intensifying the pain.

She held a cloth against his jaw. The tangy scent of herbs sharpened in his nostrils before he registered the sting of pain and drew a hiss of air between his teeth.

"Shh…" she whispered. "Keep still."

She took his hand and lifted it to the poultice.

"Hold this."

Henry complied, his body too weary to argue.

His heart also.

His skin tightened at the delicate brush of fingertips against his chest. Closing his eyes only served to heighten his other senses, her floral scent not completely masked by the woody aroma of the salve.

"Henry…"

The almost inaudible whisper caused a ripple of sensation to course through his body. It was not the lust he battled with each time she was near, but another enemy threatening to break through the barriers he'd constructed around his heart.

Love.

He dropped the poultice and took her hands.

"Henry, your jaw. You must…"

"Hush." He pulled her close and pressed his mouth against hers. He sought entrance with his tongue, and with a whimper, she welcomed him. Moisture glistened in the corners of her eyes and a low groan bubbled in her throat.

She was a woman starved. He was the one who'd starved her, yet now, he gladly quenched her hunger, a simple kiss expressing more love than he ever could with words.

Jeanette. His Jeanette. She belonged to him. Only him. Like a warrior, she'd stepped into the fray and defended him, even though Oakville had been the more deserving. What would his life be with such a woman by his side? What might she become if she knew he was beginning to love her?

She must never know. Love was a weakness. He must pack her off to Sussex before he succumbed. She might view Ravenwell Hall as a prison, isolated from the world, but at least she'd be safe there thinking, as the world thought, that he cared nothing for her.

CHAPTER TWENTY-ONE

DURING THE RIDE to Sussex, Jeanette's husband returned to the cold dispassionate man of her wedding day. What had happened to the tender moment they'd shared last night? Her heart and body had melted as he'd kissed her for the first time since their marriage, then carried her to bed. Reverently, he'd peeled off her clothes before claiming her body, worshipping her with his hands and mouth.

Whispered words of love had turned into hoarse cries of passion until he shouted his release and pulled her close while his body shuddered with the aftershocks of his lovemaking.

And lovemaking it had been. His eyes had never left hers, their dark blue depths baring his soul. After finishing inside her, he'd nestled his head against her chest, murmuring her name while his mouth once more sought her breast, his warm sigh caressing her skin as he fell into a contented sleep. But in the morning, she'd woken with only the memory of his tenderness and the imprint of his body on the bed.

The carriage drew to a halt and tipped sideways as Henry shifted his weight to climb out. Jeanette followed and stepped onto the gravel in front of Ravenwell Hall.

It was the biggest building she had ever seen.

Pale gray stone stretched across her eyeline, window after window three stories high. To the left, a neatly clipped lawn stretched into the distance where an intricate pattern of bushes had been trained into a maze. To her right, a path led to a lake across which the call of moorhens echoed. Beyond the lake, the driveway stretched back through the park.

The metallic taste of salt in the air caught in her throat. The hall was close to Brighton, the Regent's seaside town of debauchery. Would Henry join him there, to indulge in whoring after he'd deposited Jeanette in her prison?

A stiff row of servants led toward the main doors. Jeanette moved along the line, addressing each one until she reached the housekeeper, Mrs. Barnes, who stood next to her husband, the steward. Though he paid Jeanette due reverence, his attention was constantly focused on his wife, the devotion evident in his eyes and the way he touched her arm unconsciously.

How she envied Mrs. Barnes at that moment! The loveless existence of a marchioness paled in comparison to the honest partnership between a man and a woman in service.

The formalities concluded, and Henry ushered Jeanette into the building. "I'll leave you in Mrs. Barnes' capable hands, my dear. You'll understand my anxiety to return to London."

"You're leaving? Now?"

"This very moment."

"Then go," she said coldly, no longer able to temper her frustration. "I care not."

The steward exchanged a look with his wife, then addressed Henry.

"May I have a word, sir?"

"Not now, Barnes."

"It's important."

"I said, not now!"

Mr. Barnes colored and exchanged another glance with his wife. Was Henry so eager to rid himself of Jeanette that he'd stoop to insulting the staff?

After the carriage disappeared between the trees, Jeanette turned her back and sighed.

"You must do something, John," Mrs. Barnes whispered.

"I've never seen him in such a temper. Why did he leave so swiftly?"

The couple glanced toward Jeanette, and Mrs. Barnes dropped a curtsey.

"If you'd like to follow me, your ladyship, I'll show you to the parlor in the west wing where you can take tea."

⟫⟫⟫⟪⟪⟪

THE CARRIAGE SWAYED from side to side as it retraced its path along the driveway. Henry winced at the sound of the driver's whip cracking, but they needed to maintain a swift pace to reach London before nightfall.

Better that than remain in Sussex. His family home reeked of memories of a loveless childhood exacerbated by the oppressive presence of dismal portraits of his ancestors which haunted the corridors. It would always serve as a mausoleum to mark the absence of love, an estate neglected while Father spent his time and money elsewhere.

He couldn't even escape after he'd been packed off to Eton. Two years into his schooling, he'd been forced to return mid-term to bury his parents after they had been killed during one of Father's brief visits to Sussex. Killed when their carriage overturned in a rut.

Henry couldn't blame Mama for his parents' failed marriage. The epitome of aristocratic perfection, she had possessed the qualities a marquis needed in a wife, including an absence of passion. The capacity to truly love had been bred and schooled out of her.

Were it not for Mrs. Barnes, Henry would have assumed all wives were devoid of feeling toward their husbands. But the steward and his wife displayed a love not seen in society marriages, an equal partnership, strong in their own right, but united, an indestructible force. Witnessing them on the threshold of Ravenwell Hall only served to remind him of the relationship he could never have.

He closed his eyes only to be assaulted by Jeanette's cold expression as she had dismissed him.

Go. I care not.

Better he remain detached; the price of falling in love was too great.

The wheels hit another rut, and Henry almost lost his seat as the carriage pitched sideways. The road was sorely in need of repair, but Henry knew better than to ask Barnes why he hadn't seen to it. He glanced out the window as they passed a series of buildings, farms in various states of disrepair, others abandoned.

What better evidence was there of the price of love? At least in London he wouldn't have to be confronted with it.

⇥⟫⟪⇤

THE FOLLOWING MORNING, after a solitary breakfast, Jeanette instructed the footman to show her to Henry's study, then send for Mr. Barnes. To his credit, the footman's expression hardly changed at such an unladylike request. But the time had come to assert herself.

She might not understand the duties of the lady of such a large estate, but it was no different from a business with assets, liabilities, and employed staff. Her existence here might not be completely pointless.

Henry's study was as masculine as she'd expected. Dark oak panels lined the walls, the smell of ink and tobacco lingering on the furnishings. She settled into the studded leather chair behind the squat, rectangular desk and ran her finger along the carvings adorning the perimeter of the surface. Not a speck of dust. Someone tended to the room daily.

"Lady Ravenwell?"

The steward stood in the doorway. Jeanette gestured to the chair in front of the desk.

"Sit down."

The leather creaked around his body as he complied.

"Mr. Barnes, I wish to understand the running of the estate as soon as possible."

"Forgive me, but that's the province of Lord Ravenwell."

"Who chose to return to London without fulfilling his duty to it."

"That may be, your Ladyship, but I cannot discuss the estate with anyone but him."

"Because he's a man?" She leaned forward. "At least tell me the problem. And don't deny it. I may be a woman, but I'm no fool."

He hesitated. "I…"

"I won't leave this room," she interrupted, "or permit *you* to leave, until you explain what's wrong. So, I'd advise you to speak now to save both our time. Given my husband's lack of business acumen, I suspect the problem is financial, yes?"

A spark of respect lit his eyes. "Our income has been falling, but costs are increasing."

"Then let's start with the income."

"Very well," he said. "Tenants have struggled to pay their rent."

"And why's that?"

"Illness, mostly. Some of the farmers are no longer producing an income."

"And what do you do?"

"What we've always done. Evict them."

"Why not send a physician to tend to them?"

"Physicians cost money. His Lordship would never sanction the expenditure."

"What do you do with the properties? Find other tenants?"

"No, they remain empty."

How senseless! Did Henry think turning out tenants was the prudent thing to do, whether or not he cared for their welfare?

"Why not let them remain? They can accrue arrears and pay rent when they can afford it again. Better that than have empty properties fall into ruin."

"What if they cannot pay their arrears?"

"They could work for it. There must be some service they can perform."

The steward shook his head. "Their sort would take advantage. They're a different breed to the rest of us…"

He lowered his gaze. "I'm sorry, my lady. I didn't mean…"

"You didn't mean me? My father has worked hard all his life. People of his class work hard, some through necessity, others through a desire to better themselves."

"You must admit there are those unwilling to work."

"In my experience, the laziest creatures belong to my husband's social class, not mine."

The steward's lip twitched, as if suppressing a rush of amusement.

"Give the tenants a chance, Mr. Barnes," Jeanette said. "A little compassion and the opportunity to improve their lives will secure their loyalty. If we can restore the estate's income, my husband can congratulate himself on having such a clever steward."

"And if we fail?"

"He can commiserate himself on having such an interfering wife."

Mr. Barnes smiled. "I think he's made an excellent choice of wife."

"You're very kind," Jeanette smiled. "And now, if you could oblige me, I'd like to inspect the ledgers."

"But Lord Ravenwell…" The steward paused, then smiled, "…is not here. Very well, I'll bring you the ledgers for the past year."

"The past ten, if you please."

Mr. Barnes let out a laugh. "Yes," he said, "an excellent choice of wife, indeed."

It seemed Jeanette had an ally.

>>>><<<<

BY THE TIME Jeanette had finished, the sunlight had faded. Rays of light which had stretched across the rug in Henry's study had long since been replaced by shadows. She dropped the final book onto the floor, and it landed with a puff of dust. Amid her coughing, the steward entered the room.

"Shall I ask Mrs. Barnes to bring more tea?" He looked pointedly at the teacup on the desk, still full, its contents stone cold.

"No, thank you." She gestured to a chair. "Would you sit?"

"Forgive me, Lady Ravenwell, but I have to see..."

"It wasn't a request, Mr. Barnes."

Understanding flashed across his face. "You've found something?"

"I believe I have," she replied. "It dates back eight years."

His body stiffened. But the accounts had been prepared honestly, the steward demonstrating, as she'd told Henry during their first encounter, that he was more deserving of an Oxford education than his master.

"I'm not implying foul play, Mr. Barnes, but certain patterns in the accounts seem to have been overlooked."

"Patterns?"

"Subtle at first," she said, "but over a sustained period they've compounded to have a detrimental effect on the estate's financial position."

"For example?"

"You said tenants have been failing to pay their rent. This seems to have begun eight years ago. Did anything specific happen then?"

He looked to one side, as if recalling a memory. "The year 1807; a harsh winter, if I recall. What have you discovered?"

"After a sustained period of increase, the tenancy income fell in the year seven and has continued to fall. At first, the reductions were almost too small to be noticed, but then the income began to fall by larger increments, presumably representing the evictions."

"Hardly enough to bring the estate into ruin."

"Not in isolation, but the estate, like a business, resembles a living organism. Each part, and person, performs a function on which the others rely. The loss of tenants doesn't just affect the cashflow; one must consider the other benefits the tenants bring to the estate."

"Such as?"

"Goods and services, Mr. Barnes. The farmer who cannot tend to his crops or livestock is unable to supply the household."

"A single farmer can't bring an estate into ruin."

"But he has a family, sons who work the land—builders, foresters. He has daughters, women who work in the household, family ties which keep him loyal. Evict him, and others will follow. From what I've seen, ten families have left the estate in the past two years alone."

"How can ten families have made such an impact?"

"*One* family can make an impact when the accounts are balanced so delicately," she said. "Take the farmers, for example. The land hereabouts is ideal for cattle, yet according to the ledgers, there hasn't been a livestock farm here for seven years. Mrs. Barnes has all the beef and mutton sent from London."

"You're suggesting we stop ordering beef and mutton?"

"Of course not, but have you considered the impact, over seven years, of buying supplies which the estate previously produced? A London merchant is a fool if he adds anything less than fifty percent profit over the market price of his beef. Add the costs of transportation from London, it's plain to see why the estate is losing money. You're lining the pockets of merchants, where a farmer would have charged you considerably less and also yielded rent."

"What makes you think merchants are overcharging us by such a margin?"

"My father made his fortune selling to the idle rich who couldn't be bothered to put their own estates to good use. The prices in your ledgers exceed what Papa used to charge per pound by twenty percent."

"What do you propose, Lady Ravenwell?"

"Do any farmers on the estate have experience with livestock?"

He drummed his fingers on the desk. "There's Robert Milton. His father, old Mr. Milton, had a herd."

"Where's old Mr. Milton?"

The steward colored and shook his head. "Patterns."

"What do you mean, Mr. Barnes?"

"He died eight years ago; shortly after, his herd all but died out. Why didn't I notice?"

"Sometimes we're too close to the points of detail to spot the link between them." She pushed back her chair and stood. The steward followed suit.

"Will you take supper now, my lady?"

"Yes, thank you," she said. "Then tomorrow you can take me to Robert Milton."

"But he's a farmer! Wouldn't you rather I brought him to you?"

"No, I wish to see his farm."

"But you're..."

"...the *daughter* of a farmer, Mr. Barnes."

He smiled before opening the study door to let her through. "And, I might add, a better prospect for Ravenwell than the daughter of a gentleman."

CHAPTER TWENTY-TWO

T HE DEEP, THROATY caws of the rooks echoed through the trees as the gig drove past and a cloud of birds burst through the treetops, disturbed from their roost. Shortly afterward, a stone farmhouse came into view. Several slates were missing from the roof. Some had been patched, but to Jeanette's eyes, it was yet more evidence of neglect. A skilled roofer would not have left such large gaps through which rain would seep and frosts would penetrate.

Beside the farmhouse were a number of outbuildings, including a squat stone building with a steep, sloped roof and the tell-tale charring around the windows typical of a smokehouse. In the field immediately behind, tufts of wheat moved to and fro in the breeze with a fluid, rippling motion. The fields beyond were empty.

A man leading two bullocks along the perimeter fence waved and called out. Mr. Barnes raised his hand in response.

The gig drew to a halt at the farmhouse beside a painted wooden door, framed with a climbing rose bush, dotted with delicate pink blooms. A thin, dark-haired woman opened the door, a baby in her arms. On seeing Jeanette, she shrank back.

"My husband's in the field."

Her voice held an undercurrent of apprehension. And well it might. A visit from the steward was usually the precursor to an eviction. The previous quarter day, Robert Milton had only been able to pay half the rent due. Last year, his brothers had been evicted.

"Mrs. Milton, I must commend you on your beautiful roses," Jeanette said. "Forgive me for the imposition, but may we sit in your kitchen?"

The woman dipped into a curtsey. "Of course, your ladyship. Let me put the baby down before I show you."

She turned to leave, and Jeanette caught her arm, her heart clenching as the woman flinched.

"Please wait with us," Jeanette said. "I have no wish for you to be parted from your child on our account."

»»»—«««

ROBERT MILTON WAS a giant of a man. He had to hunch his shoulders to avoid his head brushing the top of the doorframe. On entering the kitchen, he ran his hands through his thick, red hair before wiping them on a cloth tied to his belt.

"Ma'am." He bowed to Jeanette before casting a wary glance at his wife. She shook her head, and Jeanette saw a slight relaxing in his shoulders.

"Are ye wanting tea, your ladyship?"

"No, thank you, Mr. Milton, I won't keep you long."

"We're here to discuss the farm," Mr. Barnes said. The farmer's stance stiffened again.

"Please don't be alarmed," Jeanette interjected, "your tenancy is secure. But I'd like to know more about your family, and your farm."

"What do ye want to know?"

She nodded toward the baby. "How many children do you have?"

"Three," he replied. "Two sons and baby Lily there."

"How old are your sons?"

"Robert, our eldest, turns fourteen this year, and Stephen is twelve."

"Old enough to help you on the farm?"

"Aye."

"What livestock do you have?"

"Two head of cattle."

"The bullocks I saw in the field," Jeanette said. "If I'm not mistaken, they're Sussex cattle, yes?"

The farmer's eyes widened. "Ye know about the Sussex?"

"Aye, I do. Originally a draught breed but prized for their versatility in being able to produce profitable quantities of both beef and milk. My father bred Herefords, but he said the Sussex were far superior. He once read a journal in which they were described as being unquestionably ranked among the best in the kingdom."

The farmer's face brightened into a smile. "I read that journal myself. My father…"

He broke off, his smile disappearing.

"I understand your father had a herd?" Jeanette said. "Did you help him?"

"Aye. My brothers and I grew up tending to the herd. After he fell ill, I tried to run the farm for him."

"So you know how to farm livestock?"

"Aye, both cattle and sheep."

"Excellent! Then I have a proposition for you, a herd of your own."

The light in his eyes dimmed. "I couldn't afford it."

"That's where I come in," Jeanette said. "I can provide you with sufficient funds to purchase, say, ten head of cattle as a start?"

"A new herd wouldn't yield much in the short term."

"I understand that, Mr. Milton, which is why I've asked Mr. Barnes here to make inquiries locally for employment. It'll be harvest time soon, and the neighboring estates would pay handsomely for any labor your family could provide."

"It'd be too much work for me. Robert and Stevie can only help me so much."

"What about your brothers, Mr. Milton? If they returned to the estate, your family can be reunited."

"Forgive me, but I cannot take charity from a lady."

"Consider it a loan," Jeanette said. "As for being a lady, I'm a farmer's daughter first and foremost. What better purpose could I put my pin money to than investing in a farm? I confess, I'd relish the prospect of attending a cattle market again."

The steward choked on his water, and Mr. Milton arched an eyebrow. "Ye'd want to come with me to Chichester?"

"Mr. Barnes's constitution would not entertain it," Jeanette laughed.

The farmer and his wife exchanged another glance, and Jeanette rose from her seat.

"We've imposed on your time long enough, Mr. Milton," she said. "I hope you'll consider my proposition. I'd like nothing more than to see your farm restored. I'll leave Mr. Barnes to make the arrangements. Perhaps you could attend him when you've decided."

The rush of hope in the farmer's eyes told her he'd already made his decision.

JEANETTE SETTLED INTO a routine at Ravenwell. Managing the household took little effort thanks to Mrs. Barnes. The estate was a different matter, but after Jeanette set her plans in motion to restore the fortunes of Milton Farm, the fruits of her labors injected a new enthusiasm into Mr. Barnes who took an active interest in the other tenants, securing paid employment for them in neighboring estates.

A month after Jeanette's proposal, Robert Milton purchased ten head of Sussex cattle at the Chichester market, including a bull he was able to put to use as a stud together with a small flock of Southdown Sheep. Riding past the farm in the gig, Jeanette heard laughter echoing across the fields. Robert's younger brother had returned with his family. Sounds of hammering drifted across the air as the brothers toiled to repair the smokehouse. With luck, the nucleus of hope, which had breathed life into one small holding, would initiate ripples of prosperity throughout the estate.

Aside from the servants, Jeanette had no company except for the portraits of Henry's ancestors which dominated the corridors. Shadowy expressions followed her each time she walked past a painting, eyes hard with disapproval at how she tainted their ancestral home. The finely bred features of the women offset the stern, square jaws of the men. Soon, Jeanette's own portrait would accompany them, an imposter among the aristocrats.

Ye gods, no wonder Henry sought solace among the London lights!

Jeanette turned once more to her music. A Broadwood grand resided in the music room, overlooked by another portrait. The woman in the picture looked a similar age to Jeanette. Her face bore a secret smile, soft gray eyes twinkling as if engaged in mischief.

Jeanette settled on the piano stool and pulled out the sheet music she had been practicing. She ran her fingers over the keys, relishing the melodies which soothed her soul.

After the last note of the final aria of the Goldberg Variations faded away, a deep female voice made Jeanette jump.

"I've not heard that Bach since I was a little girl."

Dressed in black, the woman in the doorway stood almost six feet tall, supported by a cane, her fingers curling claw-like over the tip. Eyes the color of steel focused with sharp intensity on Jeanette.

Henry's maternal grandmother, the dowager duchess.

"Your Grace." Jeanette rose from the piano stool, then dipped into a curtsey.

The woman nodded toward Jeanette's left hand. "My emerald. You must be the commoner my grandson married."

Jeanette straightened her stance. "My name is…"

"Yes, yes, I know who you are." The woman waved a dismissive hand at her. "What I want to know is what made him too ashamed to invite me to the wedding. The cursed boy saw fit only to send me a brief handwritten note."

"He hasn't told you what happened?"

"Henry possesses little sense, but he knows better than to tattle. I loathe gossip myself, but tales always have some element of truth at their core. I heard the upstart daughter of a farmer purposely ruined herself to entrap my grandson. Does the prospect of being a duchess encourage all ladies of your birth to risk their dignity?"

"I have no wish to be a duchess…"

"Yet you married a man who'll inherit a dukedom. My grandson is no easy catch. You succeeded where countless women of superior birth and fortune have failed."

Jeanette's cheeks warmed at the insult, but given Henry's contempt of her, she could hardly expect his nearest relation to welcome her into the family.

The duchess moved further into the room. "How did you snare Henry?"

"I didn't," Jeanette said. "His friend Viscount Oakville ruined my reputation so I challenged him to a duel."

"I'd heard that was Viscount De Blanchard."

"No, *him,* I punched on the nose."

"Dear God," the duchess said. "What was the boy thinking offering his hand to you?"

"I'd suggest you ask him yourself, but he's in London. Would you care for some tea?"

The old woman shook her head, and a ray of sunlight illuminated her face, the color of her eyes sharpening to ice-cold steel.

"No, thank you. I'll write to Henry myself if he lacks the courage to face me. Don't bother to show me out."

꧁꧂

As the tapping of the old woman's cane faded into the distance, Mrs. Barnes appeared at the door.

"Is the duchess not staying?"

"No."

"A pity," Mrs. Barnes said. "I'd hoped the two of you would become friends." She gestured to the portrait above the pianoforte.

"Is that her?"

"Quite the beauty, wasn't she? Mr. Davie's father captured her likeness to perfection back then. Mr. Davie will do the same for you for he's inherited his father's style and talent. You'll see for yourself tomorrow when he begins. He's adept at capturing the unconventional. She was an outsider herself, too.

"She disapproves of my being an outsider," Jeanette said. "As soon as I told her I punched a viscount, she couldn't leave quickly enough."

"Perhaps she's afraid of your right hook." Mrs. Barnes's eyes shone with mirth. "She's forgotten what she once was. The old duke's family despised her for being the daughter of a mere country squire, and her antics did nothing to recommend her. Shortly after she married, she rode a horse up the main staircase of Marcham Hall. If you look carefully, you can see a hoofprint in the wall by the fifth step. But fifty years as a duchess have taken their toll. Her freedom of spirit was eroded years ago."

"I won't let that happen to me, Mrs. Barnes."

"One must adapt to survive. You have proven more than adept at directing the management of the estate; society should be easy in comparison. Why not host a house party? His lordship usually holds one this time of year, so I'm sure he'd approve if you planned one yourself. It can be achieved at relatively little cost to the estate, especially if the tenants who have benefited from your efforts help with the arrangements."

Perhaps Mrs. Barnes was right. What better gratification could Jeanette take from playing society's worst snobs at their own game? She would show Henry that she could fulfill the role of Lady Ravenwell on her own. And there was nothing so desirable to a man such as Henry as a woman who was not in need of him.

⇶⇛⇚⇚

HENRY DROPPED THE letter on his desk. Good heavens, he hadn't expected his wife's transformation into the materialistic society lady to happen so quickly. A house party! Yet more expense on top of the cost of that bloody portrait.

Very well. Let her play the part of the hostess. She wanted him to return to Sussex, did she? She had no right to make demands of him. Women were supposed to obey their husbands, not the other way round. But he'd do exactly what she asked of him, and he would take an additional guest with him.

Perhaps that would teach her a lesson in obedience, and in knowing her place.

CHAPTER TWENTY-THREE

"I FAIL TO understand why Lord Ravenwell isn't here."

Jeanette picked up her glass to disguise the tremble in her hand. Lady Anne Almondbury leaned forward, her elegantly dressed shape coming into view, dark blue silk stretching across an over-ample bosom. Couldn't the woman have waited until after dinner?

Eight couples adorned the dining table, including Lord and Lady Holmestead. The model of discretion, Lady Holmestead had greeted Jeanette as one might greet any acquaintance. With a wry smile, she had thanked Jeanette for her invitation, adding that she hoped Henry's dueling pistols were safely under lock and key. With the exception of Sir Daniel Winters and Charlotte, Jeanette didn't know the other guests, but Mrs. Barnes had assured her they were the usual guests Henry invited, even if he hadn't bothered to return to Sussex to receive them.

Further down the table, Charlotte smiled at her. Encouraged, Jeanette set her glass aside.

"What a thoughtful remark, Lady Anne! My husband is occupied in London."

"What with?"

A hush descended over the party. Were they waiting to see her humiliated over Henry's infidelity?

"I've no idea," she replied. "Some wives waste their lives pining for their husbands' company, but it's a sorry woman who thinks her life must be defined by a man."

Lady Anne resumed her attention on her soup, but not before hissing at her husband.

"Why should we suffer the company of that upstart if her husband does not? She's even invited that doxy, Lady Winters."

"Hush, my dear. The Ravenwell name…"

"…is being dragged through the mire."

A door slammed in the distance, interrupting Lord Maybury's diatribe on animal husbandry. Jeanette's body reacted even before the dining room door flew open.

Henry stood in the doorway next to a boy about ten years old. A plain, coarsely-woven jacket hung on the child's thin frame. His face was dark with dirt, cheeks streaked with moisture, mouth set in a scowl.

But his eyes! Two bright blue gems stared around the room. The familiarity of their shape and color matched the triumphant smile on Henry's lips.

The boy needed no introduction.

"Forgive me for being late," Henry said. "Let me introduce you to Edward." His knuckles whitened and he eyed her as if in challenge.

Lady Anne craned her neck to get a look at the boy, a sneer on her face.

How could Henry treat her like this! But now was not the time for anger. The child needed to be removed from this den of wolves as quickly as possible, for his own sake.

Jeanette addressed the footman.

"Fawkes, my husband is hungry. Please set a place for him and take the young gentleman to the kitchen. Mrs. Pratt will have something for him there."

"No," Henry said, "I want *you* to take care of the brat."

"Of course." She stood and addressed the guests. "Please excuse me. My husband can take my place, and I'll join you for breakfast in the morning."

"Well, really!" Lady Anne hissed.

Jeanette marched toward Henry. Fixing him with a cold look, she took the boy's hand, sticky with dirt, and led him out of the room.

As soon as the door closed behind her, the boy began to struggle.

"Let me go!"

"No."

"Let go, you bloody woman!"

He flinched as if expecting a blow. When Jeanette didn't react, he swore again.

"Bloody, bloody hell!"

"Very good," she said, "we've established you can curse, though your repertoire is limited."

"I drink, and play poker, too!"

"Then you take after your papa," she said crisply. "Do you also sleep with whores?"

"Don't call them whores!" the boy cried. "You bloody lords and ladies think you're so much better, but you're not!"

"Then don't curse in my home."

"I'll curse all I bleedin' like!"

Jeanette spun him round to face her.

"Then you must do better than that, love." She lapsed into her regional accent. "I could drink ye under the table. As for poker, I'll see your bloody and raise you two buggers and a fuck."

The boy's eyes widened, then he giggled. "I'll meet your two buggers and a fuck and raise you a shit."

"Very good," she laughed. "You'll fit in here marvelously."

"No, I won't. I don't fit in anywhere."

"Who told you that?"

"Papa said I wouldn't be welcome here. But I have nowhere else to go." The boy's eyes glistened with vulnerability.

"Where's your mother?" Jeanette asked.

"His mother was a prostitute."

The boy flinched at the deep voice. Henry stood in the hallway, arms folded.

"I didn't ask what she was," Jeanette said. "I asked where she was."

"She died giving birth to him."

Henry's face twisted into a sneer, though whether his contempt was for the boy's mother or Jeanette herself, she didn't know. She pulled Edward into a protective embrace.

"Finish your meal, husband, and tend to our guests. I'll take care of the boy."

He opened his mouth as if to reply, then turned his back and returned to the dining room.

"Come along, Edward," she said. "Let's get you something to eat."

⊱⊰

JEANETTE SAT ON the bed and stroked Edward's forehead. The child had demolished Mrs. Pratt's stew as if he'd not eaten for days, mopping the remnants up with slabs of bread, his bony fingers cramming the food into his mouth.

He had fallen asleep while she'd bathed him, soaping his limbs and taking care to rub gently over the bruises and weals which covered his skin. He had jerked awake, crying, before shrinking back as if he'd expected her to beat him. The product of a brief, sordid liaison between a marquis and a doxy, Edward had already exceeded the average life expectancy for an abandoned, unloved child.

She had drawn him to her, water seeping into her clothes, then she'd wrapped him in a blanket and led him to the bedchamber Mrs. Barnes had prepared for him. Finally settled in bed, the creases in his forehead disappeared as Jeanette kissed him on the cheek.

Jeanette rose and returned to her bedchamber. Let Henry deal with the guests. She had no time tonight for a society which overlooked the suffering of those less fortunate.

Once inside, she leaned against the door. Thank goodness the day was over.

"My wife seems indisposed."

Henry stepped out of the shadows.

"Where have you been?"

"Tending to your son. At least, I presume he's yours."

"My wife is angry."

"Not at all."

The aroma of male spices grew stronger as he moved toward her.

"Your body betrays you, as it does on other occasions."

She stepped back. "Perhaps my husband might explain why he thinks his wife is angry."

"Because I brought my son to your society dinner."

Self-satisfaction slithered all over his expression. He raised his eyebrows in challenge, but she refused to react.

"What?" he asked. "Is the Holmestead Harlot affronted by the appearance of her husband's *natural* son?"

"Unfeeling brute," she hissed, "to shame that poor boy in front of our guests!"

"Your guests. *You* invited them."

"Had you been a proper husband, you'd have been here to receive them. And had you possessed any humanity, you would not have brought the child here."

"I'm his father. I can do what I damned well like with him. He's lived in that whorehouse with little or no discipline. He needs a good thrashing."

"Is that your answer for everything? Physical strength, exerting authority? He's a child!"

"He's the son of a prostitute."

"Maybe his poor mother had no choice."

"She spread her thighs for half the men of London."

"Then shame on them!"

He strode toward her, eyes darkening, nostrils flaring as he draped his gaze over her damp gown. "This talk of loose women has whetted my appetite."

She covered her body as her breasts began to pebble under his hungry gaze.

"Come here," he growled, "and do your duty."

Fighting the longing which pulsed within her, she moved to the door. Before she reached it, he was upon her, his lean, hard body trapping her against the wall.

"Let me go."

"Not until I've had satisfaction."

"Very well," she snarled. "Take your pleasure, then go."

His lip curled into a smile, his hooded eyes black with lust. "Oh no, my dear, I'll take your pleasure first."

A whimper of need erupted in her throat. Recognizing the invitation, he grasped her shoulders, and his hot, hard mouth crashed against hers. A fire ignited deep within her, a dark red glow which danced to a slow rhythm before bursting into a bright golden flame.

She buried her fingers in the soft material of his jacket and drew him closer, primal need conquering rational thought. With a movement borne from years of practice, he dipped his hand into the front of her gown. The material, still wet from the child's bath, clung to her skin. With a hiss of frustration, he tugged at it and the material split, tearing against her skin to expose her breasts.

He claimed a breast and nipped her skin with his teeth, marking her. Her body responded, and she arched her back, offering herself to him.

He clasped her buttocks and lifted her up, teasing her thighs open, and she wrapped her legs around him. The source of his desire bulged against the center of her need. She squirmed against him, the yearning to ease the pressure between her thighs too great to resist. In response, a rumble vibrated in his chest and he thrust his tongue deeper into her mouth, swallowing her cries.

He stepped back and collided into the dressing table. Gripping her shoulders, he spun her round until she faced the mirror, her back to him. He swept aside the contents, and bottles and phials fell to the floor, the musical notes of splintering glass overshadowed by his breathing which grew hoarse with need. He grasped the front of her gown and ripped it apart. A rush of cold air tightened her skin before his hands claimed her body once more. He squeezed her breast, playing the distended nipple with his thumb, the sweet agony intensifying until she could bear it no longer.

"Henry!"

"Do you beg me?" The low rumble of his voice swirled inside her mind.

"I…"

"Do you beg me to take you?"

He dipped his hand between her legs and teased her thighs open. The jolt of pleasure forced air into her lungs as he moved his expert fingers against her flesh which was already slick.

"Your body cannot lie, sweeting. There's nothing so arousing as a woman who is ready for her man."

"Oh!" She cried out as his finger slipped inside her.

"Look at me," he growled, "I want to see your face when you come undone."

In the mirror, her face was flushed a deep red. The man behind her moved into view, his eyes glittering with need. He drew a circle across her flesh before he found the sensitive little bud of nerves at her center. She shuddered as the wave swelled inside her.

"That's it, Jeanette, come for me."

He withdrew his fingers, then plunged into her. The wave crashed, shattering her body with the force of her climax, and she clung to the table as he pounded into her. He threw his head back, the tendons taut in his neck. Mouth open, he issued a low cry which swelled into a bellow of triumph as he drove into her with a final thrust.

The long absence of intimacy had magnified her hunger for him which now took its toll. She collapsed forward, aftershocks threading through her body. Warm arms wrapped around her, and he pulled her to him. His chest heaved with exertion, his breath a gentle whisper in her ear.

"Jeanette, oh, my Jeanette."

CHAPTER TWENTY-FOUR

"WHERE'S YOUR WIFE this morning, Lord Ravenwell? Tending to the brat?" Lady Almondbury sipped her tea, the innocent inquiry belying the malice in her eyes.

Henry had never liked the woman, yet another embodiment, and a fat one at that, of the aristocratic wife.

"She'll join us presently."

Given his behavior, he didn't know whether Jeanette would join them. She had acted admirably last night, taking care of Edward, even defending the boy. And what had Henry done in return? Not content with humiliating her in front of their guests, he had taken her roughly. Her body might have been willing, but his conscience still pained him.

Her expression had been peaceful when he'd left her at first light, her goodness radiating from her body which rose and fell with each breath as she slept. He had placed a hand on her cheek and traced the outline of her mouth with his thumb, closing his eyes and whispering her name as her warm breath caressed the skin of his hand.

She deserved better than him. Her anger last night had not arisen from indignation at Edward's appearance, but outrage at Henry's lack of compassion toward the boy. What a fool he was to have thought her similar to other ladies of society! The concern in her eyes and tender regard for the boy set her apart from the rest of the world— Henry included.

"Ah, Lady Ravenwell. How pleasant to see you."

Charlotte could always be relied upon. Henry nodded in her direction, then turned his attention on his wife. Jeanette gave him a quick, tight smile before she sat at the opposite end of the table.

"Where's the bastard?" Lady Anne whispered. To his credit, Lord Almondbury shushed her.

Metal clattered against porcelain. Jeanette leaned forward, her fork resting on her plate.

"I didn't catch what you said, Lady Anne. Would you be so kind as to repeat it?"

No answer was forthcoming.

"Never mind," Jeanette continued, "let me enlighten you all."

She pushed back her chair and stood. With the automatic reaction of male aristocracy, the men moved to stand likewise, but she waved her hand.

"Stay seated, please. Doubtless you're wondering about the identity of the child my husband brought here last night. He's his natural son."

A few gasps rippled along the table, female sensibilities unable to withstand such brutal honesty.

"His mother is dead," she continued, "so he's *my* son now. His name is Edward, and he'll join us for breakfast later. Before he arrives, if any of you have anything to say or ask about him, please do so now."

A few of the men shook their heads. Undeterred, Lady Anne spoke up.

"Might you explain *how* he came to be here?"

The woman had gone too far. Henry rose from his seat.

"Jeanette..."

"No, Henry, I can explain. The boy is, after all, my responsibility."

Jeanette turned her gaze to Lady Anne. "You're a married woman, are you not? Then unless your unfortunate husband is overly squeamish, I'm sure you understand the process by which a child enters the world without my having to draw a diagram for you."

Lady Anne's face turned a shade of puce and she coughed nervously. "I have no idea of what you speak, Lady Ravenwell."

Jeanette nodded to the footman. "Fawkes, please bring my sketchbook."

A ripple of amusement threaded through the men. Charlotte let out a snort, disguising it by sipping her tea.

"Forgive my wife," Lord Almondbury said, "she spoke out of turn."

"Of course," Jeanette replied. Mouth set in a straight line, she cast her gaze across the company, issuing a silent challenge to each guest. Her gaze lingered on Henry, and heat rushed into his cheeks. *He should have defended the boy.*

"I'm sure no malice was intended," she said. "A simple misunderstanding which I trust I've resolved." Her voice hardened, and she threw the gauntlet at her guests' feet. "And I expect *not* to hear a certain word uttered in my son's presence. I believe you know enough of my reputation to appreciate I shall not take such insults lightly."

Her face broke into a smile. "Ah, Edward, dear. Come sit by me."

The boy stood in the doorway, shifting his weight from one foot to another. Dressed in fresh breeches and a jacket, his face pink and clean, Henry would not have known him save for the expression in his eyes. The very look which had given him a jolt of recognition the moment he'd first laid eyes on the child.

The boy turned his large eyes to Henry, his lower lip trembling.

Henry nodded to his son. "Go sit by your mama, sir."

Edward took Jeanette's outstretched hand and slipped into the place beside her. His eyes widened into saucers as the footman ladled food onto his plate. He shoveled food into his mouth with his fingers, the frantic motions of one who must take what he can because the next meal might never arrive.

Rather than show disgust, Jeanette placed a protective hand on the boy's shoulder and waved the footman over.

"Fawkes, when our guests have returned to their rooms, would you be so kind as to send for Mrs. Barnes to help Master Edward?"

Henry rose from his seat and addressed the guests. "Come, *mes amis*, the day waits for no one."

After dispatching the guests to their rooms to change for the day's excursion on the estate, he returned to the breakfast room. Mrs. Barnes knelt beside the boy, helping him to eat while Jeanette showed him the array of utensils on the table, explaining the purpose of each.

"But it's so silly!" the boy exclaimed. "Why not have one fork for everything? Why must they all be different?"

Jeanette laughed. "I asked my papa the same question, and do you know what he said? The idle rich, having nothing worthwhile to occupy their time, must fill it with useless rituals to convince themselves of their superiority over the rest of the world."

The housekeeper snorted.

"Mrs. Barnes," Jeanette said, "when Master Edward has finished, would you send Mr. Barnes to see me later?"

"Very good, ma'am."

The housekeeper took her leave. When she spotted Henry, he placed a finger to his lips and moved into the room to watch his wife and son unobserved.

Jeanette tucked a stray lock of hair behind the boy's ear. "Did you enjoy your breakfast, Edward?"

"No, missus. None of them lords and ladies liked me."

She took his hand. "I'll tell you a secret. Nobody likes me either. But, as they're our guests, they have to be polite. I must admit a certain wickedness in taking pleasure from watching them struggle to maintain civility."

"I'm afraid of them. I've seen that lady before. She keeps watching me."

"Take no notice of Lady Anne! If you fear them, I have a little trick you can use."

"What's that?"

"Picture them in their undergarments. The men in frilly drawers, preferably pink ones."

"I find Papa frightening."

"Maybe not as much in pink drawers?"

The boy giggled. "I'll do my best, missus."

Jeanette took him in her arms. "It's 'Mama' now, Edward. I can never replace your mother, but I'll do my best to look after you if you'll let me."

The boy leaned into her embrace. Unwilling to spoil the tender moment, Henry stepped back and knocked a side table. Jeanette looked up; their eyes met.

She patted the boy's hand. "Run along, Edward. Mrs. Pratt said something about packing sweet buns for the picnic, and I'm sure she'll let you taste them before we set off. Can you remember the way to the kitchen?"

"Yes, Mama." The boy scrambled off his chair and disappeared.

Jeanette rose from her seat. "If you'll excuse me, husband…"

"Stay."

Her body stilled at his soft command. He moved closer and caught the scent of her. The floral notes of lavender combined with the earthy undertones of her desire which, last night, had driven him almost mad with the need to brand her as his.

He took her hand, and his skin tightened, the ache building in his breeches once more as his manhood stirred at the memory of being inside her.

"You're mistaken," he whispered.

The spark in her eyes dulled, and she turned her head away. "Does my husband find fault in his wife's behavior?"

He lifted a hand to her face and traced a curve across her forehead before following a line down her cheek and along her jaw. His fingertip outlined her mouth, and he cupped her chin and drew her to him. Her lips parted, her breath sweet and warm against his mouth.

"No," he replied, brushing his lips against hers. "You were mistaken when you said no one likes you. There's one here who likes you. Very much."

He claimed her in a lingering kiss. With a soft cry, she responded, her tongue entwining with his. He slipped his hand inside her gown to find she was ready for him.

"Henry…"

Good God, what was he doing? He'd already treated her badly, and now he was about to rut her over the breakfast table when his house was milling with guests.

She deserved better. Releasing her, he stepped back. "Forgive me. I must be going."

"Going?"

"Back to London."

"Why?" she asked, her voice thin with hurt. "Why do you keep doing this? Do you take pleasure in torturing those you deem to be inferior?"

"No, but I would ask you to trust me."

Her shoulders slumped with defeat. "Do what you want, Henry. Nothing I say will make a difference."

He couldn't risk telling her his business in London, not with her inquisitive nature. Better she hate him than spoil his plans and place herself in danger. He sighed and left the room, turning his back on his wife.

If he stayed, he was in danger of succumbing to the inner voice telling him he was in love with her.

Chapter Twenty-Five

T HE MEN DISAPPEARED to enjoy a morning's shooting, leaving the
women to picnic in the grounds. Edward, who had been trailing
the men from behind, joined Jeanette and Charlotte who sat apart
from the other ladies.

"Come, sit by me." Swallowing a brief wave of nausea, Jeanette
held out her hand.

"Charlotte, I don't believe you've been formally introduced to my
son."

Charlotte held out her hand. "Charmed, I'm sure."

The boy stiffened.

Jeanette nudged him. "Edward, shake hands."

The boy shook his head.

"Come on, Edward," Jeanette said, "if you're to become a gentleman like your papa, you must learn your manners. Lady Charlotte is
someone worth befriending."

The boy took Charlotte's hand, and she curled her fingers around
his. Her eyes narrowed as she studied him, perhaps looking for the
family resemblance.

"I've seen you before, missus."

Charlotte dropped his hand and laughed. "I doubt it, young man."

"I'm no liar." The boy's tone grew sulky.

"Edward! Charlotte isn't accusing you of anything," Jeanette chided.

"No matter," Charlotte said. "All ladies must look the same to him, as all guttersnipes look the same to me."

Edward continued to sit close to Jeanette until the picnic finished. After, he disappeared into the house as soon as Jeanette gave him leave to go.

"Forgive him, Charlotte, he has much to learn."

"I've quite forgotten, I assure you." Charlotte smiled. "I admire you taking him in, considering his background."

"I wonder why he thought he knew you."

Charlotte's smile slipped. "He's mistaken."

"He grew up in a bawdyhouse. Perhaps someone there bought some of your silks?"

"What nonsense! Daniel would never trade with those creatures." Hatred laced Charlotte's voice.

Jeanette took her friend's hand. "Surely your background enables you to understand them?"

"No." Charlotte snatched her hand free. "*I* had no choice. They willingly sell themselves. They're content to service men who are governed by lust."

She lowered her voice. "Tread carefully with that child, Jeanette. He's known the very worst of society. For your own sake, you must take no heed of what he says. Teach him to be a gentleman and banish all memories of the whorehouse."

She linked her arm through Jeanette's. "I counsel you as a friend. I'm not blind. I see the way you look at Henry. Turn his son into a gentleman and remove all traces of the London streets from the boy, and Henry cannot fail to fall in love with you."

IN THE WEEKS following, the winter clutched the landscape with icy fingers. Edward showed progress with his studies, but almost every morning Mrs. Barnes told Jeanette the chambermaids had discovered his bedsheets to be soaked. Some nights she woke to hear him crying. But when he accompanied her as she posed for Mr. Davie in the music room, he grew calm, sitting cross-legged beside the fireplace, watching the artist as he applied paint to the canvas, bringing her image to life.

She wrote to Henry regularly with news of Edward's progress. Each time her hand hovered over the page, poised to express her concerns for the boy. But would Henry care? The soulless words in his brief, infrequent responses spoke of a man who'd abandoned them both. Each time he sent a reply, she tore it open, hope fueling her until she read the terse words. It seemed he was too occupied in London to spare her more than a few written words, let alone a visit.

In one aspect, he seemed pleased. The estate accounts forecasted a profit next quarter-day. Robert Milton had paid his rent arrears and many of the once-empty houses were occupied with the prospect of an increase in rental income for the first time in eight years. Henry's letters to Mr. Barnes were full of praise for the steward's talents.

As quarter-day approached, Henry wrote asking if there were sufficient funds to make a large withdrawal. The shame-faced steward confirmed Jeanette's suspicions that sums of such a size typically signified the patronage of a new mistress.

As WINTER PROGRESSED, Jeanette began to suffer bouts of fainting. Her courses had not come since the house party; since the night Henry had taken her over her dressing table in a wild, frenzied mating. Her body burned with shame at the memory of her cries of pleasure. She had relished it.

And now she was expecting his child.

December marched on, and the artist finished Jeanette's portrait. Skilled with a paintbrush, he'd captured the image of the woman she yearned to be. The woman in the portrait glowed with contentment, her skin pink and healthy compared to the gray pallor which confronted Jeanette in the mirror each morning. The emerald in the portrait winked at her. Jeanette lifted her hand and rotated it. The sunlight caught the facets which glowed with a flame from within, as if it possessed a soul.

"I always swore that emerald was alive."

Jeanette turned to face the owner of the voice. The duchess stood at the parlor door.

"To what do I owe the pleasure, Your Grace?"

"Mr. Davie tells me the portrait is finished. I'm anxious to see whether his skill matches that of his father, and to learn more about the subject."

"I thought you'd made it clear you had no wish to acquaint yourself with me."

"I may have been hasty." The duchess' mouth curled into a smile. "Mr. Barnes approached my steward last month to discuss several propositions regarding Henry's tenants. Given it's the first time he's done so, I suspected another hand on the reins." She lifted her hand at Jeanette's protest. "No need to worry, my dear. I've said nothing to Mr. Barnes, and will say nothing to my grandson. I'm not so old as to be devoid of understanding. You fear Henry will be angry if he knows his wife meddles in the affairs of his estate."

The duchess approached Jeanette and took her hands. The papery skin and protruding blue veins belied the steel within her grasp. But her handshake was one of cordiality.

"My dear, I can only apologize for my earlier rudeness. Perhaps now I understand why my grandson chose *you* among that ocean of fortune hunters."

"Well, I can't," Jeanette said. "He's told me repeatedly I lack the attributes of a lady."

"Such as?"

"Wealth and breeding."

The duchess snorted. "Do you want Henry to value you for what you were born with or for what you do?"

"Why would you care what he thought of me?"

The duchess nodded toward her portrait. "Fifty years ago, the daughter of a country squire was not expected to secure the attentions of a duke. Edward adored me, but I spent the first years of my married life trying to fit into a society that despised me for what I was. I valued their opinion too much. I tempered my behavior and schooled my own daughter into the perfect society lady so that she would never have to endure their contempt."

"I see," Jeanette said.

"What should have been my greatest triumph was my biggest regret. My child was a debutante to be proud of but incapable of tenderness, toward my son-in-law or my grandson. Forgive me, it has made me overly protective of Henry, which means I must ensure he always has what he needs, even if it's not what he thinks he wants. So, if my grandson is foolish enough not to appreciate what he has, it's time we taught him the error of his ways. As I have seen the error of mine. If you'll be so obliging as to accommodate me, might I suggest we indulge in a small sherry while we discuss the matter further?"

"Of course, Your Grace."

"And we can stop that nonsense," she said. "I insist you call me Augusta."

Jeanette had to smile. The woman's sharp-worded mannerisms hid her guilt well. She was offering the hand of friendship. The tap-tap of Augusta's cane tattooed across the floor, and Jeanette followed in her wake. She stopped at the morning room door and brandished her cane at Jeanette.

"Where's my great-grandson? Don't deny it; Henry has never been good at hiding his indiscretions from me."

"He's with his tutor."

"Good. You can tell me about him over sherry."

Breezing past her, the formidable old woman tap-tapped her way to the morning room. As Jeanette sat beside her, Augusta frowned.

"Are you all right, my dear? You look dreadfully pale."

"I'm quite well."

"How long have you been pregnant?"

Did her bluntness know no bounds?

Augusta's mouth twitched into a smile. "I've not given birth to seven children without recognizing the signs. Does my grandson know?"

"He's much too occupied in London."

Augusta clicked her tongue. "Infuriating boy! But you must tell him. He has a right to know you're carrying his heir."

"He takes little heed of my letters."

"Then go to London and tell him in person. He can hardly turn you away."

Augusta was right. Jeanette must confront her husband. But in one aspect she was wrong. If Jeanette went to London, there was every chance Henry would refuse to admit her.

But she had to try.

HENRY LEANED BACK in the chair. The letter lay on the desk in front of him, his wife's bold, even hand filling the pages with bland words about Edward's progress with his tutor, minutiae about his mathematical abilities. A whole page had been dedicated to an account of the portrait, an overly descriptive detail of colors and tones.

But behind the words was distant notes of pain. Jeanette wasn't the type to fill empty spaces with mere remarks. The words she spoke came from the heart, each one to be valued and cherished. The desperation lingering among the mass of triviality in her letter would be unnoticeable except to those who knew her well, as if she wanted to fill the page with any piece of information in the hope it might elicit a response from him.

He jumped at a knock on the door and called out. Sanderson slipped through and closed the door behind him, body heaving with exertion, his face red.

"You're late."

"Be thankful I'm here at all," Sanderson panted. "I had to take a detour via Holborn."

"What on earth for?"

Sanderson gestured to a chair, and Henry nodded. The servant sat and took a few deep breaths before continuing. "I was followed, all the way back from the docks. I'd heard of a house where women were being held before they were sold."

"A breakthrough! Do you have an address?

Sanderson shook his head. "Only a description. But before I could find it, I spotted two men watching me, so I left, thinking I'd come back when it was dark. But they followed me. I wasn't going to lead them here, so I went to the Holborn house. But someone was watching the door."

Henry shook his head. "Dear Lord."

"It's time we gave up," Sanderson said, his voice grave. "The danger's too great. Leave it to the Runners. Or Guy Chantry. He has political influence and a conscience, not qualities often seen in the same man. Let him deal with it."

"Don't tell me you've lost your nerve."

"Not at all, sir, but consider what might have happened had I led them here? We already know they'll not stop at murder to silence those who ask too many questions."

"So you think I've lost *my* nerve?" Henry asked.

"No, I know you don't mind risking your own neck, sir, but what about those close to you? Do you think Lydia's murder was a coincidence?" Sanderson looked to one side, but not quickly enough to conceal the glint of grief in his eyes. Lydia had been strangled like the others, but unlike them, the coroner's report told of other damage. Before she died, each of her fingers had been dislocated.

Someone had tortured her.

"At all costs, you must keep *her* out of London. My Lydia was killed because of me. I can't prove it, but I know. In here." Sanderson placed his hand over his heart. "Even the meanest simpleton will work out you're involved, that I'm acting under your instruction."

Henry's skin tightened with fear at Sanderson's meaning. He looked down to see his fingers digging into the desk, his knuckles white.

"Take my advice, sir," Sanderson said. "Do everything you can to keep your wife away from here, unless you want her to share Lydia's fate."

CHAPTER TWENTY-SIX

THE ROCKING OF the carriage had long since lost its soothing properties. Bile rose in Jeanette's throat, and she pulled the window down and took a breath. Frost clung to the ground, but the cold air soothed her lungs, dissipating the fog of nausea.

The carriage jerked to a halt. Curses echoed from above, two masculine voices and a third, lighter voice, cut short at the crack of a whip.

"Get your bleedin' hands off me, ouch!"

The footman appeared at the window, holding a squirming, cursing figure.

"Edward!"

"I caught this ruffian hiding beside your trunk, your ladyship. He needs a good thrashing. We'll have to turn back."

"No!" she cried. Nausea had thinned her courage. If they returned to Ravenwell Hall now, she'd never leave. "Bring him inside."

The boy stumbled through the door, and she drew him to her. Cold seeped through her gown as she held his stiff little body.

"Edward, you're freezing! Don't you realize how dangerous it was? What possessed you?"

"I heard you were leaving."

"Yes, for London."

"What if you don't come back? Like Papa?"

"You think I'd abandon you?"

The boy remained silent.

"We should go back," she said. "I can't take you with me."

His fingers tightened around her hand. Though he turned his head away, she caught a glimpse of his lower lip wobbling and sighed.

"Perhaps you can come with me, this once."

His body relaxed as she gave the order to continue to London.

⤜⤛⤛

JENKINS OPENED THE front door. His eyes widened as they focused on Edward, before his usual bland expression took over and he gave Jeanette a stiff bow.

"I wasn't aware you were coming, your ladyship."

"Is Lord Ravenwell at home?"

"No."

"Of course not, how foolish of me. The evening must be in full swing at the bawdy houses."

The butler's mouth twitched. He'd never excel at poker; his 'tell' was too obvious.

"Could you send someone to tend to Master Edward? He's tired from the journey."

"Of course, my lady. Would you like some tea?"

"No, thank you."

The butler bowed and disappeared. Why did everyone think tea a cure for everything? Her stomach swirled. If she expelled the contents on the Aubusson rug, news would spread among the downstairs inhabitants of every house on the street. She could only be safe from prying eyes in her bedchamber.

Padding across the passageway to her chamber, she stiffened at a familiar voice coming from Henry's room. Sanderson, the servant who'd witnessed her debauchery in Henry's second townhouse, the house where he entertained his mistresses.

"You must tell the master she's here," Sanderson said. "He'll be

228

sore angry."

"I'll tell him when he returns from Betty's."

The second voice was the butler. Was he also involved?

"When will that be? Bawdy houses never close."

"He always returns before first light," Jenkins said. "We have your Miss Rosaline to thank for that. I'll wait up."

"No sleep for the wicked?"

"Do you refer to myself or the master?"

"Both, I imagine, Mister Jenkins." Sanderson issued a deep sigh. "How many women is it now?"

"More than fifty."

"And none have been found?"

"Seven bodies. Six whores, the seventh, the daughter of a merchant. The authorities think she eloped."

"Where did you hear that?"

"From the master."

"He's risking too much."

"I know, Sanderson, which is why he'll be furious to find her here. Why can't she do as she's told and stay hidden away in the country like wives are supposed to?"

"You said yourself, Jenkins, she's not a lady by birth."

"Good God! You suppose she's at risk?"

"You've seen enough of her to realize she won't be contained."

"She's got the child with her."

"Christ! What's she playing at?"

"I don't know, Sanderson, but the sooner they're returned Sussex, the better. The master's convinced the boy suspects something. He's not safe here."

The floorboards creaked. Jeanette shrank back into the shadows as the door opened.

"Did you hear something?"

"Check the brat. I'll find *her*."

The two men disappeared toward Jeanette's bedchamber. Something was afoot, but she needed to keep a cool head and make a show of ignorance. Body tightening with fear, she fled to the drawing room and hurried over to the piano. Fingers trembling, she began to play a simple sonata by Mozart, a cheerful tune to mask her fear.

Closing her eyes, she focused on the music and took deep breaths, her chest expanding and contracting to the rhythm of the music. When Jenkins found her, he would see his mistress sitting calmly at her pianoforte without a hint of the dread spreading through her veins.

Footsteps approached, a steady gait to match her heartbeat, followed by the rattle of the doorknob and a long, slow creak as the door opened behind her. Her skin tightened as a warm breath caressed her neck.

Soft lips touched her skin and a voice crawled inside her mind.

"Jeanette..."

A hand clamped her shoulder and she jumped, her hands crashing onto the keys in a distorted chord.

"Oh Jeanette." Henry turned her to face him. His eyes glistened in the candlelight, brow furrowed as if in pain. "Why are you here?"

"I wanted to see you. I've something to say..."

A finger pressed against her lips. "No talking."

"But..."

He silenced her with his mouth. Hot, hard lips marked his territory before a rumble of anguish reverberated in his throat.

"Come with me."

He scooped her into his arms and carried her upstairs to her bedchamber and placed her on the bed.

"Don't move."

He lifted her gown over her head and unlaced her undergarments. Her bare skin tightened at the rush of cold air.

"Lie back."

Obeying the command, she sank into the mattress, desire banishing her conscience as his skillful hands elicited cries of pleasure from her lips. Though his touch was gentle, it was the mark of a man not to be denied. Slowly but insistently, he nudged her thighs apart. The air thickened with the sweet scent of her own need.

"Always so wet, just for me." His breath tickled against her flesh as he placed a light kiss on her stomach, the deep rumble in his chest vibrating into her body. With a cry of embarrassment, she moved her legs to stem the surge of moisture, but he tightened his hold.

"Be still. Let me savor what's mine."

He placed a kiss on the inside of one thigh, then dipped his tongue in, sending a shudder of pleasure through her. With a growl of approval, he moved closer to the source of sweet agony swelling inside her until he found the secret bundle of nerves at her center.

Her body bucked against the exquisite torture. Pain became pleasure, and she cried out as her body shuddered.

"Henry!"

Riding her climax, his lips grew gentler as she drifted back. He peppered her body with feather-light kisses to the rhythm of the aftershocks which rippled softly through her.

The bed shifted under his weight. His heat prickled against her skin, and he came down full upon her. His mouth claimed hers once more, the sharp taste of her pleasure on his lips as he nudged her thighs wider apart with his knee.

"Henry, I can't…"

A hard thrust and he became her whole world, claiming his complete ownership of her. He withdrew slowly, then slammed inside her. The action drove her body into another climax, and bursts of fire exploded within her. She clawed at his body, pulling him toward her, fueled by her need.

His body burst with life, and he shouted her name. She wrapped her legs around him, drawing him deeper in. Henry continued to thrust, his body desperate to fill her completely. His movements grew weaker until his voice diminished to a whisper of pain and need.

He buried his head in her shoulder and held her close. Still inside her, he drifted into sleep, her name on his lips.

"Oh Jeanette. My love."

WHEN JEANETTE WOKE, she was cocooned in a warm embrace. Her husband lay draped over her body. One arm curved around her front, his hand cupping her breast.

He murmured her name and his body tensed, his breath quickening as sleep left him. The bed shifted, and he issued a curse. A rush of cold air clawed at her skin. Soft footsteps moved away. After the telltale click of the door, silence fell except for the sound of her own breathing.

Moments later, the door re-opened. The familiar aroma of musk and man teased her senses, followed by a deep sigh.

"Get up." The coldness of the voice belied the warmth of his body which had yet to dissipate. She rubbed her eyes and sat up.

Henry stood before her, fully dressed.

"You need to leave."

"Henry, there's something I must tell you."

"I don't care. You shouldn't be here."

"What about last night?"

"Last night was a mistake."

He looked away, a flicker of uncertainty in his eyes.

"You don't mean that, Henry. You *can't*."

He leaned forward, nostrils flaring. His eyes dilated, the blue turning almost black. He blinked and sighed, his breath warming her skin. An invisible thread connected them, drawing her closer until their lips met.

"Henry."

"What do you want?" he said, his voice almost inaudible.

She kissed him, taking the lead as he parted his lips, stroking them with her tongue until he granted her entrance.

"You want me, Jeanette?"

"Yes."

The bed dipped under his weight, and her skin tightened as his hands caressed her breasts.

"Lie back."

Her body obeyed and her nipples pebbled under his gaze.

"Always so responsive."

He moved his hand along her body until his fingertips reached the curls at the juncture of her thighs, already damp with her need for him.

"Part your legs."

HENRY SAT BACK, straining to conquer the urge to bury himself inside the willing woman on the bed—the wife who, despite his treatment of her, needed him as much as he yearned for her.

What the devil was he doing? Now was not the time to surrender. Her safety must overshadow his selfish desire for gratification.

He closed his eyes. If she noticed the smallest shred of concern—or even love—for her in his expression, she would demand she remained by his side. To fight, not only for the cause of the women he sought justice for, but for him. She would fight for him. Her intelligence and insight which he'd once ridiculed as traits rendering a woman undesirable not only made her unique among women, but placed him in danger of revealing his biggest weakness.

His need to be loved.

For her sake, he must barricade himself with armor thick enough to withstand her scrutiny.

"Henry?"

He opened his eyes to reveal the image he had dreamed of from the first moment he'd seen her. As if she understood his notion of paradise, she lay before him, open and ready, unashamedly offering him her body.

Digging his fingernails into his palms, he replaced the vision of paradise before him with an image of hell in his mind's eye—Jeanette, floating face down in the water, dark lesions on her neck.

It worked. Anger and fear swept through him, bringing the edge of steel into his voice.

"Jeanette, you should leave."

"You don't mean that!"

"Dear God, woman, must I repeat myself?" he cried.

Her eyes widened at his outburst, and she closed her legs and pulled her nightdress down to cover herself. She turned her head away but not before he glimpsed the shame in her eyes.

But now was not the time to comfort her. He would take her in his arms and beg forgiveness once the danger had passed.

If she forgave him.

"Take the child with you," he said. "I've sent someone to get him up. I want you out of the house in an hour. Believe me when I say it's better for you both if you comply."

She climbed out of the bed. A loose scrap of lace hung from her nightgown, and she fisted it in her hand and ripped it off. She held it to her mouth then turned to face him, and his heart tightened.

Her face was an expressionless mask, her eyes cold and hard.

"You are, of course, correct, sir," she said. "Rest assured, sir, I shan't waste your time, or mine, by coming here again."

Turning her back on him, she moved to the dressing room door and rang for her maid.

As the door closed behind her, the scrap of lace fluttered to the floor. Henry waited for her to make a sound or burst back into the bedchamber, but she did not. Eventually he heard voices. Her maid had arrived, and she would be occupied for some time.

Though her final words had been delivered coldly, base notes of pain lingered within her voice, mirroring the hurt in her eyes. He should have rejoiced that she still cared, that she had not rendered herself indifferent to him. But the gratification of being able to elicit such feelings in his wife yielded to self-loathing in the face of the evidence that she suffered almost as much as he.

He crossed the room and crouched beside the door, picking up the scrap of material. He fingered the delicate pattern of lace which a seamstress would have spent several hours tatting, her eyes straining over the intricate design. Now it lay discarded and rejected. He stood and returned to the bed, pocketing the lace in his jacket where it rested over his heart.

He placed his palm on the bedsheet, tracing the imprint of her form where an echo of her body heat still lingered. Picking up the pillow, he held it against his face and took a deep breath, inhaling her scent.

The voices next door grew louder, and he dropped the pillow. A bead of moisture stood in the center, glistening in the sunlight before it dissolved into the material, leaving the faintest of marks. By the time his wife returned to the bedchamber, it would have dried completely.

CHAPTER TWENTY-SEVEN

J EANETTE DESCENDED THE stairs toward Edward who stood waiting by the front door, fidgeting with his overcoat, a footman by his side.

"Wait outside, Edward. I'll be with you shortly."

The boy's lip wobbled. "Does Papa not want us?"

"He's busy, dear."

Henry had already dismissed them from his mind. They weren't even worth the trouble of a simple goodbye. But Jeanette had no intention of leaving without telling him exactly what she thought of him.

She addressed the footman. "Is the master still at home?"

"Yes, your ladyship, but he asked not to be disturbed."

"I'll be happy to disappoint him."

As Jeanette crossed the hall, she heard voices coming from the library.

"We need that list, Oakville."

"Betty won't give it up willingly, Dray. Half of Parliament is on it."

"Sanderson tells me it's widely known that Betty's client list contains the names of those responsible for the slavery ring. It *must not* fall into the wrong hands."

"*Your* name is on the list, Dray."

"As is yours. That's why I'll go to any lengths to get my hands on it."

"What about your wife?"

Jeanette froze.

"Jeanette doesn't suspect a thing."

"Are you sure? She's no fool. If she's heard anything…"

"That's why I've sent her away. She even brought my son here, Oakville! Did she think to disgrace me by parading the fruits of my debauchery around London?"

"Perhaps she misses you."

"You still want her, don't you? But she's mine. Till death do us part."

"Good lord, Dray, don't tell me you want a dead wife on your hands!"

Slavery, death…

Cold fingers clutched around Jeanette's throat, and she fled to the carriage, ignoring the blast of winter air as she almost tripped down the steps.

Tales of murdered prostitutes, women disappearing…

A dead wife…

A needle of pain pierced her heart. The man she'd grown to love had revealed his hatred of her. But a fear far greater than a broken heart clutched at her soul; the fear that the man she loved was a murderer.

⋙⋘

THE CARRIAGE STOPPED outside the familiar door with its brass nameplate.

Allardice, Allardice and Stockton.

"Edward, this is where I leave you," Jeanette said. "The carriage will take you to Sussex."

The boy's eyes widened. "I won't go back there."

"You can't stay with me. London is dangerous."

"You think I don't know that? London's been my home more than that bloody great house in the country!"

She took his hand. "I must find out what's happening. And for that, I have to find somewhere to stay, then I must get into Betty's. You don't understand the danger."

"I *do*. It happened to my Aunt Lydia."

"Aunt Lydia?"

"She looked after me at Betty's; she brought me up. When she disappeared, Papa told me she'd run away, but I overheard him tell Betty she'd been found. Strangled."

"Oh, Edward, I'm sorry."

"If you're going to find who killed her, I want to help you."

"You're a child! I want you safe, and so would Lydia."

"I'm nearly a man, and I want to do it for her. If you need something from Betty's, I can get it for you. I used to live there." He squeezed her hand tighter. "I don't want to go in that carriage on my own. What if something happens to me?"

A cold hand clutched at Jeanette's stomach. What if an accident, or something more deliberate, befell him on the journey to Sussex? Sanderson had said the boy knew too much.

"Very well," she said. "Perhaps you're safer with me."

"MR. STOCKTON DIDN'T say how long you'd be staying."

The owner of the boarding house, a woman almost as wide as she was tall, ushered Jeanette toward a room at the back of the building.

"Is that a problem?"

"Not at all, Mrs. Smith. He's paid me till the end of the month."

"Thank you, Mrs. Taylor."

The woman held up her candle and cast her gaze over Jeanette.

"What's your husband done?"

Good lord, were Henry's activities common knowledge among

London's underbelly?

The woman's expression softened, and she patted Edward on the head.

"No matter," she said. "We've battered wives aplenty here. Mr. Stockton knows I'm discreet."

She pressed a key into Jeanette's hand. "Keep your door locked."

After turning the key in the lock, Jeanette took off her cloak. Uncle George's housekeeper's old cloak, moth-bitten and frayed. She opened the valise and inspected the contents—two plain dresses, with spare clothes for Edward. Dear Uncle George! Her godfather had cancelled his appointments and spent most of the day securing her a place to stay in secret.

She drew the curtains to shut out the night, grimacing at the small movement on the floor in the corner of her eye; movement which matched the faint scuttling noise.

"Come on, Edward, time for sleep."

WHEN JEANETTE WOKE, her skin itched. During the night Edward had cried out, pleading to be left unmolested. Later on, more cries had echoed outside the chamber, screams of the other inhabitants, women seeking refuge from brutish husbands, wives of murderers perhaps?

Murderers...

Henry's eyes had penetrated her dreams, pale blue glaciers staring into the eyes of his victim, the whites of his eyes glowing in the dark, matching his knuckles which whitened as he crushed her throat. He peeled back his lips to reveal sharp, pointed teeth, a low hiss of triumph as he flung the body into the water.

Jeanette's head pulsed with pain. Pinpricks of light sheared her mind as the pressure on her throat increased. When she'd sat up, the nightmare had dissolved, but the curses outside continued, a male voice demanding to be heard, followed by shrill female cries.

Which of her fellow inmates had been disturbed? Would she go home, forgive her husband, ignore the alcohol on his breath and blame herself for her beatings until once more she appeared on the doorstep of a stranger, begging for sanctuary?

Images of bruises and corpses dissipated, and she roused Edward. Time to visit Betty's.

⇛⟫❬⟪⇚

JEANETTE CHECKED UP and down the street, as if expecting Henry's carriage to appear any moment. Pulling her hood over her face, she took Edward's hand. Betty's whorehouse was only a short walk away.

As they approached their destination, a voice called out.

"Jeanette?"

"Mama..." Edward tightened his grip.

"Hush, Edward, let's move a little more quickly."

Footsteps hurried toward her. "It *is* you! What are you doing dressed so shabbily?"

A hand clasped her shoulder.

"Charlotte. How did you recognize me?"

"I didn't. I recognized the boy."

Edward's body stiffened.

"Are you following someone?" Charlotte asked. "Henry, perhaps?"

"Why would you think that?"

Pity shone in Charlotte's eyes. "I hear he's taken a mistress. He won't respect you for following him." She took Jeanette's hand. "Go home. I counsel you as a friend."

Jeanette shook her head. "I'm here for another reason. But don't tell him you've seen me."

Charlotte's eyes narrowed. "What are you doing?"

"I can't say, it's too dangerous."

"I'm your friend. Who can you trust if not me?"

Charlotte was right. Jeanette must place her trust in someone.

"Somebody's murdering prostitutes."

Charlotte shook her head. "Whores die every day; why concern yourself with them? Men are murdered on the streets as well. If women live in a world as equals, they must die also. Those of us striving for equality must accept the dark as well as the light."

"I must at least find out what's happening."

"And put yourself at risk? You won't achieve anything. Take the boy and go home. You know I speak sense."

"I know you mean well, Charlotte, but I must try. If I have no luck at Betty's, I'll go home."

Charlotte's eyes narrowed, and she opened her mouth as if to respond before she stepped back and smiled.

"If you have any trouble, my dear, come straight to me. Promise?"

"I promise."

The skirt of Charlotte's gown swished from side to side as she walked away, the sunlight picking out flashes of bright blue trimming.

A sharp pain spiked in the center of her palm. Edward stood still, body stiff and erect, his fingers curled into a claw, the nails digging into Jeanette's flesh.

"Edward, are you all right?"

"The lady. I'm frightened of her."

THE MAIN DOOR of Betty's whorehouse was painted a discreet shade of green, belying the activities which took place inside. The frontal façade boasted nine windows, nine rooms where the women serviced their clientele. How many of them had Henry visited? Had he taken pleasure in every room?

Jeanette knocked, and the door opened with a loud creak. A thin face looked out, dark rings of fatigue under her eyes. At night a prostitute's face might seduce and tempt, but in daylight, it showed her age, each line in her skin relating tales of sins and suffering.

Jeanette held out her hand. "Are you Betty?"

"What do you want?" Hostility seeped from her tone.

"I'm looking for work."

"What's your name?"

"Frances. Frances Smith."

The woman cocked her head to one side, then opened the door more fully. "Come in."

The entrance hall reeked of promiscuity. Red drapes adorned the walls, the odor of male musk and cheap perfume permeating the air like a thick fog. On closer inspection, the drapes had frayed edges, the gilt covering the wall sconces peeling off in places.

Betty blocked Jeanette's path.

"You may be dressed as a whore, but I'm no fool. I recognize the brat, and I know his father. What do you want, Lady Ravenwell?"

Jeanette stepped back. "I want to know what happened to Lydia."

Betty stiffened. "She died."

"I heard she was murdered."

The woman glanced at Edward. "The brat has an overactive imagination."

"Do you think me a simpleton?" Jeanette hissed. "I heard she'd been strangled, and she wasn't the first. Why has nothing been done about it? Don't you care?"

Betty's hostility thawed a little. "Sometimes a girl disappears. A hazard of our profession."

"Do you suspect anyone?"

"A patron, most likely, but I can't turn them all away. My girls know the risks, and I do my best to keep them safe."

"Like you did for Lydia?"

"That's enough!" Betty's face twisted in anger. "You dare judge me? Do you really care about those women, or are you just another pathetic wife come to whine about all the women her husband is fucking?"

"No, I..."

"Get out!" she yelled, "and take the brat with you. Stay away from here!"

Before Jeanette could respond, the woman shouldered her out the door. Her foot caught on the step and she tripped onto the pavement.

Edward followed her and held out his hand. "Come on, Mama."

"I'm sorry, Edward," she said. "Perhaps we should go home."

"There's another way in," the child said.

"It'll be impossible to get that list if Betty's in the house."

"What list?"

"A list of her clients. It might help identify who killed your Aunt Lydia."

The boy nodded. "Betty hides it in the kitchen, among the oats. I heard her say that if she was raided, it's the last place anyone would look."

"How do you know that?

He shrugged. "I hear all sorts of things. People forget I'm around. Nobody notices me, except you."

Jeanette struggled to her feet, her breath catching in her throat at the spike of pain in her ankle. Edward led her into an alleyway between two houses. At the end, a gate led into a narrow passage in almost total darkness.

A warm hand took hers. "I used to hide here all the time. When the men looked at me, Aunt Lydia told me to hide."

"Good God, Edward, what kind of life have you led?"

"Hush!" the boy hissed, "I hear something."

Footsteps approached, and Jeanette heard a cough followed by hawking and spitting, then silence.

A lifetime of hiding in the shadows had taught Edward self-preservation. Huddling together, they shrank back against the walls of the passageway.

Lighter footsteps joined the first. Murmured voices rose, the hoarse tones of a man and the lighter voice of a woman, coaxing, giggling. Soon, the rhythmic sounds of flesh against flesh accompanied female moans and male grunts, culminating in shrieks of pleasure. After a moment of silence and a rustle of fabric, the footsteps receded.

"That'll be Rosaline," Edward said.

"Rosaline?"

"Aye. Betty hadn't had her long when I left. She was shy at first but soon settled in. Betty was always complaining about her taking a fancy to some of the clients over others. She said she liked to give free samples to her favorites."

Was this the same *Miss Rosaline* that Sanderson had spoken of? Was that who Henry had established as his mistress?

"Follow me, Mama." Edward's matter-of-fact tone disturbed her. Witnessing two fornicating savages must have been an everyday occurrence for him.

"It's a dead end."

"No, it's not. We're at the back of the brothel. I know a way in."

Jeanette could make out a door, but when she tried the handle, it was locked.

"No," Edward said. "Look down."

He pointed to a hole in the ground. Jeanette couldn't see anything inside. It could be three feet deep or thirty. She sniffed at the smell of damp and dust, and something else, a metallic odor which reminded her of sitting on Papa's knee by the fireplace back at home.

A coal cellar. Edward lowered himself into the hole. It was barely large enough for him to squeeze through, and Jeanette would never fit.

"Wait by the door."

He disappeared, and a minute later, the bolts drew back. With a creak of protest, the door swung inward to reveal Edward's face, smeared with coal dust. With a grin, he pulled her into a small hallway. No longer in use, the windows had been boarded up. Slivers of light picked out silvery threads where the spiders had done their work over the years. Dust motes swirled in the air, as if angry at the intruders disturbing their rest.

"Nobody's about," Edward whispered. "The women sleep during the day, and the cook doesn't come till sundown. Only Betty stays awake, and she spends her time in the parlor with her gin."

Edward gestured toward a door.

"That leads to the front hall. The one next to it leads to the kitchen."

Before Jeanette could answer, she froze at a familiar voice. Edward's sharp intake of breath told her he'd also recognized it.

"Go to the kitchen, Edward," she whispered. "I'll follow in a minute."

She crouched at the hall door and peered through the keyhole. Her stomach churned at the sight before her. A man and a woman stood together, bodies molded into an embrace. The woman gave a hoarse moan of pleasure, her body heaving with lust.

"Oh, Lord Ravenwell," she purred. "Has your wife driven you into my arms at last? I thought you loved her."

Henry grasped her by the neck. "I've never loved her, Betty, and I never will."

"Why did you marry her?"

"Out of pity," he replied. "Marry in haste, repent at leisure. I've repented from the moment I shackled myself to her."

He gave her a swift, brutal kiss. "I've not come here to talk about a whore. I'm here to do business with one. And I won't leave unsatisfied."

He took Betty's arm and pushed her out of Jeanette's view. A door slammed and silence fell.

How could Jeanette have been so blind? In her naiveté, she'd hoped to confirm he had nothing to do with the disappearing women, that he loved her. In her folly, she'd clung to his isolated, occasional acts of kindness as a drowning man reaches out for driftwood. But nothing could save her; hope sunk to the riverbed, buried under the silt and debris of reality.

Edward looked up as Jeanette entered the kitchen. He held his hand up, a dog-eared piece of parchment between his fingers. *The list.*

She unfolded it and read the names. Henry's was there, of course, and his friends. De Blanchard's name came as no surprise, neither did Guy Chantry's, and her other dinner guests. But a name near the bottom of the list made her breath catch.

"Sir Daniel Winters!"

"Aunt Lydia talked about him all the time," Edward said. "She was his favorite—tipped her extra special."

Poor Charlotte! Did she know Sir Daniel, with all the mild-mannered demeanor of a devoted husband, cheated on her as much as the rakes she had once serviced?

Jeanette folded the piece of paper and tucked it into her bodice.

When they emerged from the kitchen, a hush had descended over the house. Holding her hand up for Edward to be quiet, Jeanette pushed open the door to the hall.

A body lay on the floor.

"Betty!" Edward ran toward the lifeless form.

The whore's limbs were twisted at grotesque angles as if she had engaged in a wild, savage dance. Her face bore an expression of shock and betrayal. Mouth open, her tongue protruded from between her teeth, thick and swollen where she had bitten through it. Dark lesions adorned her throat.

She'd been strangled.

CHAPTER TWENTY-EIGHT

J EANETTE STEPPED BACK and collided with a solid mass.

"What do we have here?" A male voice chuckled and thick arms circled her waist.

"Mama!"

"No, Edward!" she screamed. "Run, remember what I said!"

"Get him!"

Jeanette kicked against her assailant who grunted as her foot came into contact with his shin. Edward sprinted across the hallway and slipped through the main door.

Twisting herself free, Jeanette curled her hand into a fist and rammed it between her assailant's thighs. With an airless gasp, he doubled up and collapsed onto the floor, clutching his groin. Seizing her chance, Jeanette sprinted out the front door and into the street. Her lungs ached as she drew in air, and a metallic taste rasped in her throat, but she maintained her pace as the footsteps behind her drew closer.

A man appeared to her right, blocking her route to Mrs. Taylor's. With luck, Edward had managed to reach there, but Jeanette had no wish to lead them to him, so she continued along the street.

A carriage stood at the end of the street. The window lowered and a familiar voice called out.

"Jeanette!"

"Charlotte?"

The door opened and Charlotte ushered her in.

"You look terrible!"

"Charlotte, someone's after me. I must get away."

"You poor dear!" Charlotte rapped her hand against the side of the carriage, and it set off with a lurch.

"Jeanette, what's happened?"

"Murder," Jeanette choked. "Oh, Charlotte! I believe Henry's involved."

"How dreadful! You're sure?"

Jeanette nodded, "I heard him speak of it, and I saw him at the whorehouse."

"Damn him!" Charlotte's face twisted in anger before pity and compassion glossed over her eyes. "Let's take you home."

"There's no time," Jeanette panted. "I must tell the authorities. I have a list of names and have to hand it to them."

"We need to take care of you first, Jeanette." Charlotte lifted her hand to interrupt Jeanette's protest. "You know yourself what little heed the men who rule this world pay to the account of a woman." Her eyes hardened for a moment before she blinked and the cold expression disappeared. "Once you're cleaned up, and with Daniel and I by your side, they cannot fail to listen to you."

"We must find Edward first," Jeanette said. "He's alone and in danger."

"Let's get you safe, Jeanette," Charlotte said, "then I'll send someone for him. Where is he?"

"We've been staying at a boarding house, Mrs. Taylor's on Vine Street."

When the carriage drew to a halt, Charlotte ushered Jeanette into a townhouse. Ignoring Jeanette's protests, she summoned her housekeeper and instructed her to bathe her friend. The woman nodded, wrinkling her nose at the stench of dirt and sweat on Jeanette's clothes. Charlotte was right. If servants treated Jeanette with disdain, what prejudices would the authorities have in a world where appearance mattered over substance?

Daylight was fading when Jeanette finally joined Charlotte in her parlor, dressed in one of Charlotte's old gowns, which was a little tight around the waist.

The room had been decorated in feminine pastel shades. The soft furnishings shimmered in the light, the fruits of Sir Daniel's exploits in the silk trade. A delicate floral aroma lingered in the air, melting into the warmth from the fire which crackled in the hearth.

"You look *much* better!" Charlotte exclaimed. "Sit by the fire."

"Where's Edward?"

Charlotte's eyes narrowed. "He's with the authorities."

"Shouldn't we go?"

"There's plenty of time, and I'm expecting Daniel any moment. Why don't you tell me everything, then we can agree how best to present it to the authorities. You've nothing to lose by taking some tea first. You must be thirsty."

She poured a cup and handed it to Jeanette. "This will make everything better."

Jeanette took a sip, wrinkling her nose at the bitter taste.

"How silly of me!" Charlotte exclaimed. "You'll need sugar for the shock."

Before Jeanette could respond, Charlotte snatched her cup and dropped three sugar lumps into the liquid, swirling the cup before handing it back.

"Now, tell me what's happened."

Sipping her tea, Jeanette related the events at the brothel. Betty's murder, together with Henry's declaration. The very act of relating his words cemented the truth in her mind. At best, Henry was a man who loathed her, at worst, a murderer and slave trader.

"You think Henry capable of murder?"

"I saw him!"

"Well, you're safe now," Charlotte said. "Daniel and I will deal with it. Neither of us condone slavery."

Had Jeanette mentioned slavery? Her mind receded, trying to recall what she'd told her friend. Patterns of thought spiraled into ever tighter circles. They burst into shards, pulsing with the heat of the fire, then dissolved into blackness.

Her throat began to burn. "Thirsty…"

"Drink your tea."

Charlotte's voice seemed distant as if muffled by a blanket. She moved closer, filling Jeanette's vision with a wall of blue silk which pulsed to a slow, languid heartbeat. The furnishings vibrated in unison with the heartbeat, and the room pitched sideways. The pain in Jeanette's ankle dissolved. Her legs crumpled and the floor collided with her body. A splintering crash exploded to one side and droplets of tea splattered her face.

A silk slipper appeared before her eyes.

Jeanette's tongue thickened in her throat. "What…"

"That'll be the laudanum, my dear," Charlotte said. "I'm disappointed in you. I thought you had greater perception than the others."

"I- I don't…" Jeanette croaked.

"Why should you assume that a *man* was behind it all?"

The colors faded to black, the last vision in her mind that of two blue pinpoints, the eyes of the child she had grown to love, who she'd unwittingly betrayed, as she herself had been betrayed by her friend.

"Edward…"

Charlotte's laugh sliced through Jeanette's senses. "You've really fallen for the little bastard, haven't you? He'll fetch an excellent price. Some of my clients pay handsomely for sweet, young flesh. Take a good look around you, Jeanette. After you're sold, you'll never see English soil again.

The slipper shifted sideways before a blow to the head sent Jeanette into oblivion.

➤➤➤✦◄◄◄

"FOR FUCK'S SAKE, Sanderson, she can't have disappeared into thin air!"

"London's a big place, sir, and it's a bleedin' maze round the docks. There's only so many houses we can search, even with the help of the Runners."

"Where the devil is she!" Henry banged his fist on the desk.

"Smashing your knuckles won't help." Oakville pushed a brandy glass toward him. "Try this instead."

"I don't want a drink. I want my wife!"

"We must narrow down the possibilities," Sanderson said. "We'll not be able to search every house in time."

"In time for what?"

"The auction. The spring tide is a little before midnight tomorrow, so the auction must be happening shortly before then. The buyers won't want to hang around with their purchases before sailing. They'll want to scatter as soon as possible."

Fingers of dread gripped Henry's heart. Jeanette was about to be auctioned off like cattle and transported into slavery to goodness knew where, subject to the whims and lusts of creatures whose tastes were too depraved even for whores to endure. Africa, America, anywhere in the world.

If he didn't find her by midnight tomorrow, he might never see her again.

CHAPTER TWENTY-NINE

JEANETTE OPENED HER eyes. Watery stains spread across the ceiling above her. Light strained through a window, obscured by smears on the glass. Hard floorboards dug into her back. She pushed herself to a sitting position and winced as a splinter sliced into her palm.

Sounds of activity came from outside, shrill cries of men and women, drunken laughter, and the screech of seagulls. The air reeked of stale sweat. A flood of nausea overcame her and she leaned forward, retching. Pain shot through her scalp as a hand grasped her hair and yanked her head back.

"Stupid whore!"

A hand slapped her cheek.

"Don't expect me to clean up after you."

"That's enough!" another voice spoke. "Leave her face alone."

"The bitch caused a mess."

"We don't damage the merchandise."

"Women are easily replaced."

"Not that one. She's worth more than the rest put together."

"She needs a lesson," the first man said.

"Maybe the boss'll let you bed her before the auction."

The first man growled with lust. Hot, sour breath slithered across her neck.

His companion stood in front of her, arms folded, head to one side as if sizing up her monetary value. Beyond, an open door led into a corridor. He glanced behind before smiling coldly.

"There's no point crying for help. Nobody will hear you."

Heavy footsteps approached, and a third man filled the doorway, holding the body of a woman. He dropped her onto the floor as if discarding rubbish.

"Stop dawdling, you two, we've work to do."

The men grunted in response. Footsteps receded, and the door slammed shut, followed by the metallic scrape of bolts sliding into place.

Jeanette crawled toward the woman. Gaudy paint covered her face, cheeks smothered in rouge to attract the attention and the coin of men wanting cheap gratification. She was young, barely out of childhood. The unadulterated skin at the edge of her face still possessed a youthful glow, missing the telltale sags of the older women.

Her eyes creaked open, dulled with pain. Soft amber irises widened, her pupils shrinking to pinpoints. A groan bubbled from her throat.

Jeanette cradled her arm round the woman's shoulders. "Let me help."

"What's your name?"

"Rosaline."

"Do you know who those men are?"

"The traders. They've been rounding us up for months. Sometimes weeks go by when nobody is taken, sometimes many are taken in a single night. Betty said to be careful. Which house do *you* belong to?"

"I'm not a whore."

The girl's lips lifted in a hard smile. "You must be new if you've yet to accept what you are. But it matters not." She sighed. "I suspect they'll take us abroad after we're sold."

Resignation bled through her voice. "I hope my new owner will be kind."

She turned her eyes to Jeanette, "I hope yours will be, too."

Had she already accepted her fate?

"We can't let that happen!" Jeanette cried. "We can escape."

"Don't you think others tried to escape?" Rosaline said. "Those who did were murdered, strangled. They said they'd cut my face and break my fingers if I didn't do what they said. And who will bid for me then? I'm as good as dead if I don't attract a buyer."

"There are some fates worse than death," Jeanette said. "Why do you think men are willing to risk arrest at a slave auction when they could spend their money on a courtesan instead? I assure you, it's not from the kindness of their hearts."

"Does it matter?"

"Of course! If nobody knows your whereabouts, you become invisible, disposable. Your owner can treat you how he likes, with no fear of retribution."

"You don't know what you're saying."

"I was raised on a farm," Jeanette said. "I saw how some farmers treated their livestock, creatures who cannot speak for themselves or fight back. What makes you think your fate will be any different?"

"A man willing to pay to own me will want to take care of me if I'm good to him."

"But will he be good to you, Rosaline?"

"I'll give him what he wants."

"What about *your* wishes?"

"Nobody cares about my wishes," Rosaline said, her voice dull. "Nobody gives a damn about us."

Jeanette shook her head. "There's the authorities…"

"You think they care about a few whores?" Rosaline laughed. "I'd thought *he* could be trusted, but Betty told me to trust no one, especially not Lord Ravenwell."

Jeanette's body contracted and she drew in a sharp breath. "Ravenwell?"

"He'd been asking questions, came to Betty's all the time. He seemed kind, he bought me for a whole night once. Betty said a whore always has to feign her pleasure. But with *him*, my pleasure was real."

Jeanette swallowed the bile threatening to coat her mouth. "Some men are skilled at making you fall in love with them and convincing you they can be trusted."

"Betty said the same. She'd been making her own inquiries about the abductions when Lord Ravenwell started questioning her. She thought he might be testing whether she knew too much. I tried to tell her he's not the type. But she called me a naïve little fool, a lovesick girl whose vision of a man, a monster, was clouded by romantic sensibilities."

Salty moisture stung Jeanette's eyes. A naïve little fool. Rosaline had just unwittingly described Jeanette herself.

"I won't go back," Rosaline whispered. "I've nothing to go back for."

But Jeanette had Edward, and her unborn child.

"I can't stay here, I have my son. And someone has to stop these men."

"The door's locked."

"Then I'll try the window."

The window was unlocked. Jeanette pushed it open and looked out, her stomach heaving at the stench of stagnant water and waste matter. A narrow street of grimy buildings stretched ahead. Beyond the rooftops, masts poked toward the sky, moving up and down to a gentle rhythm. Which one of those ships would transport her to her fate?

None. She would not let them take her.

"Come with me, Rosaline."

The girl shook her head. "They'll catch you, they always do. And even if they don't, I'll suffer for it. Stay here, I beg you."

Jeanette opened the window more fully and squeezed through.

The drop below must be about fifteen feet. As a child, she'd learned how to jump from trees, to bend her legs at the moment of impact. She gripped the edge and lowered herself until her body hung in midair, arms locked, bearing her full weight, then she let go.

A brief moment of weightlessness, then the impact shuddered through her bones as the ground met her feet and a hot flame ignited in her ankle. She curled her body into a ball to absorb the impact and rolled sideways, cradling her belly.

Jeanette struggled to her feet, biting her tongue as she bore her weight on her right foot, and limped along the street. The darkness would be her salvation, shadows to hide among.

A bulky shape appeared before her and she collided into a solid wall of muscle.

"Devil be damned," a familiar voice said. "It's you!"

Hair hung over his brow in unruly wisps, framing a face taut with anger. Dark eyes glittered with rage.

"Sanderson!"

"Foolish woman! Why can't you do what you're told?"

"Women are being taken, murdered, sold..."

"You think we don't know that? You're going to ruin everything we've been doing!"

He shook her until her teeth rattled. "You've been nothing but a bloody nuisance. If it were up to me, I'd throw you in the river myself, but you're worth too much to the master."

Henry... Good lord, did he plan to sell her in a flesh market?

"It's time you were properly restrained."

A man emerged from the shadows. "That won't be necessary, Sanderson."

Henry.

He moved his right hand. Something smooth and round glittered in the moonlight. The muzzle of a pistol, pointed directly at her.

>>><<<

RELIEF FLOODED THROUGH Henry at the sight of his wife's face, her eyes round with terror. He tucked his pistol into his belt, then gestured to Sanderson.

"Get her out of my sight before she ruins everything."

Before Sanderson could move, Jeanette darted toward him and snatched the pistol from his belt.

"Where's Edward?"

Brave as she was, now was not the time. Henry held out his hand. "Troublesome woman! Give me the pistol."

"Get away, both of you!" she cried. "Or I'll shoot!"

Sanderson cursed and drew his own pistol. Henry battled with memories of the duel, of his wife's broken body on the ground.

"Jeanette," he said, fear tightening his voice. "Stop this. Now. You of all people should know the damage a loaded pistol can do."

"Then I'd advise you to do as I say, *Henry*."

"For the love of God, woman!" Henry roared, giving in to his frustration. "Why couldn't I have married someone who'd do as they were bloody told!"

Sanderson advanced on her. "Women are cowards, sir. She'll never shoot."

An explosion tore through the night. A blue cloud burst into the air and the astringent odor of gunpowder pricked at Henry's eyes. Sanderson dropped his weapon and fell to his knees.

"Shit!" Henry leaped toward his servant. "You fool, Jeanette!" he cried, "you stupid little fool!"

He picked up Sanderson's pistol and aimed it at her. If she wouldn't respond to words, he'd have to resort to force. "You're coming with me, Jeanette. It'd be far better for you without a bullet in your foot, but right now, I'm beyond caring."

She turned her back and fled, but a figure appeared and blocked her path.

Charlotte.

She raised an arm, and Henry heard the distinct click of a pistol being cocked.

"Put the gun down, Lady Winters."

A laugh burst from Charlotte's lips. "Why so formal, Henry? I remember how you used to cry my name when you climaxed."

"Charlotte, be quiet."

"Why?" Charlotte said. "You think this creature you married out of pity doesn't know your reputation for bedding every woman in town?"

"I *said* put the gun down!"

Charlotte laughed. "Don't tell me you've grown fond of her? Henry, darling, have your standards sunk so low?"

Dear God, had he betrayed his feelings for his wife? After denying them to society, to her, to Betty, and even to himself?

Charlotte aimed her pistol at Jeanette. "The Holmestead Harlot's nothing but a runt in society who should be killed to keep the rest of the herd pure."

"You're not so pure yourself, Charlotte." Henry's hand shook as he gripped Sanderson's pistol. "How many men have you given yourself to in order to further your husband's business?"

"I did what I had to!" she cried. "No man would do business with me otherwise. I learned years ago that the only way to control a man was with my sex."

"You sold yourself," Henry said. "But it wasn't enough, was it? You wanted more, so you decided to sell others. Do you hate your own sex that much, Charlotte?"

"No!" Her face twisted in anger. "It's you I hate! Men! Your lust for power, your insatiable greed to assert your mastery over everything in your path, including me."

"Lower your weapon, Charlotte," Henry spoke more softly. "By now, the authorities will be rounding up your men. Surrender and you'll be treated leniently. A man would hang for this, but a woman can elicit compassion. I can speak on your behalf."

"You'd love that, wouldn't you?" Charlotte snarled. "Have me degrade myself by accepting the benevolence of a man. I won't subject myself to that again."

"Charlotte, you're my friend," Jeanette said. "Can't you see what you've done is wrong? I understand your feelings toward the men who might have treated you badly, but what about the women who are suffering to fund your lifestyle?"

"Don't be a simpleton, Jeanette! The reason men rule the world is because women let them! Whores are nothing, only fit to serve the men. It's all they know and all they crave. Men are tools I can use to further my own ends. Even your husband; you let him treat you like dirt and he relished it! He stayed with me longer than anyone. Whereas he grew tired of you the first moment he stuck his cock in you."

"Leave my wife alone," Henry growled.

Charlotte sneered. "You *love* her, don't you?"

At all costs, he needed to divert Charlotte's attention away from Jeanette.

"Of course not," he said. "I've never loved any woman, least of all *her*."

"Then you wouldn't mind if I shot her?"

"Do what you will, Charlotte," he said, forcing his voice to sound calm. "You've only got one bullet, so it's a choice between her and I. Personally, I'd rather stay alive."

Jeanette turned to face him, her eyes wet with tears. "Henry..."

Charlotte laughed. "I'll enjoy killing her and the little bastard."

"Edward!" Jeanette cried. "What have you done to him?"

Charlotte shook her head with a snort of disgust. "You really are stupid, aren't you? I didn't mean Henry's bastard, I meant the brat in your belly."

A jolt reverberated through Henry's body as if he'd been punched in the gut.

Charlotte gave a shrill laugh. "Didn't she tell you she's with child? The bet book at White's must be full of pledges as to who the father might be. Men are such simpletons; to think you believed a *man* could run my operation! Could a man understand the particular needs and desires of my clients? I cater to their tastes because I observe them. Give a man what he wants and you control him completely." Her teeth gleamed with a predatory smile. "Is that why you despise Jeanette, because she couldn't give you what you wanted?"

She raised her arm. "Say goodbye, Henry, to the wife you never wanted."

"No!" With a roar, Henry leapt in front of Jeanette. A brief flare illuminated Charlotte's face, a twisted mask of hatred, before the puff of gunpowder dispersed into the air. Jeanette screamed, but to Henry's relief, she looked unharmed. Charlotte had missed.

He moved forward to take the spent pistol from Charlotte's hand. A pinpoint of heat pricked at his chest and he looked down. A dark red stain was already spreading across his shirt. Before he could register the pain, he pitched forward as darkness claimed him.

Charlotte hadn't missed.

CHAPTER THIRTY

JEANETTE DROPPED TO the ground beside her husband. Sticky red liquid soaked his shirt and his eyes were narrow slits of pain. His body grew limp, and the weapon in his hand clattered to the ground.

"What a waste," Charlotte sneered, "a marquis sacrificing himself for a whore."

Jeanette picked up the discarded pistol, but Charlotte merely laughed.

"Oh, Jeanette! Everybody knows you're a terrible shot. You couldn't even shoot straight to defend your honor in a duel. Henry and I spent hours laughing about that. You think shooting me will restore your dignity? You had none to start with."

"My dignity I can do without," Jeanette said, her hand shaking under the weight of the pistol, "but it won't stop me avenging the man I love."

"But he doesn't," Charlotte nudged Henry's body with her foot, "or *didn't*, love you."

"You think that matters? True love isn't conditional, Charlotte. I've known of his indifference from the day we married. But I love him still."

"Then you can join him."

Charlotte drew a knife and rushed toward Jeanette. Gripping the pistol firmly in her hand, Jeanette pulled the trigger.

This time, she was ready for the recoil. Charlotte screamed and clutched her chest. Blood oozed between her fingers. She swayed to one side and her legs collapsed beneath her. She gave a cough, spluttering more blood, her final breath leaving her chest in a hoarse rattle.

"Bloody hell!"

Jeanette looked up. Four uniformed men stood before her.

"Murderess!"

Jeanette had shot her friend at point-blank range and the authorities had witnessed it. Her neck began to itch, her body's instinctive anticipation of the fate which now awaited her. Such a crime carried only one punishment.

The gallows.

Rough hands hauled her to her feet.

"Please, you must help my husband."

"Be quiet!"

Her captor addressed his colleagues. "She's murdered one of the women. With luck, Peter's rounded up the rest."

"Why not shoot her now? It'd save the paperwork."

"Lady Winters must be questioned. Lord Ravenwell expects us to…"

"I'm not Lady Winters!" Jeanette cried.

"Liar," he snarled, "you'll say anything to save your skin."

"Stop!" a voice called out. A recognizable voice. Rupert stood beside Sanderson who was struggling to his feet, clutching his arm and cursing.

"Viscount Oakville, what do you want?"

"Unhand Lady Ravenwell," Rupert said, "or her husband will have your head."

"Lady Ravenwell? Then Lady Winters…"

"…is lying dead at your feet, if I'm not mistaken."

"Rupert…" Jeanette fought for breath. "Henry…"

Rupert knelt beside Henry's body. "He's breathing but he's been shot."

"It was Charlotte," Jeanette sobbed.

Rupert probed the wound. "The ball's lodged between his ribs. He's been lucky; an inch above or below and she'd have got his heart. We must get him to a surgeon."

A deep groan rumbled in Henry's chest.

"Foolish bastard," Rupert hissed. "I *said* your bloody heroics would get you killed."

"Go to hell..." the words rattled in Henry's throat, and he coughed, his body spasming with the effort, culminating in a cry of pain.

Jeanette's chest tightened at the sound. Henry, always so strong, lay broken and crumpled. Shame crushed her heart that she could have believed him capable of murder. Instead, he'd been risking his life to save countless women who society cared nothing for. Her love for him, which had warred with her fear and mistrust, burst within her. But it held no value, because he didn't love her.

And now he was going to die.

"Rupert..." the words choked out of her body. "Help him."

"How many times must I tell you to be quiet?" Jeanette's captor tightened his grip.

"Unhand her." Rupert barked.

"Don't tell me what to do, Oakville. We saw her shoot Lady Winters. She's guilty of murder."

"For God's sake, man!" Rupert roared. "She's a darn sight braver than you, and she's Ravenwell's wife. Let her tend to him."

"You've no right to..."

"I have every right! Were it not for Ravenwell and I, those slavers would still be trading right under your noses."

The Runner gestured to his companion.

"John here will help you carry Lord Ravenwell to your lodgings. We'll send a surgeon there."

Oakville held out his hand to Jeanette. "Come with me." His hand trembled, and he lowered his voice to a whisper. "Please..."

"I can fend for myself, Lord Oakville," she said. "Or do you think me a weak woman incapable of facing danger without swooning in fear?"

"Why do you insist on battling your femininity?" he sighed. "I see no fear in you. Instead, I see much to admire."

He curled his fingers around her wrist and drew his thumb along her skin in the ghost of a caress. "If anything, I'm afraid for myself." Uncertainty filled his face and he lowered his voice to a whisper. "I'm afraid of disappointing you. Let me prove myself by taking care of you now."

His expression hardened as he focused on the man holding her.

"Let her go." His words carried a backbone of steel, the voice of a man not to be denied. "Now."

Her captor released her and backed away.

"Jeanette," Oakville said, "above all, I want to be worthy of a word of praise from you."

She flinched, but he pulled her closer. "I don't expect anything, not after what I did to you. But if I can do something to merit your regard, then I'll find some peace."

"You've earned your praise, Lord Oakville." She entwined her fingers in his.

Oakville's nostrils flared as he took in a sharp breath.

"Call me Rupert," he said, the need for approval glistening in his eyes.

"You've earned your praise, Rupert."

His face illuminated into a smile, so different from the smiles he'd bestowed while courting her, calculated to snare a woman in a game of seduction. It was the honest smile of that rarest of beasts, a good-hearted man.

"You'll never know how deeply I regret my behavior, Jeanette. I could have married the finest woman in England. I cannot comprehend the enormity of what I've lost. Made all the greater for knowing my loss was at my own hand."

"We would never have been happy together."

He cupped her cheek. "Why not?"

"Because I don't love *you*."

Rupert drew his arms around her, and his voice rumbled in his chest, his breath tickling her ear.

"Ravenwell is damned lucky."

Her body tightened, the mention of his name reigniting the fear.

"Dear God, Rupert," she choked, "he might die."

"I'll do my utmost to prevent that, Jeanette. For you. I'd rather die than see your heart break."

⇶⫷

DARK GRAY SHAPES shifted in Henry's vision, voices muffled as if he were under water. A hand touched his chest and an explosion of agony burst through him.

"Shit!"

A male voice spoke. "He's alive."

"Good lord," another voice interjected, "if that's the diagnosis of an expert, you can call *me* a surgeon."

His manhood stirred at the familiar female timbre. Something cold and hard nudged his lips open. Liquid spilled into his mouth and he swallowed involuntarily.

"Keep him still, can't you?" the first voice barked.

"Just do your job." Oakville's face swam into view.

"I can't operate while he's still awake."

"Wait much longer and he'll bleed to death on the table."

Despite the pain which covered every inch of his body, Henry's mouth twitched into a smile. When under duress, her regional accent always broke through. What had once been evidence of her low birth had now become soft music to soothe his pain and fulfill his dreams.

Perhaps it was because her accent came to the fore when she cried his name as she climaxed. The French called it *"la petite mort"*, the little death. He had never understood its true meaning before. But at that single moment in time, each time he took her, he died. His mind and soul entered the unattainable paradise which parsons preached about in order to convert the unbelieving. Before he returned to life, reborn with the love he bore her.

He loved her.

How unfashionable for a man in his position to love his wife. But she was no ordinary woman. Rather than reduce her status to that of a biddable female, she stood up for what she believed in, even if it placed her life in danger.

What a relief to know she was safe! The Runners had rounded up the whores, delivering them to the townhouse Oakville had rented, where they were being interviewed. But Henry had wanted to collect Jeanette himself. He'd recognized one of the women, a pretty little thing. Sanderson had taken quite the shine to her, not surprising, for she was a charming creature. What was her name again? Ah yes, Rosaline.

"Rosaline…"

Jeanette's face swam into view. The flame in her eyes dulled and she looked away.

Oakville's form materialized beside her. "Don't listen to him, Jeanette. He's in pain."

Jeanette, how dare he show such familiarity!

"Don't defend him," she said. "Pain hampers a man's ability to deceive. Torture has always been the most effective method of securing the truth."

"No." Henry croaked. The words stuck in his throat as the laudanum took effect. His tongue thickened in his mouth and the world dimmed until only his hearing remained.

"Get that woman out of here, Viscount Oakville."

"I'm not going anywhere. You think because I'm a woman I can be ordered about?"

"Jeanette, perhaps you should leave. You've been through a lot."

"Not you, too!"

"For the love of God, get her out! An operating table is no place for a woman, especially a marchioness."

"I'm the daughter of a farmer. I'm capable of withstanding the sight of blood."

"But he's still in danger of death."

"Then stop bloody arguing and let me help."

She was still cursing when Henry slipped into oblivion, not knowing if he'd wake again.

CHAPTER THIRTY-ONE

WHEN JEANETTE WOKE, a bright ray of morning sunshine stretched across the room. The previous night, she had yielded to Oakville's insistence and her own exhaustion, and let him escort her to a small bedchamber overlooking the docks. The surgeon had left some hours before, a pile of blood-soaked linen the only evidence he'd been there.

"You're awake early," a male voice said. Oakville stood in the doorway with a broad grin on his face.

Hope ignited within her. "Is Henry awake? Has he asked for me?"

"Not yet. But I've a surprise for you." He looked behind him. "Come in, she's waiting."

A small figure appeared at his side. Clear blue eyes widened as they recognized her.

"Edward!"

Jeanette fell to her knees, her fears for him dissipating into paralyzing relief as he ran into her arms.

"Mama!"

"Oh, Edward, my precious son! I was so worried about you. Are you hurt?"

"He's fine." Oakville knelt beside her, placing a hand on her arm. "We rounded up the rest of the traders and the women last night. I found this little man among them."

"*You* found him?"

Oakville smiled. "I told you I hoped not to disappoint you."

She kissed the boy's forehead. "Edward, dear. Let's get you fed and rested. You look exhausted."

"Where's Papa?" the boy asked. "I want to see him. Lord Oakville told me about his bravery."

"Your papa is still asleep," Oakville said. "I'll take you to him when he wakes up. But for now, you must listen to your mother."

>>>><<<<

JEANETTE STROKED EDWARD'S head. His breathing eased and he relaxed into sleep. So much had happened since the night she'd first tucked him into bed, the night Henry had brought him to Ravenwell Hall. He'd done it to punish her, then affirmed his contempt by rutting with her like a beast before abandoning her the following morning.

Other than physical exhaustion, Edward seemed unaffected by his ordeal. Had a life on the streets of London rendered him immune to a world of slavery and murder?

Oakville entered the room. "Henry was awake a few moments ago."

"Has he asked for me?"

Relief and hope warmed her body which he crushed with his response.

"No."

"Has he asked for *her*?"

"Rosaline?" Oakville hesitated. "It meant nothing when he said her name. He only saw her once."

"But he saw her after he married me, didn't he?"

Oakville colored and looked away. Jeanette sighed and turned her attention to the sleeping child. His features were so like his father's. Would he grow to despise her also?

"If I ask you a question, Rupert, will you answer it honestly?"

"Of course."

"Does Henry love me? Did he ever?"

Oakville opened his mouth, and she lifted her hand.

"Don't try to foist niceties upon me, Rupert. You owe me honesty. Does he love me, to the exclusion of all others?"

Oakville's eyes flinched, betraying his answer even before his lips formed the words. "He's not said as much, but he's a good man."

A good man, yes. He cared enough about the world to help those who society ignored. But, to him, Jeanette would only ever be someone he'd married in a momentary fit of charity.

She placed a hand over her stomach. Henry had bred with his wife; time to give him leave to love his mistress. She had no wish to become one of those bitter, shrewish society wives she despised. She would leave while she still could, with her dignity intact.

"Rupert, can you arrange my passage to Sussex?"

"Henry would never permit it."

She turned away from the sleeping child. "He wanted me out of sight and mind while he enjoyed life in London. Help me to leave, and he'll thank you for accomplishing his desire at so little trouble to himself."

A warm hand closed over hers, the soft skin of a man who had never done a day's labor in his life.

"Stay for him, Jeanette. You can make him happy."

"What about *my* happiness?"

"Then stay for Edward. You've done so much for him."

"If it weren't for me, he'd be safe in Sussex, not subjected to a slave auction."

"If it weren't for you, Jeanette, he'd be motherless. Few women would take in the child of a prostitute. Because of you, he has a mother now. Don't take that away from him."

"He has his father."

"He needs a mother's love, Jeanette. Don't let your pride get in the way of what's best for him."

"I'm not leaving out of pride."

"Then what? You think because you love someone, they must love you in return? Or that if you're not loved yourself, you must refrain from loving others? Love isn't a commodity for you to withhold as you see fit." He sighed. "Forgive me, but over these past months I've grown to understand much about unrequited love. But love for a child is something more. Don't be the next person to abandon Edward. He deserves better from you."

Jeanette blinked away the moisture behind her eyelids and hardened her voice. Oakville's words threatened to melt her heart, and she couldn't afford it, not when her resolve was already weakening.

"I didn't ask you to give me a lecture, Lord Oakville. I asked if you could arrange my passage to Sussex. I want to leave this house. Tonight."

Oakville sighed. "If I refuse, you'll only find someone else. I happen to know Mister O'Reilly's at home. He has a townhouse overlooking the docks."

"Theodore? And Andrea?"

"I assume she's with him. Shall I take you to him?"

To think Oakville, the man who'd masterminded her ruination, was now her key to freedom; freedom from a husband who had never loved her.

"Thank you, Rupert."

"Don't thank me for something I know to be wrong."

She bit her lip. "Tell Henry I won't trouble him if he wants to divorce me. I'll ask only a small stipend to ensure a comfortable existence."

"God's teeth, woman, you're serious?"

"Perfectly. Let Henry find a wife more suited to his taste and status."

"You're making a grave mistake, abandoning your family."

"I'm not abandoning them."

"Yes, you are." He lowered his voice. "When I first laid eyes on you, you had such spirit. Fresh, funny, passionate for what you believed in, and determined to do the right thing. So much so, it nearly ruined you. Did Henry and I destroy that spirit?"

His words picked at her heart, peeling off the protective layers she'd fashioned around it. But she couldn't afford to show weakness now.

"Promise me you'll look out for him, Rupert. Both of them. Edward will need someone after I'm gone."

A small cry made her look round. A pair of dark blue eyes stared up at her, laced with despair, anger, and hatred.

Edward had heard every word.

⫸⫷

A FOG OF pain formed a thick, hot spiral inside Henry's mind before sharpening into focus deep inside his chest.

Good grief, is this what *she* endured when Oakville had shot her?

"Oakville…"

"Hush," a female voice spoke, low and seductive, tempered by concern. A voice he recognized; the pretty creature Sanderson had taken such a shine to.

"Rosaline."

He opened his eyes and a shaft of light pierced his skull.

"So, you're awake at last," Oakville said. "Bloody fool."

"Hush, my lord!" Rosaline's face swam into view.

Sanderson stood behind her, a look of adoration on his face.

Jeanette. Where was she? The woman he'd instinctively thrown himself into the path of a bullet to protect?

Or had he failed? His heart jolted at the notion that she may be dead.

"Jeanette…"

Oakville sat beside the bed.

"She's gone."

A wave of nausea rippled in Henry's stomach. His heart threatened to shatter with grief. "Dear Christ!"

"No, no, you misunderstand me. She's left you."

Relief dampened by abandonment tightened the clamp on his heart. She lived but wanted nothing to do with him.

"I suppose you arranged it, Oakville. How convenient."

"What would you have me do? She wanted to leave."

"You could have kept her here! Aren't you man enough to contain one woman?"

"You're the one who humiliated her and sent her away. You should have told her the truth about what you were doing, not let her expect the worst. And now you've let her go."

Anger and jealousy surged in Henry's veins and he struggled to sit up. "What the hell could I do? If you hadn't noticed, I've been bloody unconscious!"

A soft hand touched his forehead. "Lord Ravenwell," Rosaline said, "this isn't helping."

"Tell it to Oakville." Henry grumbled. "It's his doing."

"Leave her alone, sir," Sanderson growled, placing a protective arm around the woman's shoulders. "Lord Oakville only did what your wife asked him to." He lifted his hand at Henry's protest. "I don't blame her for leaving. She's no soulless lady who only cares for fine gowns and grand carriages. She's a flesh-and-blood woman who craves an equal partnership in life."

"Not you, too," Henry rasped, before a cough racked his body. "Damn! Help me up, can't you?"

"Get yourself up," Oakville said. "There's nobody to blame for her leaving but you."

"I was protecting her!" he cried. "That's why I sent her to sodding

Sussex!"

"Dray, we both know there's no point forcing your wife to do anything. Jeanette isn't the biddable mannequin society expects a marquis to marry. She knows her own mind and will act upon it. By letting her go on her own terms, I could at least ensure she was safe. With someone who'll protect her."

"Who?"

"O'Reilly."

The privateer. The American who'd blighted the ballrooms of London and set both courtesans' and debutantes' pulses racing. A fortune and a piratical appearance had made O'Reilly a fierce competitor for female attention during the past season, until he had offered for the prim Miss Elliott, after which he'd had eyes for none other.

A coy smile spread across Rosaline's lips. Had O'Reilly patronized her?

Henry snorted. "That man is a rogue."

"Nonsense," Oakville scoffed. "He merely has the appearance of one. You might have an ancient name to lend respectability, but you're as much of a rogue as O'Reilly."

"And now he has my wife."

Oakville shrugged. "You should have trusted her."

"There's a bloody lot more I should have done, Oakville," Henry sighed. "Help me up. I must follow her."

"You need to rest; you've lost a lot of blood," Oakville said. "Besides, your chances of winning her back will be much improved if you're strong enough to handle her."

Oakville was right. Jeanette was safe with O'Reilly. Henry could win her back as soon as he'd recovered.

And win her back he would. It was time to cast off the shackles of his past, and his cowardice. Time to declare to the world that he loved his wife.

CHAPTER THIRTY-TWO

JEANETTE OPENED THE window. The taste of salt stung her lips, and the noise of the docks—captains bellowing orders and sailors chatting animatedly in anticipation of a prosperous voyage—warred with the harsh cries of the birds circling overhead. She closed her eyes and the image overtook her—blue eyes dark with despair, anger, and abandonment.

Edward's last words to Jeanette had shredded her heart. Even when she had offered to take him with her, he'd refused, accusing her of deserting Henry. He didn't understand how she couldn't bear to live with a man who didn't love her.

By acknowledging Edward as her son, Jeanette had set him up for another betrayal. She was worse than the ruffians whose mistreatment he'd endured all his life, for she knew better but had abandoned him anyway. Edward couldn't hate her more than she hated herself.

Would she let her unborn child down also?

A gray shape circled above her, then descended in a spiral to land on the windowsill. Stretching its wings, the seagull squawked before turning its expectant eye on her.

"I've nothing for you."

The bird cocked its head to one side, ruffled its feathers, and stood its ground.

"Talking to the birds, Jeanie?"

Andrea appeared at her side, a smile of amusement on her face, and waved a gloved hand at the bird. With a screech, the gull launched upward, flapping in earnest to gain height before it picked up an air current and began to soar, ascending in a wide arc to join its companions.

"Where else would I find intelligent conversation, Andy?"

Andrea snorted with laughter. Life with a privateer had destroyed some of the inhibitions society had bred into her.

A cacophony erupted above them, a rush of wings as the seabirds dove toward a ship which was drawing into dock where a deckhand threw scraps over the side.

Jeanette drew in another lungful of air. "Do you suppose seagulls have accents? Are French gulls distinguishable from English?"

"I've no idea, Jeanie."

"Some of those birds will have followed that ship across the water. But perhaps they're turned away when they approach the English coastline for not fitting into society, their squawks too coarse for English sensibilities."

Andrea rolled her eyes. "We're not speaking of seagulls, are we?"

A deep voice rumbled from behind. "Ah, my favorite shipmates."

"Theo, darling."

His chocolate-brown eyes crinkled into a smile. His tanned skin and hair curling over his shoulders made him look every part the rogue. He placed an arm around Andrea's shoulders. His arm muscles bulged gently, strength concealed under the soft linen of his shirt.

Had Jeanette not known him, she'd have thought him the worst sort of ruffian. As a privateer, he'd have to deal with enemies on the ocean as well as hold command over his crew. The first sign of weakness and the laws of the beast would prevail. Yet his fingers entwined with Andrea's in a tender, loving gesture.

The love they shared was rare indeed. It was the passion a man shared with his mistress together with the affection and respect he shared with his wife, united in the same man. It was a love Jeanette had yearned for since she'd understood the concept. A love she could never have.

Theodore kissed Andrea full on the lips, and in response, she lifted her hands and buried them in his hair, pulling him close with a soft moan.

He broke the kiss and admonished his wife gently.

"Later, Andrea, my love."

He smiled at Jeanette. "I trust you're comfortable, Lady Ravenwell, and recovered from your ordeal?"

"I'm capable of weathering captivity and slavery, Mister O'Reilly."

"But not a marriage?"

His gaze, loaded with perception, turned toward her and the heat rose in her face.

"I can't thank you enough, Mister O'Reilly, for offering to take me to Sussex.

"Viscount Oakville persuaded me, but even if he did not, it's my pleasure to be of service."

"Oakville," she sighed. "It seems I misjudged him."

"As you misjudged your husband?"

Andrea nudged him, but he shrugged. "Would you have me lie to her, my love?"

"No, you're right," Jeanette said, "I was wrong about Henry."

"Then isn't it a mistake to leave him?"

"No," she replied. "I was wrong to think him involved in those abductions, but I'm not wrong in leaving. There's more than one definition of liberty, Mister O'Reilly."

"Running away doesn't mean you've liberated yourself."

Jeanette shook her head. "I'm sure you have the best intentions, but *you* love your wife. Henry may be a good man, but that doesn't mean I'll be happy with him, or he with me. I could better withstand his contempt of me if he was an evil man. Knowing he's a good man, willing to endanger his life for others, yet still despises me, has destroyed my heart."

"Then you're a fool."

"Theo!" Andrea exclaimed. "That's enough. Leave her alone."

"As you wish." He bowed to Jeanette. "My carriage is waiting. The driver will take you anywhere you wish to go. I shall await you outside."

The door closed behind him, and Andrea shook her head. "I'm sorry, Theo spoke out of turn, Jeanie."

"No matter."

"But he's right. Your place is with Henry."

"Even if he doesn't love me?"

"Are you sure he doesn't?"

"He couldn't dispose of me quickly enough," Jeanette said, "spiriting me away to Sussex while he indulged himself in London and established a mistress."

Andrea sighed. "A mistress is something of a fashion statement." She lowered her voice. "Shortly before we married, I learned Theo had a mistress."

Jeanette recoiled. "And still you married him! Did you not have any self-respect?"

"My love for Theo surpasses any personal desire to be admired. We resolved the issue by talking to each other."

"But a *mistress*, Andrea!"

"They were lovers long before he and I met. After she secured a new patron, Theo and she became friends. She's much older than Theo and has little chance of finding a patron now. But in recognition of their friendship, he pays her a small stipend and visits her occasionally as a good friend, nothing else."

"Aren't you concerned that he and she, that they..." Jeanette's voice trailed away, her cheeks warming with embarrassment.

Andrea laughed. "Of course not. I trust him. I've even met her. She treats him like a younger brother, with indulgence and gratitude."

Her expression sobered and she took Jeanette's hand. "All men have a past, Jeanie."

"I can forgive Henry his past deeds," Jeanette said. "It's his present thoughts I cannot endure."

"Have you discussed it with him?"

Jeanette sighed. "The last time we spoke, he turned me out of the house. I heard him tell a whore in her own house how much he regretted our marriage. What more evidence do I need?"

"I'm not referring to an argument in the heat of the moment or an overheard conversation in a bawdy house," Andrea said. "Surely you of all people understand the best form of communication is a rational, direct conversation. Or are you afraid of what he'd say if you asked him how he felt?"

How perceptive Andrea had become! Was it the benefit of an honest marriage with a man of the world, a life on board ship where the niceties of social convention deferred to the rules of survival? Had Jeanette fled Henry to avoid an open admission that he didn't love her?

"No matter," Andrea said softly. "You've been through an ordeal. Now's not the time to speak of it. The carriage is waiting. Would you like me to come with you?"

"No," Jeanette replied. "If I'm to accustom myself to being alone, I must begin as soon as possible."

Theo waited for them by the carriage. Behind him, the ship had docked. Figures ran along the water's edge, the gaudy colors of the prostitutes' dresses as they gathered in eagerness at the prospect of fruitful trade. Men cheered from deck, eager to part with their coins in exchange for a warm pair of thighs. A crowd gathered as the ship drew to a halt, spectators jostling to get a better look.

The crowd parted to reveal the darker hues of men in uniform. Soldiers approached Theo's house and formed a semicircle around Jeanette and her friends.

"Lady Ravenwell?"

Theo's body stiffened at the voice, and he moved in front of Jeanette, as if to shield her body from the man who pulled out a sheaf of paper from his coat pocket.

"Jeanette Frances Drayton, Lady Ravenwell. You're to come with us."

A cold hand of fear brushed her skin at the grave tone of his voice.

Theo placed a protective hand on her arm. "For what purpose?"

"This woman is under arrest for murder. Stand aside or we'll take her by force."

Theo cursed. "You cannot be serious! Who the devil is she supposed to have murdered?"

"My wife." The soldiers parted, and another man appeared. Elegantly dressed in a dark green coat, the normally mild-mannered man shook with hatred.

Daniel Winters.

"Do you deny you killed her?"

Ignoring Theo's warning glance, Jeanette shook her head. "Sir Daniel, I'm sorry…"

"You bitch!" he cried. "She was your friend, and this is how you repay her? My Charlotte could never hurt anyone, and you murdered her." He turned to the soldiers.

"What are you waiting for? You heard her confess!"

Theo pushed her aside and drew his pistol.

"Theo, no!" Jeanette cried. The soldiers were armed. To avoid bloodshed, she had to surrender.

"Jeanette, you're innocent."

"I shot Charlotte," she said. "I took a life. I must pay for what I did."

"But…"

She bit her lip to prevent her voice catching with fear. "If you try to stop these men, they'll shoot you down. Lower your weapon, for Andrea's sake."

"No!" Andrea cried out. "Theo, can't you do something?"

Jeanette placed her hand on Theo's arm. "Don't provoke them; they outnumber us. Either way, they'll take me. I'd rather you survived it."

Theo uncocked his weapon. "This isn't over, Jeanette. I'll go to my lawyer directly."

"That'll make no difference," Sir Daniel said. "Nothing can bring my Charlotte back, but I'll at least have the satisfaction of seeing that bitch swinging from the hangman's noose."

Strong, unyielding hands took Jeanette's arms and dragged her away from the house. The last thing she heard before she was hauled away was Andrea's sobs, punctuated only by the screech of the seagulls overhead.

CHAPTER THIRTY-THREE

DAWN BROKE, CASTING a cold gray light onto the walls of Jeanette's cell. Eager voices rumbled outside as a crowd began to gather. One of her fellow prisoners was to hang.

Thick mucus glistened on the stones. The damp air provided a nurturing ground for mold and disease. If she stayed here too long, she wouldn't have to fear the gallows; sickness would get her first. Her stomach twitched, and she caressed her belly. Her poor child would never see the world.

Sir Daniel's words rang in her ears. *You murdered my wife! Did you begrudge our happiness? I loved her, but your husband despises you. And so he should. You're evil, nothing but a filthy whore!*

"You'll be next."

The jailer's face appeared at the window in the cell door, grinning to reveal a row of rotten teeth.

"Leave me alone."

He laughed. "They won't even give you a trial seein' as you confessed. You're not a fancy nob anymore; you're one of us. About time one of you lot swung from a gibbet."

His eyes glittered with fervor. "Do you know what hanging is like? The rope tightens round your neck, then they drop you. If you're lucky, it'll be a long rope and your neck will snap on impact. If not, the noose will cut into your throat until you choke for breath. You'll jerk and dance as you try to break free, but it'll only work tighter and tighter."

He licked his lips. "I've paid the executioner well. He'll ensure the rope is short enough so you entertain the crowd before you die. Ye'll dance like a maggot on a fish-hook."

"Hey! What are you doing?"

At the new voice, the jailer's stance turned from predatory to deferent.

"Begging your pardon, sir, I…"

"Unlock that cell."

Keys jangled in the lock before the door swung outward to reveal a liveried soldier.

"Come with me, ma'am."

Fear spiked in her body and a needle of pain jabbed at her stomach.

"Are you going to hang me?"

"Not without a trial. I'm to take you to the magistrate."

As JEANETTE WAS ushered through the door to the magistrate's house, a familiar figure waited for her in the hallway.

"Uncle George!"

"What on earth have you been up to, my dear?"

Unwittingly, he mirrored the words he'd spoken the day she had visited him after her ruination, the day Henry had taken her back to his townhouse and she'd given herself to him and sealed her fate.

He drew her into his embrace. "It was a rhetorical question, my dear. Mister O'Reilly's told me everything."

"That I'm to be tried for murder?"

He huffed with exasperation. "Bloody fools should never have incarcerated you. Sir Daniel can be very persuasive when he wants to be. Understandable, I suppose, given he's mourning his wife, even if she was a murdering whore."

"Uncle George, she's dead. And she couldn't help her background."

"Nevertheless, if it wasn't for her, you wouldn't be in this predicament."

"What's going to happen to me?"

"Today we're meeting Earl Stiles, the magistrate. It's quite common for the accused to attend the magistrate in a less formal setting. He'll decide whether there's a case to answer. The evidence points to self-defense, but Winters is likely to say some unpleasant things, so I'd warn you to guard your tongue. I know Stiles; he's a client of mine. But that won't garner us any favors. He's renowned for his fairness, but he won't stand any nonsense, especially not from a woman."

A door creaked open.

"The earl will see you now."

⫸⫷

JEANETTE STARED STRAIGHT ahead while Uncle George pleaded her case. Earl Stiles was a formidable man. Deep brown eyes radiated a keen intelligence, together with insight and understanding. He wasn't a man one could lie to with any hope of success. His lithe, muscular form filled his jacket, and he sat at his desk with an air of authority as if the whole world could bend to his will.

He tapped his forefinger on the table, a slow, steady rhythm as Uncle George delivered his address, continuing while Oakville related his account of events.

When Sir Daniel came forward, the tapping increased in pace. Stiles cast his gaze about the room, taking in each player in the game where the prize was Jeanette's life and liberty. When his gaze fell on her, his eyes hardened and the tapping stopped.

"Mister Stockton, I cannot avoid the fact that your client took a life."

Jeanette's body spasmed with fear. She glanced toward the soldiers standing guard by the door, and a sharp spike of pain jabbed inside her belly.

"However," Stiles continued, "it's my view she had reasonable cause to fear for her life, given that Lady Winters had injured Lord Ravenwell. Given the evidence presented in reference to her activities in the flesh trade, exploitation of the weak is to be abhorred, and I applaud Viscount Oakville's efforts in investigating this matter."

His expression softened and he glanced at Jeanette. "Bravery in a woman is to be commended. I apologize for your incarceration. It shouldn't have happened unless I deemed there to be a case to answer. I don't believe there is, and therefore, declare this case dismissed."

"No!" Daniel Winters cried. "She killed my Charlotte! Murdering bitch!"

Stiles barely reacted apart from a slight lift to the eyebrows. What horrors had he faced to render such stoicism?

"Remove that man," he said, his voice calm and cold. Still protesting, Winters was hauled away by two of the soldiers.

"You'll pay for this! My Charlotte would never have done those wicked things!" His cries turned into sobs which faded into the distance. A door slammed, then silence fell.

Uncle George sighed. "He's in denial but it won't last. He reminds me of some of my clients when presented with evidence of their wives' infidelity."

"Poor man," Jeanette whispered, "he really loved her. Why couldn't she have been content with what he could give her, rather than wanting more for herself?"

"Like you, Jeanette?" Uncle George said.

"I don't know what you mean."

"Yes, you do, child. What's this I hear about you leaving your husband?"

Oakville let out a little cough.

"Viscount Oakville should learn to keep matters to himself," Jeanette said.

"A divorce would hardly be a discreet matter." Uncle George's tone was that of a disappointed parent.

"Have you quite finished?" A stentorian voice boomed across the room. Stiles seemed to have grown in stature, his back ramrod straight, eyes dark with cold anger as he fixed his stare on Jeanette. "Where's your husband?"

Yet another man deemed her to be the property of another.

"It's no business of yours…"

"What my client meant to say," Uncle George interrupted, "is that he's presently indisposed and they'll be reunited later."

"No…" Jeanette protested, but a sharp dig in the ribs stopped her.

Stiles leaned forward, his knuckles whitening. "A woman's place is with her husband. You do not have the right to abandon your responsibilities. Lady Winters was, by all accounts, the very worst example of a woman who refused to accept her place in the world."

His eyes narrowed, as if in pain, and he sat back.

"Your client is free to go, Mister Stockton. Remove her before I change my mind."

"Thank you, sir," Uncle George said. After a moment's silence, he nudged Jeanette, but she remained tight-lipped. He took her hand and led her out of the room.

"You were damned lucky," George said as they crossed the hall. "For a moment, I thought Stiles was going to change his mind. Why couldn't you have kept your mouth shut?"

"Why should he care whether I leave Henry or not?" Jeanette asked.

"His fiancée abandoned him. She was not unlike you, Jeanette, an outsider, clouded by scandal. He's been looking for her this past year but with no success. Even *I* could tell he was deeply in love with her. He understands your husband's position well."

"It's not the same," Jeanette said. "Henry doesn't love me and never has."

A footman opened the main doors. Blinking, she stepped into the sunlight.

"Daughter! *Ma fille!*"

A warm body collided with hers. Soft arms enveloped her with a rush of floral scent. Mama broke into a torrent of rapid French while she rained kisses on Jeanette's cheeks.

"Oh, Jeanette!"

Her voice was not that of a woman desperate to gain a footing in society but a mother, overjoyed at seeing her child again. It transported Jeanette back to her home, the farmhouse where she'd spent her childhood, when society belonged to another world and Mama cared only for her happiness.

"Mariette, love, let the lass breathe."

"Papa…"

Papa took Uncle George's hand. "What was the outcome?"

"The charges have been dropped. She's free to go."

"*Dieu merci!*" Mama kissed Jeanette on the cheek once more before releasing her and holding her at arm's length.

"My poor darling, what you've endured! Papa and I will take care of you now."

"But…"

"I'll not hear another word on the matter," Mama said. "You're coming home with us. You're braver than I could ever hope to be. You risked your life to save others, and that makes you a daughter to be proud of."

Jeanette's stomach twitched and a sharp agony erupted inside her, radiating outward, and she pitched forward.

"What's wrong, Jeanie love?"

"Robert, Mariette, she's bleeding." Uncle George's usually stoic voice held a note of panic. "Get her into the carriage. Quickly!"

"My baby…"

Another burst of pain ripped through her body. Mama's cries faded as Jeanette slipped out of consciousness. She might have gained her freedom, but she would still reap the rewards of her sin. In exchange for taking Charlotte's life, fate had demanded the life of her unborn child.

CHAPTER THIRTY-FOUR

"CHRIST, MAN, LEAVE it alone!" Pain thrust into Henry's chest as fat fingers prodded his ribs.

The surgeon ignored his demand. "If you want to recover, do as you're told and stop hurling abuse at me. I've better things to do with my time."

"Who do you think you're talking to?"

Oakville's face swam into view, concern etched onto his features.

Unlike the surgeon, Henry would have refused to let Doctor Lucas treat him, but he'd been unconscious throughout the journey to Mayfair. The bullet wound had festered, necessitating a second operation during which he'd almost died. Sanderson had said it would have served him right. His own servant, a bloody servant, had lectured him, while he lay sick and in pain, about how he didn't deserve his wife. Rosaline had even tried to speak to Jeanette, but Lady Claybone refused to admit her.

"If you will indulge in illegal dueling," the surgeon said, "it's only a matter of time before someone puts a bullet in you. Bloody idle rich."

His bedside manner hadn't improved since their last encounter at Holmestead Hall.

"Lord Ravenwell hasn't been dueling, Doctor Lucas," Oakville protested.

"I'm no fool." The surgeon secured a knot in the bandage. "I take no pleasure in serving people who risk their lives for the gratification of waving a pistol about. I recall performing a similar service on that harlot."

"How bloody dare you!" Henry sat up, ignoring the thrust of pain which constricted his lungs. "The lady you refer to is my wife."

"That's enough, both of you," Oakville said. "Doctor Lucas, you're paid to treat my friend with discretion, to employ your skills as a surgeon, not a wordsmith. And Dray, no matter what Doctor Lucas says, shut up and let him do his job."

Since when had Rupert grown a pair of balls? Had everyone in Henry's acquaintance changed?

Not her. She was just as admirable as she'd always been.

The surgeon completed his work, then issued instructions as to when Henry should be permitted to rise. Rupert's stern expression and dominant stance told him he wouldn't be leaving the house any time soon. Even Sanderson, sporting his own bullet wound, had ordered Henry to stay in bed. *Sanderson issuing commands! What was the world coming to?*

Like a lamb, he drank the medicine Rupert offered, then sank into the pillows.

⋙⋘

JEANETTE OPENED HER eyes. A ray of sunlight caught the pattern of the curtains, evoking memories of childhood. Gold letters sparkled on the spines of books which lay in a pile on a table beside the window, untouched since the day she'd left for the Holmestead house party. Now she had returned to Papa's townhouse, a discarded wife, a murderess, and now a failed mother who'd lost her child before it had even been born.

The door opened, and two young women appeared, one holding a teacup, the other, a plate laden with a slice of cake.

"Doctor Farrell said you were waking up."

"We thought you might like this."

Jeanette's sisters had changed since the summer. With dark hair and silvery eyes set within delicate features, Susan had always been the prettiest, having inherited Mama's well-bred looks. But now she had turned into a beauty, easy prey for the men who prowled society's parlors and ballrooms. Jane still possessed the soft, round features and youthful enthusiasm of a puppy. She bounded across the room and sat on Jeanette's bed.

"Jane!" Susan admonished.

"Oh, hush, Sue, you silly cake." Jane took Jeanette's hand. "Are you all right now, Jeanie? You were talking such nonsense when Papa carried you in here last week."

I can't begin to understand how you survived it, Jeanie," Susan said. "You've weathered the biggest scandal of last season and endured marriage to a rake, slavery, murder, and the threat of the gallows."

"And there's that Winters business!" Jane exclaimed. "Fancy him shooting himself."

Jeanette froze. *"What?"*

"By all accounts, Lady Charlotte amassed a fortune right under Sir Daniel's nose, and he was too smitten to notice. Fancy a woman meddling with her husband's finances! When confronted with the truth, Sir Daniel turned a pistol on himself."

A ripple of nausea threatened to engulf her and Jeanette's breath caught in her throat.

"Jeanie?"

Jane held the teacup out. "You've gone white as snow, Jeanie. Drink this. It'll help. Doctor Farrell says you must get your strength back for the sake of the baby."

"The baby?"

"Yes," Susan replied. "He told Mama the baby's fine and prescribed complete rest. He said laudanum was the only way to keep you quiet."

"Actually," Jane interrupted, "he said a damned good dose was needed to prevent you running about the streets like a bloody pirate."

"Jane!" Susan exclaimed.

"Oh pooh!" Jane replied. "You curse more than I do. Besides, I'm proud to have an adventuress in the family. I don't care what the papers say."

Jeanette closed her eyes, and their warring voices faded. She reached under the bedsheet and caressed her stomach. Her baby was alive.

"Jeanette, drink your tea."

Yet more tea! But her sisters meant well. She took a sip and recoiled at the taste.

"Sugar, for shock," Susan said. "That's what the cake's for, too. We promised Mama we'd make you eat it after we told you about Daniel Winters."

"We were among the first to hear of it," Jane said.

"Jane!" Susan interrupted. "It's not something to relish." She took the teacup back. "Uncle George told us all about it. He's been with Viscount Oakville for most of the week."

"Ooh, Viscount Oakville!" Jane repeated in a high-pitched voice.

Susan's face flushed a delicate shade of rose. "He's pleasant company, that's all."

"Stay away from him," Jeanette warned. "He's a rake."

"He's a hero, Jeanie."

"I'll admit he's not as bad as I first thought," Jeanette said, "but I'll be damned if either of my sisters is put at risk of having their hearts broken."

"I've no intention of doing anything about it," Susan said, "not after the shocking way your husband treated you, handsome though *he* may be. Given Papa's improved prospects, I've no need for a wealthy husband. I'm going to help him run the business."

"I can't understand why you'd want to bury your nose in Papa's ledgers, Sue," Jane laughed, "though I intend to capitalize on it. Mama cannot refuse my request to come out this season if you prefer to remain indoors."

A stab of envy needled at Jeanette. Susan would enjoy the life Jeanette had been denied ever since Papa's baronetcy. But last time she'd spoken to her father, his business had been floundering following the dishonest actions of the employee who'd replaced her.

"I thought Papa's business was in trouble."

Susan nodded. "Earlier this year, Papa acquired a partner. Well, I say acquired, but someone invested enough to clear Papa's debts.

"A partner?" Jeanette's heart sank. "What do they want in return?"

"That's the beauty of it," Susan said. "According to Uncle George, they want nothing apart from anonymity and a reasonable dividend. Papa can run the business as he sees fit and I'm to reap the rewards."

Jane snorted. "Rewards! To be locked in a study rather than attend balls and parties? I'll never understand you, Sue."

The sisters' chatter turned into an indistinct murmur as Jeanette's mind spiraled with question after question. Who was the anonymous investor? Perhaps it was Oakville.

But even if it was, it would never be enough for her to trust him with her sister's heart.

And where was Henry? Now he was rid of her, was he with Rosaline?

Jane's voice cut through her thoughts. "Say what you like, Sue, but we both know the viscount will call today." She turned a mischievous smile on Jeanette. "He calls every day and always asks after you, Jeanie. Now you're awake, your presence might encourage him to keep calling. Didn't he court you last season?"

"And that ended in disaster," Jeanette said.

"But there's nothing so attractive as a penitent man," Jane said.

Susan snorted. "You're a hopeless romantic, Jane."

Hoofbeats clattered on the street outside. Jane leapt off the bed and ran to the window.

"It's not Oakville's carriage. I don't recognize the crest." She lifted the bottom sash and leaned out. "Oh, it's a woman," she said, disappointment in her voice. "She's very beautiful."

Susan joined Jane at the window and gave a noise of exasperation. "It's *her* again, and she's got that servant with her." She glanced at Jeanette, then pulled Jane back. "Don't let her see you."

"Who is it?"

"Just some tart."

"Of course!" Jane exclaimed. "That's the Ravenwell crest. Is that his mistress?"

Her hand flew to her mouth. "Oh! I'm sorry."

"That's enough, Jane," Susan snapped. "Don't worry, Jeanie. Mama will send her away again."

Mama's voice floated up from the hallway, sharp tones overpowering the plaintive voice of their visitor. The front door slammed followed by the clatter of hooves which faded into the distance.

At length, footsteps approached and Mama entered the room.

"Ah, *cherie*, you're awake."

"Has she gone?" Susan asked.

Jeanette set the teacup down. "Was it Rosaline?"

Mama nodded. "That woman shall not set foot in our home."

Jeanette closed her eyes to stem the tears threatening to burn her eyelids. The bed shifted beneath her, and soft, warm arms enveloped her.

"Shh, *ma petite*, Mama is here. You and your child will always have a home with us. Henry doesn't deserve you."

WHEN HENRY WOKE, his fever had eased. He rang for Sanderson who helped him to dress. The world shifted as he stood, the combined effect of the drugs and the infection. But now was not the time for male pride, and he let his manservant support his weight as he limped downstairs.

A large package dominated the center of the morning room.

"It arrived yesterday, sir. Your grandmother sent it."

Henry sank into a chair. "Open it."

Sanderson tore the paper from the package.

It was a portrait of a woman. She sat on a chaise lounge, hands folded demurely on her lap. Her eyes portrayed a sense of mischief as if she knew she didn't fit into her surroundings but didn't care. The background reflected accents of color from her gown, scandalously bright tones of red and green mirroring the green of her eyes.

Her character could have come across as arrogant, yet she looked as if she had no expectations from the world.

The woman was Jeanette. Not the disgraced creature he'd married out of pity, nor the commoner he resented, but the woman who had captured his heart, accepted his son as her own, and risked her life for him. The woman he loved exactly as she was.

"Bloody hell, sir." Three words that conveyed the manservant's opinion of Jeanette, and of himself.

"There's a note."

"Read it," Henry commanded.

Henry closed his eyes, but the image of the portrait remained.

The paper crackled as Sanderson unfolded the note.

"My dear Henry. I trust this finds you well after your escapade, though if you died of a bullet wound, it might teach you a lesson. I have no idea when you'll grace the shades of Ravenwell Hall again, and have therefore taken the liberty of sending this to you. At least the portrait—she's underlined that word, sir—won't reside in exile while you continue to enjoy London society. Rest assured, you've not shouldered any part of the cost. I paid for it myself. I trust you'll take better care of the portrait than you ever did the subject."

Grandmamma's unique tone of disapproval shone through her

words, even though they had been articulated in Sanderson's rough accent. Henry's gaze turned to the wall facing the door, the wooden panels against which he'd taken Jeanette's virginity. The tryst had been the desperate act of a woman doomed to a life of condemnation, only asking that she be granted the brief moment of pleasure which society had assumed she'd already taken.

In offering Jeanette his hand, he had won himself a prize—the finest woman in all England. He'd be damned if he let her go. If he had to break down the door to her father's townhouse to win her back, then so be it.

⟫⟫⟫⟪⟪⟪

WINCING WITH PAIN, Henry rapped on the door to the Claybones' townhouse. He'd ventured out against the doctor's orders and his body suffered for it, having felt every bump on the ride over as if his driver had deliberately sought out every loose stone on the street.

The door opened and two pairs of feet appeared; one wearing the black shoes of a footman, buckles glinting in the sunlight, the other in feminine slippers. He straightened up and looked into the eyes of Mariette, Lady Claybone.

Rather than the deference he'd expected, she carried an air of dignified disapproval. Her eyes, which he'd once thought insipid, were the color of steel. His confidence wilted under her matriarchal gaze, and it became clear to Henry where Jeanette had inherited her backbone from.

He should have realized it from the brief interviews with Sir Robert when discussing his daughters' dowries and, more recently, when he'd visited him at Stockton's offices to discuss his business. Jeanette's father lacked the instinct to prey on others, which explained why he'd been duped to the point where his business had lingered on the brink of ruination.

"What do you want?" Lady Claybone's voice held the timbre born of hundreds of years of French aristocratic lineage.

Henry might have the superior standing in the eyes of London society, but the woman before him possessed true breeding. Why hadn't he noticed it before?

"Lady Claybone, won't you admit me?"

"What possible benefit could arise from it, Lord Ravenwell?"

"It's my right to expect an audience with my wife."

"Your right!" she muttered to herself before jabbing her finger at his chest. "You relinquished your rights to my daughter months ago."

"In the eyes of the law…"

"The law of the land, perhaps, but what about laws of decency, of humanity? You ignored my daughter's rights as your wife to be loved, honored, and cherished, and you expect me to throw her back into your lair?"

Anger bristled through him. "What of your behavior, madam? Didn't you strive to seek rich husbands for your daughters with no thought for who those husbands might be?"

"What would you have me do? Let them starve?"

"What about love?"

"Love!" she scoffed. "As if you'd understand a fraction of that emotion! As if any man would, save my dearest Robert. The chances of my daughters finding men to love them as they deserve is nonexistent. I did the best I could to ensure they would at least be spared poverty."

A shred of pain flicked across her eyes. She would have fled the Terrors in France with little more than the clothes she wore. What hardships would a young *émigré* have suffered in London, alone, with only her wits to live by? Had Sir Robert not married her, she might have met her end floating in the Serpentine or been sold into slavery; the very slavery Jeanette had risked her life to thwart.

"By your own argument, madam, you have declared my right to take my wife back, where she can enjoy the life of a marchioness."

Henry's words sounded petulant, but he'd be damned if Lady Claybone bettered him in a battle of words with Jeanette as the prize.

Her eyes hardened. "Jeanette is not a commodity for you to claim, Lord Ravenwell. Her ordeal has confirmed how wrong I was in trying to secure a society marriage for her. I will no longer force my daughters into anything. They're free to make their own choices."

"Then isn't it up to Jeanette whether or not she wishes to see me?"

"She doesn't wish to see you."

"You lie."

"Don't insult me!" She gestured to the footman. "Charles, make sure this gentleman leaves."

She turned her back on Henry and disappeared into the house.

"Sir." The footman drew close. Henry stood a good four inches higher and was very likely ten years younger. But the path to winning Jeanette back was not paved with force. He must utilize a different tactic, something which had never come naturally to him.

He would have to court her properly.

Holding his hands up in resignation, he retreated. As soon as his feet were off the threshold, the door closed.

A voice hailed from above. He looked up and saw a young woman leaning out from an upstairs window.

"I *thought* it was you! We all wondered when you'd show your face. Have you come to see Jeanie?"

"Is she here?"

"No, she's with Uncle George. If you want an audience with her, you'll have a fight on your hands."

"As I've just experienced."

The girl giggled. "Mama says you're the embodiment of the devil."

"And you?"

"I think we should draw our own conclusions rather than submit to persuasion."

She leaned out further, the sunlight catching in her hair.

"Jeanie's fond of walking, you know. She loves Hyde Park, the way the afternoon light catches the trees along the path where the rhododendrons are in bloom. I hear the light is just right around three o'clock."

"Jane!" A voice called from within, and the girl disappeared.

So, Henry had an ally in Jeanette's family. He had another in his, someone who might help him. Edward missed her so much. Surely she wouldn't refuse a plea from the boy if he begged her to see him?

You bloody coward. An accusing voice whispered in his ear at the notion an illegitimate child might have more success in securing an audience with Jeanette than Henry himself.

No, not illegitimate, but his son. A child to be loved and respected.

Christ, now his conscience had begun to echo Jeanette's sentiments! What had she done, this woman he'd married with such reluctance and grown to love without knowing it?

He climbed into the carriage and rapped on the window. "Take me home."

CHAPTER THIRTY-FIVE

"THERE'S A LETTER for you, ma'am."

Jeanette's maid held out a folded piece of paper.

"Why didn't Charles deliver it?" Jeanette cared little for convention, but Mama insisted on it. Maids weren't supposed to answer the front door.

"He came to the back entrance."

"Who?"

"The child."

Jeanette's heartbeat quickened. "Thank you, Sarah. You may go." She waited until the door closed before unfolding the note.

Mama Jeanette. Can we meet this afternoon in Hyde Park?

I miss you

E.

The hand was a little more refined than when she'd last seen it. Edward must have been practicing his penmanship.

Unlike the prose of a prospective suitor out to impress, the honest simplicity of the note did more to melt her heart than the poems Oakville had once tried to woo her with.

Oakville. Though Jeanette had seen him only once at Uncle George's offices, their conversation had been stilted and dull, restricted to remarks about the weather. Henry had been conspicuous by his absence, from both the room and the topic of conversation.

The caricature of the Holmestead Heifer had been resurrected to grace the broadsheets again, accompanied by an account of how a certain Lord R sought solace in the arms of another and a dissertation on the folly of marriages between the classes. Yesterday afternoon in the park she had experienced snubs, pointed glances, and exaggerated whispers. Perhaps if she jumped into the Serpentine again, they'd have something else to laugh at.

But she couldn't. She placed a hand over her belly. If nothing else, marriage had taught her that the carefree existence of a girl ended the moment she became a woman.

She shook her head to dispel the memory of when *he* had made her a woman, and each time thereafter when her body had shattered with pleasure at his touch.

Don't think about him, it'll only break your heart.

But she couldn't let Edward down. She had abandoned him, just like everyone else who'd been letting him down all his life. She owed it to him to honor his request.

And she missed him, the brave little soul who'd taken a piece of her heart.

She glanced at the ormolu clock on the mantelshelf. Almost three o'clock; her usual time for walking. Was it a coincidence? Or had Edward, with all his wits borne out of a life on the streets, managed to observe her unseen while she had wandered through Hyde Park?

She concealed the note under her pillow and rang the bell for Sarah.

NOT LONG AFTER she entered the park, she saw him, standing in the center of the path where it forked. His companion, a thick-set manservant, stood a pace behind him, his left arm in a sling.

With a cry, the boy propelled himself toward Jeanette. The impact knocked her backward as he threw his arms around her waist, burying his head into her chest.

"Dear Edward!"

"Mama…"

She stroked his dark locks and breathed in the scent of his hair. What was blood compared to the love which grew from experience and mutual affection? The child in her arms was her son. He would always be her son, as much as the child she carried within her.

The manservant gave a stiff bow.

"Lady Ravenwell, a pleasure to see you again."

"Sanderson." She nodded toward his arm. "I believe I owe you an apology."

His usually dour face crinkled into a smile. "It's no more than I deserved. I must ask forgiveness for frightening you. I'm sorry you had reason to think I…" He shifted his weight as if in discomfort. "Or anyone else, meant you harm."

"Be thankful I'm a rotten shot."

"Your subsequent shot was aimed rather better."

The memory of having taken a life resurfaced. She looked away, guilt consuming her.

A gentle hand touched her shoulder. "Don't think about it, your ladyship. You were instrumental in saving lives. Even if she had survived, she'd have hanged for her crimes."

Edward wriggled free from her embrace. "Mama, will you walk with us? I want to show you something."

He took her hand and pulled her toward the left fork in the path.

"Careful, little master," Sanderson warned.

"I want to show her!" Edward cried, eagerness animating his voice.

Sanderson flashed Jeanette a knowing glance. "All in good time, lad. Your mama shouldn't run in her condition."

After a few minutes, their surroundings became more secluded. Tall, thick bushes graced the path from either side, adorned by purple flowers just coming into bloom. The sunlight struggled to penetrate the vegetation and the air grew cooler, a welcome respite from the afternoon heat. Such secluded corners, where nature had not been manicured out of existence, held no attraction for London society. It was, without doubt, Jeanette's favorite part of the park.

The voice of nature ruled here, the rush of the wind in the bushes and the occasional burst of birdsong, the brighter melodies of a male perched high up in the sunshine, proudly calling prospective mates to his territory.

New voices joined the birdsong, growing louder with each step Jeanette took. They weren't birds she recognized. Perhaps a bird of paradise had escaped from a nearby aviary.

No. Not birds of paradise but the rich melodic tones of a woman. Two women, their voices uniting in perfect harmony.

The song of the zephyr from the *Marriage of Figaro*.

The timeless melody drew her in, enveloping her heart. Though the women sang about infidelity, the opera was about love. A pure, unwavering love which could withstand the machinations of those who sought to destroy it. The women in the duet plotted to thwart a lecher so the heroine could marry Figaro, her true love.

The path opened into a clearing. The two singers stood in the center, surrounded by a handful of onlookers.

A man stood underneath a tree, his features concealed in the shadows. He moved into the light, and Jeanette's heart tightened in her chest.

Henry had lost weight since she'd seen him last. His jacket, which his muscular frame had once filled to perfection, hung loose on his shoulders. But the chiseled jaw, determined mouth, and clear blue eyes were the same as she remembered.

He held out his hand. "Jeanette."

She turned to Sanderson. "What's this? Some sort of trick?"

Edward squeezed her hand. "Don't leave, Mama. Please."

The notes spiraled upward as the duet finished. A faint echo of the melody drifted into the air until it was replaced by an irregular spattering. A droplet of water splashed on Jeanette's arm, followed by another.

A murmur rose from the onlookers, women muttering about the rain as they opened their parasols, the pastel shades offsetting the dark green surrounding them. One of the men removed his jacket and draped it around his companion's shoulders.

Henry nodded to the singers. "You may leave us now. My man will see to your payment."

"Very good, Your Grace."

Your Grace?

The singers curtseyed, and Sanderson led them away.

"How romantic!" a voice spoke.

"I know," said another. "Ravenwell's the last man I'd have expected to do such a thing."

Henry moved closer until Jeanette could almost feel his body heat. His eyes darkened with need, and he lifted his eyebrows in question, asking, as all suitors ask, not to be hurt.

"Henry, please," she whispered, "this isn't fair. Return to your mistress and let me go."

He lowered himself onto one knee and took her hand.

A sigh rippled through the onlookers which morphed into gasps as she jerked her hand away.

"I'm sorry, Henry," she said. "I can't spend the rest of my life with a man who'd rather be in the arms of others."

"You're my wife, Jeanette, and you're carrying my heir."

"Is that why you lured me here? And why did those women address you as Your Grace?"

"My cousin died of consumption a few days ago."

"I'm sorry."

He shook his head. "I barely knew him."

"I see," she said. "Now you're a duke and need to maintain appearances."

"For the love of Christ, woman!" he cried. "Do you want me to beg?" He sighed and spoke more quietly, his voice filled with pain. "At least hear me out. Please, Jeanette."

The rain grew heavier, but he remained kneeling before her as droplets splashed on his eyelids and small rivulets ran down his face. He coughed, and she took his hand.

"Henry, you're not well, you must get out of the rain."

"Not until you agree to come home with me." His mouth curled into a smile. "Though I know you relish the prospect of dancing in a downpour."

He dipped his head and brushed his lips across the back of her hand. When he looked up at her, his eyes glistened with emotion.

"I think that was the moment I fell in love with you, when I spotted you dancing in the rain at the Holmestead estate. I wondered how someone could be so carefree, so totally at ease with their own company. You had no need of others to make you whole or to find fulfilment. How I envied you!"

Edward tugged at her other hand. "Please come home with us, Mama."

Jeanette sighed. "Very well. I'll come with you now, but you're mistaken if you think you can persuade me to follow a course of action which will make me miserable."

"Jeanette, my love, I have every intention of giving you pleasure, not misery."

SANDERSON STOOD BESIDE the carriage, seemingly oblivious of the rain which trickled off his hair. Henry placed his hand on the small of his wife's back. Her gown was soaked, her skin cold beneath the white muslin. Her body stiffened at his touch and she climbed in. He ushered Edward in after her, then climbed in. He reached under the seat for a rug and placed it over her knees.

The carriage left the park and turned into the London streets. Earlier that afternoon, when Henry had driven past on the way to the park, bright colors had adorned the pavement. But now the rain triumphed, rendering the streets gray and driving the people inside save for the occasional running figure caught in the downpour.

"Look at them," Jeanette said, "all running in fear of a little water. Society may believe it controls the lives of others, but it'll never conquer Mother Nature." A smile spread across her lips. "Good for her." She sighed, her breath forming a cloud of mist on the window, and she traced her initial on the glass.

Edward nudged Henry.

"Papa, why don't you do what we agreed?"

"Not yet, young sir."

His son's face creased into a frown. "But you promised, and Mama told me that a gentleman always honors his promises."

The boy had plagued him ever since Jeanette had left. He missed and loved her almost as much as Henry himself.

"Your mama is right, as always," Henry said, "but I regret to say, I've not always behaved like a gentleman."

"Then do it now," the boy urged.

Henry knelt at Jeanette's feet and took her hand. Her fingers trembled, and he held them to his lips and looked up at her. Doubt clouded her expression. But what had he done to merit her trust?

"Be my wife, Jeanette," he whispered.

She tried to break free, and he tightened his grip.

"No!" he said. "Be still!"

She froze at his command. Her breath quickened. Whether she liked it or not, her body wanted him. But now was not the time to take advantage of their mutual desire for each other.

He placed his hand against her cheek and spoke more softly. "When I first offered for you, Jeanette, it was out of compassion, even pity. I immediately regretted it, thinking you'd trapped me. So, let me ask you again, now, out of desire."

The doubt in her eyes morphed into anger. She pulled her hand free and rapped on the window.

"Stop! Sanderson, let me out!"

The carriage continued. She cried out again, and he gripped her arm, guilt stabbing his conscience at the way she flinched.

"Sanderson obeys *me*, Jeanette," he said. "Why don't you honor your vows and do the same?"

She let out a bitter laugh. "Honor my vows? Like you did? Henry, stop the carriage and let me go. I won't contest a divorce, if that's what you're afraid of. Just promise me you'll make sure your next wife treats Edward properly."

"Dear God, Jeanette, why so stubborn? Why don't you stop this nonsense and come home? You know it's the right thing to do. For me, for you." He gestured toward Edward. "Especially for him."

"Mama…"

At the boy's plea, her body seemed to deflate, the fight leaving her. She slumped back in her seat and gestured around the carriage.

"I never wanted this," she said, "and you certainly made it clear I didn't deserve it. I can't imagine anything more miserable than being married to you."

"Jeanette, don't be such a fool." He grasped her hand but she snatched it away.

"No!" she cried. "You should have let them sell me into slavery. It couldn't be worse than a life with you!"

He flinched at her words and drew back. Is this what he'd driven her to? In his attempts to protect her by keeping her at a distance, had he earned her hatred?

"I must commend you for your honesty, madam."

She turned her head away. "I was nothing to you. I had some use in the country where your tenants valued me for myself and not for my rank." She sighed, lowering her voice to a whisper and closed her eyes. "It was the only consolation I had for being married to a man who despised me. I'd resolved never to fall in love with you, but I did nonetheless."

He took her wrist, and she drew a sharp breath.

"Look at me."

"Please," she said, "let me go."

"Not until you look at me and repeat what you just said."

He tightened his grip. "Now, Jeanette. I won't release you until you do."

She lifted her gaze. "I said my consolation was at Ravenwell Hall…"

He curled his free hand round the back of her neck and pulled her close until their eyes drew level.

"Papa!"

"Not now, Edward," he said through gritted teeth. "Jeanette, repeat what you said at the end."

She held her gaze. "I said I resolved never to fall in love with you."

"But you did anyway."

She closed her eyes and nodded. He lifted his hand and brushed aside the tear on her cheek. With the tip of his finger, he traced the outline of her face.

"Then stay, Jeanette. For me."

He moved closer until their mouths met.

"No, I can't!" She pulled away.

"But you said…"

"What about what *you've* said, Henry?"

"What do you mean?"

"I heard you at the brothel. You told Betty you married in haste. I'm merely ensuring you don't *repent at leisure, Your Grace.*"

Dear God, had she heard what he'd said to Betty?

"Oh, Jeanette, I'm sorry you overhead." He took her hand. "I spent the greater part of our marriage trying to convince myself I didn't love you. When I realized my investigations into the abductions might place you at risk, I had to put you at a distance. I had to convince the world I cared nothing for you. If they knew how much I loved you, your life would have been in too much danger. Christ, woman, why do you think I did everything I could to remove you from London?"

"But you treated me…"

"Abominably, I know. I wanted you to think I despised you. It was the only way to keep you in the country. Safe." He shook his head. "Sanderson chided me so many times about it. Even Rosaline has admonished me over it. She's getting bolder every day."

Jeanette's eyes darkened. "Rosaline. Is that the woman you spent the night with at Betty's?"

"Nothing happened," he said. "I couldn't bring myself to touch another woman once I'd had a taste of you, Jeanette."

"Then what's she doing still with you?"

"I've given her a position, as upper housemaid at my Mayfair house."

"Isn't she a little young, inexperienced?"

He smiled. "That's what I told Sanderson, but he wouldn't relent until I agreed. The poor man's almost as smitten with her as I am with you."

Jeanette bit her lip and looked out of the window. "It broke my heart when you threw me out."

He stroked her thumb. "Forgive me, my love, but I'd rather see your heart than your neck broken. I've seen so many bodies, Jeanette. I'd never forgive myself if anything had happened to you. I did what I thought was best to protect you, by convincing you I didn't love you."

Salty moisture stung his eyes, but he made no attempt to wipe it away.

"I'm a fool for hurting you, Jeanette. So many women from my wilder days have died—Edward's mother, Lydia, Betty, and I could do nothing to save them. But you, the woman I love, I would do anything in my power to keep you from harm. Even confront your mother."

"Mama?"

"My severest critic where you're concerned. She's a force to be reckoned with. Your father's a man to be admired, but recently I've realized your mother is equally admirable. When I saw your father last month, we were both quaking in fear lest she come upon us and turn me out of the house. She loves you dearly, almost as much as I."

"Don't say it, Henry, not unless you mean it."

"I won't just say it. I'll spend the rest of my life showing you how much I love you."

"What did you see Papa for?"

The carriage drew to a halt, saving him the necessity of answering. The carriage door opened and Sanderson appeared.

"We've arrived, Your Grace."

He climbed out of the carriage and ushered his wife and son toward the townhouse. The rain was falling more heavily now, fat droplets splashing on the steps.

The door opened and Jenkins appeared at the threshold.

"Welcome home, Your Grace." The butler looked at Jeanette expectantly, and her brow furrowed in confusion. "His Grace has been most anxious for your return. It's a pleasure to see you home again."

Henry curled an arm around Jeanette's waist. "Speaking of pleasure, Jenkins, it's time I indulged in a little myself. Sanderson, take Master Edward to the kitchen and get him something to eat."

Jenkins colored, and Sanderson led Edward across the hallway.

"Papa…" Edward protested.

"Go with Sanderson, young sir. Cook will have some sweet tarts waiting for you to celebrate a successful expedition. I want to enjoy your Mama, and I cannot wait any longer." He winked at the servant.

"I'm sure Sanderson wishes to be reunited with Rosaline. They've been apart for at least two hours."

"Henry!" Jeanette slapped his arm, and he winced. No wonder her right hook had bloodied that lecher De Blanchard's nose so effectively.

He traced a light fingertip along her neck. Her breath caught in her throat.

"Henry..."

"Yes," he whispered, his voice hoarse. "I like hearing my name on your lips, Jeanette. I want to hear you scream it when I'm buried inside you."

"Henry!"

He moved his hips against her, and her breath quickened.

"Yes. Just like that."

"Is this how you intend to behave now you're a duke?"

His teeth grazed the back of her neck. "Aye," he whispered, "I intend to behave scandalously with you. Here in the hall, and in every room in the house."

He nipped her skin, affirming his ownership.

"Jenkins," he said. "Her Grace and I will be taking tea in the drawing room later."

"Very good, Your Grace. When would you like tea?"

"Give us an hour," Henry said, lifting his wife into his arms. "No, on second thought, make it two."

CHAPTER THIRTY-SIX

W HEN JEANETTE WOKE, for a moment she did not recognize her surroundings. She was in an enormous bed made from dark wood and a room furnished in strong, masculine colors.

Henry had never permitted her into his room before.

Her body still glowed with the memory of their lovemaking. Yawning, she stretched and sat up. The bed shifted, and her husband's warm, strong arms wrapped around her.

"I wondered how long you'd sleep." His hot breath tickled her ear. "I'm afraid our tea will have grown cold."

"What will Jenkins think of us, Henry, indulging in such scandalous pleasures in broad daylight?"

"His opinion of you will be as high as it always has been, my love. As for me, he'll think as I do—that I'm a damned lucky bastard."

Her torn corset lay on the floor. They had fumbled with the laces together to remove it and only succeeded in tightening the knots, at which point he'd cursed and ripped it apart, promising to buy her a new one, before taking her to the heights of pleasure, again and again.

"Henry…" She closed her eyes, relishing the memory.

He grazed his teeth against her ear. "If I recall, not one hour ago you were screaming my name."

"Henry!"

His body shook as he let out a low chuckle. "Yes, just like that—only much louder."

She turned to admonish him and her indignation died.

A large scar adorned the left side of his chest, surrounded by the yellowing remains of a bruise. Her heart constricted at the memory of him lying on the table in that dingy house at the docks.

What pain he must have endured!

Had he not moved into the path of Charlotte's bullet, Jeanette might have sustained that injury. Or died.

She traced an outline of the bruise with her finger. "Does it still pain you?"

"Only as a reminder that I could have lost you," he said. "But I wear it with pride and would gladly take a bullet for you again."

"Oh Henry, I..."

He placed a finger on her lips. "Let us speak of it no more, Jeanette. Now is not the time to regret the past. We must look to our future." He traced a line across her chest, his nostrils flaring as his fingertip moved across her breasts.

His expression sobered. "It's time we ended all deception between us."

"What do you mean?"

He sighed. "Since inheriting the dukedom, I felt it prudent to ask Mr. Barnes to send me the ledgers for the Ravenwell estate. He told me you'd seen them."

Her stomach tightened at the memory. The large withdrawal, the one Mr. Barnes had told her Henry had requested to establish a mistress.

"I see from your expression you know what I'm talking about." He sighed. "The day we met, you demonstrated your mathematical prowess. I should have known you'd be unable to leave the Ravenwell accounts alone."

"I'm glad of it," she said, "otherwise, I'd never have known what you'd done."

"I did it for you."

"What—wasted your money on another woman?"

Confusion stretched across his forehead, followed by recognition, and he rolled his eyes.

"You think I spent it on a mistress?" he asked. "Have you listened to nothing I've said? I gave it to your father. For his business."

"That was you?"

"It was the least I could do considering I married his finest clerk. Though I hear her replacement—Susan, is it?—is developing a similar degree of business acumen."

He gave her a sad smile. "You've every reason to think the worst of me after my behavior. Trust can be destroyed in a day, and it takes much longer to rebuild."

He placed his palm on her cheek and caressed her skin with his thumb. "What about you, my dear? Were you ever going to confess *your* deception?"

What was he accusing her of?

"My love," he laughed, "you've gone as white as this bedsheet. I refer to the unexpected restoration of the estate's cashflow and the prosperity of some of the farms thereabouts. Mr. Barnes may be an excellent steward, but he knows as much about farming as Grandmamma's pug dog. I can't tell you how proud I am of you; how lucky I feel to have such a woman for a wife."

He placed his hand on her belly. "I must work hard to make you equally proud, for your sake and that of our child. And Edward. I've been such a poor father to him, while you've been a shining example to me."

He took her hands in his and lifted them to his lips. "Will you teach me to be a better man, Jeanette, so that I might be worthy of you?"

She brushed her lips against his. "I'll do my best to teach a duke how to behave properly."

He smiled, his eyes radiating love. "I can think of no better teacher than the Holmestead Harlot."

"Why do you persist in using that dreadful nickname?"

He grinned. "It serves as a reminder that in marrying you, I saved myself from being shackled to a woman of breeding. Instead of a soulless match with the single objective of producing an heir, I have found fulfilment in a union with a woman in possession of qualities which are the very antithesis of society's ideals—wit, intelligence, kindness, and a passion for love and life."

He claimed her mouth in a kiss, then lay back, pulling her with him.

"Henry—we must get dressed for dinner," she said. "Jenkins…"

"Will, if he has any sense, be instructing the rest of the household not to disturb us until morning," he said. "The one thing I have dreamed of, save making love to my wife, is holding her in my arms while she sleeps. Would you deny me that pleasure?"

Smiling, she relaxed in his arms and drifted into a contented sleep, recognizing, at last, her good fortune in having secured the attention of a man of the ton.

The End

About the Author

Emily Royal grew up in Sussex, England, and has devoured romantic novels for as long as she can remember. A mathematician at heart, Emily has worked in financial services for over twenty years. She indulged in her love of writing after she moved to Scotland, where she lives with her husband, teenage daughters and menagerie of rescue pets including Twinkle, an attention-seeking boa constrictor.

She has a passion for both reading and writing romance with a weakness for Regency rakes, Highland heroes, and Medieval knights. Persuasion is one of her all-time favorite novels which she reads several times each year and she is fortunate enough to live within sight of a Medieval palace.

When not writing, Emily enjoys playing the piano, hiking, and painting landscapes, particularly the Highlands. One of her ambitions is to paint, as well as climb, every mountain in Scotland.

Follow Emily Royal:
Website: www.emroyal.com
Facebook: facebook.com/eroyalauthor
Twitter: twitter.com/eroyalauthor
Newsletter signup: mailchi.mp/e5806720bfe0/emilyroyalauthor
Goodreads: goodreads.com/author/show/14834886.Emily_Royal